MOR

THE STRANGE CASE OF HARRIET HALL

KATHERINE DALTON RENOIR ('Moray Dalton') was born in Hammersmith, London in 1881, the only child of a Canadian father and English mother.

The author wrote two well-received early novels, *Olive in Italy* (1909), and *The Sword of Love* (1920). However, her career in crime fiction did not begin until 1924, after which Moray Dalton published twenty-nine mysteries, the last in 1951. The majority of these feature her recurring sleuths, Scotland Yard inspector Hugh Collier and private inquiry agent Hermann Glide.

Moray Dalton married Louis Jean Renoir in 1921, and the couple had a son a year later. The author lived on the south coast of England for the majority of her life following the marriage. She died in Worthing, West Sussex, in 1963.

MORAY DALTON MYSTERIES
Available from Dean Street Press

One by One They Disappeared

The Night of Fear

The Body in the Road

Death in the Cup

The Strange Case of Harriet Hall

MORAY DALTON

THE STRANGE CASE OF HARRIET HALL

With an introduction by Curtis Evans

DEAN STREET PRESS

LOST GOLD FROM A GOLDEN AGE

The Detective Fiction of Moray Dalton
(Katherine Mary Deville Dalton Renoir,
1881-1963)

"GOLD" COMES in many forms. For literal-minded people gold may be merely a precious metal, physically stripped from the earth. For fans of Golden Age detective fiction, however, gold can be artfully spun out of the human brain, in the form not of bricks but books. While the father of Katherine Mary Deville Dalton Renoir may have derived the Dalton family fortune from nuggets of metallic ore, the riches which she herself produced were made from far humbler, though arguably ultimately mightier, materials: paper and ink. As the mystery writer Moray Dalton, Katherine Dalton Renoir published twenty-nine crime novels between 1924 and 1951, the majority of which feature her recurring sleuths, Scotland Yard inspector Hugh Collier and private inquiry agent Hermann Glide. Although the Moray Dalton mysteries are finely polished examples of criminally scintillating Golden Age art, the books unjustifiably fell into neglect for decades. For most fans of vintage mystery they long remained, like the fabled Lost Dutchman's mine, tantalizingly elusive treasure. Happily the crime fiction of Moray Dalton has been unearthed for modern readers by those industrious miners of vintage mystery at Dean Street Press.

Born in Hammersmith, London on May 6, 1881, Katherine was the only child of Joseph Dixon Dalton and Laura Back Dalton. Like the parents of that admittedly more famous mistress of mystery, Agatha Christie, Katherine's parents hailed from different nations, separated by the Atlantic Ocean. While both authors had British mothers, Christie's father was American and Dalton's father Canadian.

Laura Back Dalton, who at the time of her marriage in 1879 was twenty-six years old, about fifteen years younger than her husband, was the daughter of Alfred and Catherine Mary Back. In her early childhood years Laura Back resided at Valley

House, a lovely regency villa built around 1825 in Stratford St. Mary, Suffolk, in the heart of so-called "Constable Country" (so named for the fact that the great Suffolk landscape artist John Constable painted many of his works in and around Stratford). Alfred Back was a wealthy miller who with his brother Octavius, a corn merchant, owned and operated a steam-powered six-story mill right across the River Stour from Valley House. In 1820 John Constable, himself the son of a miller, executed a painting of fishers on the River Stour which partly included the earlier, more modest incarnation (complete with water wheel) of the Back family's mill. (This piece Constable later repainted under the title *The Young Waltonians*, one of his best known works.) After Alfred Back's death in 1860, his widow moved with her daughters to Brondesbury Villas in Maida Vale, London, where Laura in the 1870s met Joseph Dixon Dalton, an eligible Canadian-born bachelor and retired gold miner of about forty years of age who lived in nearby Kew.

Joseph Dixon Dalton was born around 1838 in London, Ontario, Canada, to Henry and Mary (Dixon) Dalton, Wesleyan Methodists from northern England who had migrated to Canada a few years previously. In 1834, not long before Joseph's birth, Henry Dalton started a soap and candle factory in London, Ontario, which after his death two decades later was continued, under the appellation Dalton Brothers, by Joseph and his siblings Joshua and Thomas. (No relation to the notorious "Dalton Gang" of American outlaws is presumed.) Joseph's sister Hannah wed John Carling, a politician who came from a prominent family of Canadian brewers and was later knighted for his varied public services, making him Sir John and his wife Lady Hannah. Just how Joseph left the family soap and candle business to prospect for gold is currently unclear, but sometime in the 1870s, after fabulous gold rushes at Cariboo and Cassiar, British Columbia and the Black Hills of South Dakota, among other locales, Joseph left Canada and carried his riches with him to London, England, where for a time he enjoyed life as a gentleman of leisure in one of the great metropolises of the world.

Although Joshua and Laura Dalton's first married years were spent with their daughter Katherine in Hammersmith at a villa named Kenmore Lodge, by 1891 the family had moved to 9 Orchard Place in Southampton, where young Katherine received a private education from Jeanne Delport, a governess from Paris. Two decades later, Katherine, now 30 years old, resided with her parents at Perth Villa in the village of Merriott, Somerset, today about an eighty miles' drive west of Southampton. By this time Katherine had published, under the masculine-sounding pseudonym of Moray Dalton (probably a gender-bending play on "Mary Dalton") a well-received first novel, *Olive in Italy* (1909), a study of a winsome orphaned Englishwoman attempting to make her own living as an artist's model in Italy that possibly had been influenced by E.M. Forster's novels *Where Angels Fear to Tread* (1905) and *A Room with a View* (1908), both of which are partly set in an idealized Italy of pure gold sunlight and passionate love. Yet despite her accomplishment, Katherine's name had no occupation listed next it in the census two years later.

During the Great War the Daltons, parents and child, resided at 14 East Ham Road in Littlehampton, a seaside resort town located 19 miles west of Brighton. Like many other bookish and patriotic British women of her day, Katherine produced an effusion of memorial war poetry, including "To Some Who Have Fallen," "Edith Cavell," "Rupert Brooke," "To Italy" and "Mort Homme." These short works appeared in the *Spectator* and were reprinted during and after the war in George Herbert Clarke's *Treasury of War Poetry* anthologies. "To Italy," which Katherine had composed as a tribute to the beleaguered British ally after its calamitous defeat, at the hands of the forces of Germany and Austria-Hungary, at the Battle of Caporetto in 1917, even popped up in the United States in the "poet's corner" of the *United Mine Workers Journal*, perhaps on account of the poem's pro-Italy sentiment, doubtlessly agreeable to Italian miner immigrants in America.

Katherine also published short stories in various periodicals, including *The Cornhill Magazine*, which was then edited by Leonard Huxley, son of the eminent zoologist Thomas Henry Huxley and father of famed writer Aldous Huxley. Leonard Huxley obligingly read over--and in his words "plied my scalpel upon"--Katherine's second novel, *The Sword of Love*, a romantic adventure saga set in the Florentine Republic at the time of Lorenzo the Magnificent and the infamous Pazzi Conspiracy, which was published in 1920. Katherine writes with obvious affection for *il bel paese* in her first two novels and her poem "To Italy," which concludes with the ringing lines

> Greece was enslaved, and Carthage is but dust,
> But thou art living, maugre [i.e., in spite of] all thy scars,
> To bear fresh wounds of rapine and of lust,
> Immortal victim of unnumbered wars.
> Nor shalt thou cease until we cease to be
> Whose hearts are thine, beloved Italy.

The author maintained her affection for "beloved Italy" in her later Moray Dalton mysteries, which include sympathetically-rendered Italian settings and characters.

Around this time Katherine in her own life evidently discovered romance, however short-lived. At Brighton in the spring of 1921, the author, now nearly 40 years old, wed a presumed Frenchman, Louis Jean Renoir, by whom the next year she bore her only child, a son, Louis Anthony Laurence Dalton Renoir. (Katherine's father seems to have missed these important developments in his daughter's life, apparently having died in 1918, possibly in the flu pandemic.) Sparse evidence as to the actual existence of this man, Louis Jean Renoir, in Katherine's life suggests that the marriage may not have been a successful one. In the 1939 census Katherine was listed as living with her mother Laura at 71 Wallace Avenue in Worthing, Sussex, another coastal town not far from Brighton, where she had married Louis Jean eighteen years earlier; yet he is not in evidence, even though he is stated to be Katherine's husband in her mother's will, which was probated in Worthing in 1945. Perhaps not unrelatedly, empathy with what people in her day considered unorthodox sexual unions characterizes the crime fiction which Katherine would write.

Whatever happened to Louis Jean Renoir, marriage and motherhood did not slow down "Moray Dalton." Indeed, much to the contrary, in 1924, only a couple of years after the birth of her son, Katherine published, at the age of 42 (the same age at which P.D. James published her debut mystery novel, *Cover Her Face*), *The Kingsclere Mystery*, the first of her 29 crime novels. (Possibly the title was derived from the village of Kingsclere, located some 30 miles north of Southampton.) The heady scent of Renaissance romance which perfumes *The Sword of Love* is found as well in the first four Moray Dalton mysteries (aside from *The Kingsclere Mystery*, these are *The Shadow on the Wall*, *The Black Wings* and *The Stretton Darknesse Mystery*), which although set in the present-day world have, like much of the mystery fiction of John Dickson Carr, the elevated emotional temperature of the highly-colored age of the cavaliers. However in 1929 and 1930, with the publication of, respectively, *One by One They Disappeared*, the first of the Inspector Hugh Collier mysteries and *The Body in the Road*, the debut Hermann Glide tale, the Moray Dalton novels begin to become more typical of British crime fiction at that time, ultimately bearing considerable similarity to the work of Agatha Christie and Dorothy L. Sayers, as well as other prolific women mystery authors who would achieve popularity in the 1930s, such as Margery Allingham, Lucy Beatrice Malleson (best known as "Anthony Gilbert") and Edith Caroline Rivett, who wrote under the pen names E.C.R. Lorac and Carol Carnac.

For much of the decade of the 1930s Katherine shared the same publisher, Sampson Low, with Edith Rivett, who published her first detective novel in 1931, although Rivett moved on, with both of her pseudonyms, to that rather more prominent purveyor of mysteries, the Collins Crime Club. Consequently the Lorac and Carnac novels are better known today than those of Moray Dalton. Additionally, only three early Moray Dalton titles (*One by One They Disappeared*, *The Body in the Road* and *The Night of Fear*) were picked up in the United States, another factor which mitigated against the Dalton mysteries achieving long-term renown. It is also possible that the independently wealthy author, who left an estate valued, in modern estimation, at nearly a million American dollars at her death at the age of 81 in 1963, felt less of an imperative to "push" her writing than the typical "starving author."

Whatever forces compelled Katherine Dalton Renoir to write fiction, between 1929 and 1951 the author as Moray Dalton published fifteen Inspector Hugh Collier mysteries and ten other crime novels (several of these with Hermann Glide). Some of the non-series novels daringly straddle genres. *The Black Death*, for example, somewhat bizarrely yet altogether compellingly merges the murder mystery with post-apocalyptic science fiction, whereas *Death at the Villa*, set in Italy during the Second World War, is a gripping wartime adventure thriller with crime and death. Taken together, the imaginative and ingenious Moray Dalton crime fiction, wherein death is not so much a game as a dark and compelling human drama, is one of the more significant bodies of work by a Golden Age mystery writer—though the author has, until now, been most regrettably overlooked by publishers, for decades remaining accessible almost solely to connoisseurs with deep pockets.

Even noted mystery genre authorities Jacques Barzun and Wendell Hertig Taylor managed to read only five books by Moray Dalton, all of which the pair thereupon listed in their massive critical compendium, *A Catalogue of Crime* (1972; revised and expanded 1989). Yet Barzun and Taylor were warm admirers of the author's writing, avowing for example, of the twelfth Hugh Collier mystery, *The Condamine Case* (under the impression that the author was a man): "[T]his is the author's 17th book, and [it is] remarkably fresh and unstereotyped [actually it was Dalton's 25th book, making it even more remarkable—C.E.]. . . . [H]ere is a neglected man, for his earlier work shows him to be a conscientious workman, with a flair for the unusual, and capable of clever touches."

Today in 2019, nine decades since the debut of the conscientious and clever Moray Dalton's Inspector Hugh Collier detective series, it is a great personal pleasure to announce that this criminally neglected woman is neglected no longer and to welcome her books back into light. Vintage crime fiction fans have a golden treat in store with the classic mysteries of Moray Dalton.

The Strange Case of Harriet Hall

The Strange Case of Harriet Hall (1936), one of the finest detective novels from the Golden Age of mystery, marked the seventh appearance in print of Moray Dalton's intelligent and empathetic Scotland Yard sleuth, Inspector Hugh Collier. Between this case and Inspector Collier's debut performance, *One by One They Disappeared*, there were five other novels in which Collier appeared: *The Night of Fear* (1931), *The Belfry Murder* (1933), *The Harvest of Tares* (1933), *The Belgrave Manor Crime* (1935) and *The Mystery of the Kneeling Woman* (1936). In *The Night of Fear*, Collier, though he initiates the investigation after the local man is sidelined by gas poisoning, soon is pulled off the case due to political pressure, leaving the truth to be uncovered by Dalton's other, shorter-lived series sleuth, private inquiry agent Hermann Glide. Beginning with *The Belfry Murder*, however, Collier acts as the lead sleuth in the novels in which he appears, with the exception of *Death of a Spinster* (1951), his final novel, where he appears only briefly near the end of the tale.

Certainly the innocent in *The Strange Case of Harriet Hall* have reason to be grateful for Collier's involvement, given the bumbling behavior of the gentry-toadying local Chief Constable, Colonel Boult. It is a strange case indeed, concerning the murder of that strangely offputting individual, Harriet Hall, at her isolated cottage outside the village of Larnwood, on the eve of the arrival of her pretty, young, down on her luck niece, Amy Steer. Why was the likeable Deene family of the Dower House at Lennor Park--comprised of elegant widowed matriarch Mary Deene and her charming children Tony, Mollie and Lavvy, the latter of whom is engaged to marry Sir Miles Lennor, son of the forbidding Lady Louisa Lennor--seemingly so in thrall to the objectionably pushing and gauche Harriet Hall? As Collier's investigation deepens, the case gets stranger still. Finally, however, the guilty are punished--though readers will have to read through to the book's final, quietly devastating chapter, so reminiscent of a P.D. James mystery, to see just how.

Curtis Evans

Chapter I
PERSONAL

STALE, THESE PHRASES employers used, employers and their agents: stale as a worn gramophone record whirring under a blunted needle.

Nothing for you to-day. . . . Move on, please, there are others waiting. You see how many there are before you. . . . The post is filled. . . . What can you do . . . I see. I like your appearance, but you must realise that there are others more qualified—

And so out again through swing doors, along corridors, down stairs, down and out. Down and out.

The queue of disappointed women, young and middle-aged, was dispersing. Amy Steer took advantage of a momentary lull in the traffic to dart across the street to the big red block of the Municipal Library. There might be something in the wanted columns of the daily papers. Oh, why hadn't her mother realised that she must be trained? What was the use of being nineteen, healthy, and willing to work?

The reading-room was crowded with unemployed men trying to pass the time. One or two glanced up with a gleam of interest as she made her way across the room, but she remained unaware of them. Someone had just left the *Daily Telegraph* stand, and a man who had been yawning over a trade journal rose hurriedly, but Amy slipped by him. He sat down again with a grunt of annoyance.

Amy felt pleased with herself. She was learning to push. You had to in London. Push or you would be left standing on the kerb when the bus started: push, or the office boy would bang the door in your face. Push!

She turned over the pages. Crisis in Bolivia. Seaplane disaster. She glanced at the picture page. The *Mauretania* in dry dock. A new inmate of the Zoo. The excavations in the Valley of Kings. Miss Lavinia Dene, elder daughter of Mrs. Dene of the Dower House, Lennor, whose engagement to Sir Miles Lennor is announced.

"She's lovely if she's like that," thought Amy with a little sigh of envy. Girls like her had everything. They didn't have to worry.

She turned back the pages.

SITUATIONS VACANT

Gowns.—Required, Saleswoman, Highest grade experience essential.

Young lady receptionist. Must be experienced.

Salesmen or saleswomen required to sell door to door.

Amy winced. She had been offered that sort of job, and another girl had told her what it meant. "Hawking. Doors slammed in your face, and you'll wear your shoes out in less than a week." She turned to another column. But mistresses advertising for working housekeepers or cook generals wanted good references.

PERSONAL

Cars bought for cash. . . .

Reduce your weight. . . .

Steer.—Any relative of the late Julius Horace Steer writing full particulars may hear something to their advantage.—Write Box 5972 Daily Telegraph.

Julius Horace. "That's Father!" she thought. There could hardly be another Julius Horace. They were both uncommon names. She could not remember her father, and she knew nothing about his family. Something to their advantage. She might never have seen the advertisement for she hardly ever looked at the Personal column. She shut her eyes for a moment, gripping the edge of the newspaper stand. She felt a little dizzy. Had her luck turned at last? Was something wonderful going to happen to her? What next? She must write, of course, and furnish the required particulars. The man who had been pretending to read the magazine for poultry-keepers jumped up as she turned away and almost thrust her aside in his eagerness to secure her place.

There was a little stationer's shop opposite the Free Library. She went in and bought a twopenny packet of note-paper and envelopes, a three halfpenny stamp, a copy of the *Daily Telegraph*. She had a pen and a bottle of ink in the bedroom that was hers until the end of the week. She hurried back to it The landlady, hearing her come in, emerged from the kitchen.

"About your room, Miss Steer. Would you be wanting it after Saturday? If you stay I'll have to raise the rent by half a crown. I've been offered that by a former tenant that wants to come back to me."

"I see. I'm not sure. Can you wait until Friday?" The landlady's eyes were hard. "She knows I'm nearly on the rocks," thought Amy.

"I can't wait, Miss Steer."

"Very well. I'll leave on Monday."

She ran upstairs. Her fellow tenants were all out at this hour. The old musician who described himself as a member of an orchestra but was suspected of playing the cornet in the streets; the girl who had a job at the Cinema; the little old lady who went out, in a feather boa that moulted all down the stairs and beaded evening slippers, to buy cat's meat to feed the gulls on the Embankment. Amy shut her door and sat down to write at her rickety little table without even waiting to take off her hat.

Julius Horace Steer was my father. He died when I was two years old. I am now nineteen. I lived with my mother at Little Benenden, five miles out of Tunbridge Wells. She died a year ago. The cottage was not ours.

The furniture was sold and I got seventy pounds. I came up to London. I got a place as assistant in a hat shop. I left there six weeks ago and I've been out ever since. I'm trying hard to get something to do. Unfortunately I can't type or write shorthand. Will you please write to Miss Amy Steer, Poste Restante, Daley Street Post Office, as I am leaving my present lodgings next Monday.

She read over what she had written, addressed the envelope, and put on the stamp. Then she went out to the pillar box. The letter fell into the box with a plop, and Amy felt her heart fall with it. She had not given herself any time to think. Suppose this advertisement was not what it purported to be, but some kind of trap? That was absurd. It must be genuine, and if she had not answered it she would never have forgiven herself. Now she would have to wait for an answer. Meanwhile there was that agency in the Strand. The man there had told her there might be crowd work at the Hertford Studio. She walked to the end of the road to get a bus.

Two days passed. On Thursday morning the young woman behind the counter in the Daley Street sub-office pushed a letter across to her. Amy's hand trembled as she took it up. She wanted to be alone when she read it, but her landlady did not like her lodgers to be continually coming in and out during the day, and she had a sharp tongue. Amy read her letter standing on the pavement.

MY DEAR NIECE,

I was very glad to hear from you. I lost sight of your father many years ago but I knew be had married and I thought he might have had a family. I gather you were the only child. I live very quietly in the country, but I am fortunate in having very good friends. I am coming up to London for the day on Thursday. If you can be in the first-class ladies' waiting-room at eleven we can have a talk. Meanwhile, I remain,

Your affectionate aunt,

HARRIET HALL.

Amy glanced up at the post office clock, thrust the letter into her bag, and ran to catch a bus. She arrived at her destination, rather flurried and out of breath, with three minutes to spare. Had her aunt arrived? There was nobody in the waiting-room who looked at all likely. In one corner a young mother was nursing her baby, and in another two subfusc females with shopping bags were nibbling biscuits. Amy went to the looking glass over the mantelpiece and stared rather anxiously at her own reflection. She knew that some people thought her pretty, but she was not looking her best. Who could, she thought, on a diet of buns and cocoa and an occasional herring.

She powdered her nose and settled her hat at a slightly different angle. As she turned away a tall woman came quickly through the swing doors, and after a swift appraising look round, moved towards her. She was well dressed in black with a long silk coat with a collar of fox furs, and her hard handsome face was heavily made up.

"You are Amy Steer? My dear child—come and sit down."

When they were seated side by side she looked down at Amy smilingly. Her bold brown eyes were thickly lashed. The chief fault of her face was the unusually coarse texture of the skin which she evidently tried to disguise by a liberal application of cosmetics. Amy found her rather alarming in spite of the friendliness of her manner and faltered a little as she said: "It was quite by chance I saw your advertisement—"

"It's been in every day for the past fortnight. You are just what I hoped for. I've a nephew, but he takes advantage—I've done with him. Your mother died? Quite alone, eh? Well, you can come and stay with me in my country cottage; it's a lodge, really, on a friend's estate. She lets me live in it rent free. She helps me in every way. And she's got two girls and a boy. You'll have plenty of fun. And if you can get off with the young man that would suit my book very well. In fact, that's what I'm asking you down for." She laughed, and Amy laughed too as this seemed to be expected of her.

Mrs. Hall wore large drop earrings that swung backwards and forwards as she moved. The two subfusc females in the corner had finished their biscuits and were eyeing her disapprovingly. Amy, who was always quick to respond to kindness, was trying not to think that her aunt seemed rather a vulgar person.

"You mustn't be shy of me," said Mrs. Hall when she had asked some further questions. "I can see you've had a thin time since you left that hat shop. Forget it. You do what I tell you, my dear, and you won't go far wrong. I've got it all mapped out for you. Now, when can you come?"

"I have to leave my lodgings on Monday."

"Monday," said Mrs. Hall briskly. "That will suit me and it will give you time to get some suitable clothes. I want you to do me credit. I daresay you haven't much—"

"No. I—"

Mrs. Hall talked on, ignoring the interruptions. "You'll need a couple of evening dresses and an evening coat or cloak. You'll be dining with the Denes and I daresay you'll get asked to other places. The elder girl has just got engaged to a big pot. A poor fish, but he's County all right. Two or three silk frocks for tennis, and a couple of woolly suits and a tweed skirt and jumpers for wet days. Then you'll want shoes for different occasions, stockings, hats—"

"Aunt Harriet—" said Amy desperately.

"Well, what's biting you?" enquired that lady with a touch of impatience. Evidently she disliked being interrupted.

"I haven't any money to buy clothes."

Mrs. Hall nodded and smiled. "I'm going to give you some. I came prepared." She opened the large red and black striped morocco bag which, with its flashing chromium-plated fittings, seemed so characteristic of her rather blatant personality, and drew out a thick wad of notes.

"I'm giving you a hundred pounds. Twelve fives and the rest in one pound notes. You must pay your fare down out of that, but you can spend the rest on pretties. I want you to make a good impression; it'll make things easier all round if you're liked. My address is North Lodge, Dower House, Lennor, West Sussex. Larnwood is the station. There's a train from here a little before three. Look it up. You can come by that. You'll be met."

"Oh, Aunt Harriet," gasped Amy, "thank you."

Mrs. Hall stood up. "That's okay," she said easily, "there's more where that comes from. I have my faults, but I'm not mean. And now I've some business to transact and you ought to start shopping. What a little thing you are—"

"Not really, Aunt Harriet. You're tall."

"Yes. I suppose it's that. Cheerio. I shall expect you on Monday."

She bent over her niece. Amy, conscious of her somewhat overpowering aura of combined Nuit d'Amour and Turkish cigarettes, tried hard not to shrink away as Mrs. Hall's painted lips brushed her cheek. A minute later she found herself standing alone, in a kind of dream, and clutching the incredible sum that had been thrust upon her.

CHAPTER II
A BIT OF A RISK

Amy spent Sunday evening packing her new clothes in her new trunk and suitcase, while her neighbour from across the landing, Miss Vanna d'Este, who sometimes played small parts in films, sat on the end of her bed and offered criticism and advice.

"I'll say it's romantic finding an aunt like that," she said. "Not that I've much use for aunts. They're generally stuffy and fault-finding. Was she your father's sister?"

Amy sat back on her heels. "Yes, I suppose so. She must have been," she said vaguely. "I'd like to hear more about him and his people. He died when I was a baby, and my mother never spoke about his relations."

"Do you think you're going to like her?"

"I—I hope so. She was very kind. But, of course, I only saw her for a few minutes. She was in a hurry, going on somewhere."

"Seems to me that you're taking a bit of a risk," said Miss d'Este. "You don't know a thing about her really. Are you sure you're wise to go down to this place?"

"She knew my father's name," said Amy. "I think it's all right. Besides, I haven't much choice. I've got to get out of here to-morrow, and I hadn't a job."

"A boy friend's useful when jobs are scarce," said Miss d'Este.

"Not for me, thanks," said Amy firmly.

"You won't be so darned particular when you've been on your own as long as I have, my dear. But if auntie's okay you won't have to worry. Anyhow you've got a decent outfit. I like that green brocade evening coat. Mind how you fold it or you'll crumple the sleeves. How much have you got left? Fifteen pounds? I think you're marvellous. Why, she told you to spend it all, didn't she?"

"I was to keep enough for my railway fare," Amy explained as she slipped tissue paper between the filmy flounces of the more expensive of her two dance frocks, "but I'll feel safer with a little in hand."

"I know," said Miss d'Este with feeling. "I always used to keep a ten shilling note sewed into the lining of my stays. I mean to say a girl never knows when she's going to get badly left. Well," she yawned, "I'm dead to the world and I've got to be at the agents' bright and early in the morning or I won't get a dog's chance. I may not be seeing you again. All of the best—"

"Thank you."

Miss d'Este was hunting for her lipstick in a rather dingy vanity bag. She carefully retraced her Cupid's bow before she resumed. "By the way, dear, I hate to ask, but I'm fearfully short of cash just now. I simply had to get a new pair of shoes. There's such a lot of walking to do in these blasted film studios. Could you lend me a couple of quid just to go on with? I'll pay you back—"

"Why, of course," said Amy, trying not to seem reluctant. She had lent her fellow lodger various small sums at times before she came to the end of her own small savings, and she had not been repaid. She took two notes from her bag and held them out.

Miss d'Este took them. "Darling, I won't forget. Oh, I say! that leaves you with thirteen—"

"Yes."

"That won't do, dear. That's horribly unlucky. You'd better give me another for your own sake—"

Amy laughed as she shook her head. "I think I'll chance that. It won't be for long."

"Well, don't say I didn't warn you. Nighty night, dearie, and thanks for the loan."

Amy locked her door when Miss d'Este had left her. If it got about that she had money she might be having a visit from the old woman who fed the gulls, or the even more mysterious tenant of the ground floor front. She was in bed by ten, but for a long time she was unable to sleep. Now that the excitement attendant on buying all her new clothes had begun to die down she was aware of misgivings. Her own mother had been quiet, gentle, self-effacing. Amy had adored her mother. Mrs. Steer had been what old-fashioned people call a real lady. Amy knew she would have shrunk appalled from Aunt Harriet with her dangling earrings, her painted lips.

Amy had not dared describe Mrs. Hall's appearance to Miss d'Este. She had not wanted to hear that outspoken young woman's probable comments. She tried to reassure herself. Lots of women who were perfectly respectable made up their faces and wore gimcrack jewellery. If Aunt Harriet had a kind heart—that was all that mattered.

She had to leave her lodgings early as the landlady wanted to clean the room before the next tenant arrived, so she took her luggage to the station in a taxi and spent the intervening hours before her train started in the Tate Gallery. The train, a slow train, for no others stopped at Larnwood, was not crowded and she settled herself in a corner seat in an empty third class compartment. But she was not to remain alone.

Just as the train was beginning to move a young man rushed up, regardless of warning shouts from porters, opened the door and dropped rather heavily on to the seat facing hers.

He caught Amy's eye and grinned. "A damned near thing, as Wellington said at Waterloo—"

"It's frightfully dangerous," she said, "if you had slipped you might have been killed."

He listened to this truism with the respectful attention a young man is apt to give to the most unimportant remarks when the utterer is as pretty as Amy looked at that moment.

"You're absolutely right, of course." It was a corridor carriage and normally, after seeing the triangular notice on the window that meant that he must not smoke he would have gone to look for another compartment. As it was, he stayed. Amy was quite willing that he should. He looked nice, she thought. The novel she had bought to read on the journey, a cheap edition of a best-seller, had slipped from her knees. He picked it up for her and began to talk about books. They discussed plays, too.

While Amy was at the hat shop she had gone to a theatre nearly every week. Sometimes there were complimentary tickets, but more often she had been in the gallery. By the time they reached Dorking they were on the friendliest terms, contradicting each other freely and the young man had said "Don't be an ass!" twice. At Dorking he bethought himself, leaned out of the window, and, after a considerable expenditure of energy, secured a tea basket for two.

"You pour out. I take two lumps. By the way, where do you get out?"

"At Larnwood."

"The deuce you do. That's my station. Do you live in those parts?"

"It's my first visit," she explained. "I'm going to stay with an aunt."

"Good," he said. "Are you taking part in the Lennor Pageant?"

"I don't know."

"You would be," he said, "if I was producing. I say, we've been talking such a lot that I haven't introduced myself. My name's Dene, Anthony Dene, better known as Tony."

He rumpled his hair with both hands. "This is a bit of luck!" he said in a heart-felt tone.

"What is?"

"Why—I thought you might be going on to Portsmouth."

Amy laughed and finished the last crumb of her cake.

"Are we nearly there?"

"Another twenty minutes. Aren't you going to tell me your name?"

"Oh, of course. I'm Amy Steer."

She was watching his clever, humorous, mobile face. He was nice looking, she thought, in spite of the horn-rimmed spectacles.

His brown eyes beamed at her almost affectionately through the slightly enlarging lenses.

"Amy. That means beloved. You see I know a bit of French. Amy. Yes, I like the sound of it. I say, can I run you home? I've only been up for the day and I left my car parked in the station yard."

"Thank you. But Mrs. Hall said she would meet me."

An extraordinary change came over him. He sat quite still looking at her. His body remained, but the spirit that informed it, the real Anthony Dene, withdrew to some illimitable distance. It was from that distance that he addressed her in a voice she had not yet heard.

"Is Mrs. Hall your aunt? I see. I—excuse me—"

He got up and went into the corridor. She gazed after him, puzzled, and more hurt than she would have believed possible.

Time passed and he did not come back. She sat, her face hot with mingled shame and anger. What had she said? It was something to do with her aunt. Dene. The name was vaguely familiar. She had seen it somewhere quite recently. He must have had a perfectly ghastly row with Mrs. Hall. There could be no other explanation of his conduct. Amy was still quivering with bewildered resentment when the train stopped again and she heard a porter shouting "Larnwood."

She got out and walked towards the luggage van. The only other passenger to alight had been young Dene and he had disappeared into the booking office. She heard a car being started up as she stood by her trunk and suitcase. The porter, who seemed to be the only member of the staff on duty, took her ticket.

It was a little country station with fields on either side of the line and no house in sight.

"Were you to be fetched, miss?"

"Yes. A lady—my aunt—"

"There's nobody here."

"I suppose I had better wait."

She waited half an hour, sitting on the bench in the hot sun. Had her aunt forgotten her or had something happened to prevent her coming? She went into the ticket office where the porter could be seen through a door marked Private, but left ajar, drinking tea from a Thermos.

"Could I hire something to take me?"

"Where to, miss?"

"North Lodge, Lennor."

He scratched his head. "I might stop the baker's van present-ly. He'd bring your luggage, I daresay," he looked at her doubt-fully, "I don't know if you could walk it."

"How far is it?" she asked.

"Round about five miles."

"I could manage that," she said. Anything was better than Waiting any longer on that station platform. "If you'll see about my trunk I can carry the suitcase. It's quite light." She listened to his long and involved directions, gave him a shilling, and started on her long tramp.

After the first two miles the suitcase began to feel heavy and she had to stop at intervals and change it from hand to hand. She was trying not to be depressed but she had been more upset than she cared to admit by the strange conduct of the young man in the train. He had been so nice to her until he learned that she was Mrs. Hall's niece.

"He hates her," she thought. "Oh, well, it can't be helped."

It was a warm, still evening and a golden haze softened the outlines of the surrounding hills. The road she had been told to follow was little more than a lane and it wound on and on inter-minably. She met nobody though once she heard the rattling of a farm wagon and the voice of the carter exhorting his team. She was hot and tired when, at last, she reached a signpost half-way across an open space of sandy ground patched with gorse and heather, and saw traces of what had once been a carriage road leading towards the enclosed woods that skirted the moor on the left and sloped down into the valley. The porter had told her to turn off here. The old road led her directly to a high wrought-iron gate set between stone posts bearing heraldic griffins.

The lodge was just inside on the right. She managed to get the gate open, not without difficulty, for it was very heavy and its rusty hinges creaked a protest. The lodge had a small patch of front garden, gay with flowers, and enclosed by low railings that had been recently painted green. It had a thatched roof and a diamond paned window screened with lace curtains on either side of the porch. It looked very spick and span standing among such neglected surroundings. The big gate had been red with rust and the gate posts stood in beds of nettles.

Amy went slowly up the brick path to the front door. Was her aunt in? Had she seen her through the lace curtains and would she run to open the door to her? What reason would she give for not having met her? Perhaps it was her fault. She might have mistaken the day. But she was sure Mrs. Hall had said Monday.

Amy noticed that the brass knocker was well polished. Either Mrs. Hall had a good maid, or was herself a notable housewife. She knocked and waited for the sound of approaching footsteps, but the silence within was unbroken. It struck her that her aunt might have gone to meet her by another road and missed her in some unexplained fashion. She knocked again. It was a good thing, she thought, that she had had tea on the train. She was very thirsty again now after her long walk and would be glad to take off her shoes and have a good wash.

After some hesitation she tried the door knob. It turned easily. She stepped into a tiny passage. The door on the right stood open. As she entered the sitting-room she noticed the scent of Nuit d'Amour and Turkish cigarettes. The room itself was quite charming, with bright chintz covers on the chairs, a fine old mahogany bureau, and a big bowl of roses on the gate leg table. The row of novels on the window-sill included some recently published and bearing Mudie's labels and others, in garish cardboard bindings, of a more doubtful character. Amy noticed a brass ash tray heaped with stubs of cigarettes with red smeared ends. The floor was of brick and in one corner it looked quite wet as if it had been recently washed.

She went back into the passage and called out, "Aunt Harriet."

There was no reply.

She opened the door on the left and looked into a bedroom. Here, too, there was good old furniture, and the bed was covered with a pink silk eiderdown. The dressing-table was crowded with pots of vanishing cream, powder, and rouge, and Amy noticed a large bottle of her aunt's favourite scent.

The black silk coat with the big fur collar which she had worn when she met her at Victoria hung from a hook at the back of the door.

She went into the kitchen. It was very neat and the cupboard was well stocked with tinned provisions. The grate was empty. It was evident to Amy by this time that her aunt had no servant. Evidently she did her cooking on an oil stove. Amy filled a kettle from the pump over the sink. When she went to light the stove she was startled to find that the oil container was quite warm. She touched it again gingerly to make sure. Yes, it was warm. That meant that it had been alight quite recently. Someone must have been in the cottage only a few minutes previously. It was odd, and rather disturbing. Probably the explanation was quite a simple one, but it didn't, as the French say, jump to the eyes.

Amy put the kettle on and went to look at the only remaining room in the cottage. Another bedroom, and she saw at once that it had been got ready for her. There was a clean towel on the rail and a cake of soap in the soap dish. The little white bed looked attractive and everything was clean and neat. She looked out of the window and saw beyond the brick paved court and wood shed a long narrow garden overshadowed by the high park wall and choked with a mass of overgrown currant and gooseberry bushes out of which a few half-dead apple trees extended gnarled branches as if appealing for help.

Amy took off her hat and coat, washed her hands and face, and went back to the kitchen where she made a meal of tea and biscuits and cleared up before returning to the sitting-room. There was a pile of illustrated weeklies on the settee and she turned them over to pass the time. Presently she saw the lovely girl whose picture she had already noticed a few days earlier in the *Telegraph*. Miss Lavinia Dene, whose engagement to Sir Miles Lennor, of Lennor Park, has been announced. Lennor. That was the name of the village her aunt had mentioned. They lived near here then. And the name of the young man in the train was Dene. He must be this girl's brother.

There was somebody at the door. She ran out eagerly expecting to see her aunt, and found two men carrying her trunk between them.

"Sorry to be so long, miss, but we had to carry'm up the lane from the road. 'Tisn't fit for no make of car."

"Are you Mrs. Hall's baker?"

"Yes, miss. I call twice a week. I was here Saturday and I'll be round again Wednesday. Will she be wanting any extra bread?"

"I don't know. She isn't in just now."

They carried the box into the back bedroom for her. She paid them and saw them go with mixed feelings. She was beginning to be oppressed by the loneliness of the place. The back of the cottage, cut off from the sun by the high wall, was gloomy and dank. She unstrapped her suitcase and took out what she needed for the night but she did not open her box. It occurred to her that her aunt might have left a written message explaining her absence, but though she looked about she found nothing of the kind. In fact, though there was a bureau she saw no letters, and the ink well was dry. She looked at her watch and saw that it was nearly eight. She re-lit the oil stove and prepared another meal, cocoa this time, and bread and butter and an apple, but she did not enjoy her food. The silence of the place was unnerving. She was beginning to be rather frightened. It was such a dear little house—but there was something about it that made her hesitate and brace herself before she opened a door. It was so quiet that the ticking of the clock sounded unnaturally loud. The tiny patch of front garden was full of flowers, but at the back was the thorny wilderness darkened by the stone wall of the park. She shrank from the thought that she would have to spend the night alone there, but it had to be faced. She decided that she would sit up until eleven. Mrs. Hall might have gone up to London. She might return by the last train. Yes. But who had been using the oil stove just before she arrived? Or had she been mistaken in thinking it was still warm?

She bolted both the front and the back door and drew the curtains before it grew quite dark, and she lit a lamp in the living room and another in the kitchen, and put candles in both bedrooms. Then she took a novel from the row on the window sill and sat down and tried to read. After a while the book slipped from her hand and she slept fitfully, a sleep broken by dreams in which she and a tall woman with dangling earrings and a wide, crimson mouth played a sinister game of hide and seek through an endless series of darkened rooms.

When she woke, aching with fatigue and numbed with cold, the lamp had gone out and the grey light of dawn was creeping into the room.

CHAPTER III

THE PERFECT FRAME

MOLLIE DENE had finished her solitary dinner and was sitting on the terrace with Binkie, her Cairn terrier, slumbering on her lap when her brother joined her.

"Tony, what an age you've been. Did you miss your train?"

He pushed one of the wicker chairs nearer to hers, sat down, and lit a cigarette.

"No. I caught the ten to three—"

"Then—where on earth have you been?"

He answered drearily. "I just drove on and on. I didn't feel like coming home. Where's Mother?"

"She's got one of her headaches. She left word with Parsons that she was going to take aspirin and try to sleep so I haven't been up."

"And Lavvy?"

"She's dining with the Lennors. Miles will bring her home. What's the matter, Tony?"

It was too dark to see her brother's face, but Mollie did not need her eyes to tell her that something had happened to upset Tony. Though, or perhaps because he was five years older, he and she had always been pals. Lavvy, fragile and exquisite, her mother's pride and darling, had always gone her own way. With her faint, aloof little smile she had withdrawn herself from her brother's teasing and her little sister's inconvenient enthusiasm. They loved her, they were loyal, but they had learned that they must not encroach. If she needed them they would be summoned. Lately she had not needed them. "Has Mrs. Hall been here to-day?"

"Not that I know of. I was down the village, at the vicarage all the afternoon, and I stayed to tea."

He dropped the end of his cigarette and ground it under his heel. A moth flying towards the lighted window behind them blundered against him. The cry of a night bird came from the wooded valley beyond the open spaces of the park.

"I wish we'd never come here," he said.

"Oh, Tony, it's lovely. And Mother always said it was a great bargain. I always remember her saying 'I've found the perfect frame for Lavvy.' And it's true."

"Yes. But I think it's costing more than she expected to keep up. She won't tell me anything, but I believe she's drawing on her capital."

"Is that what's bothering you?"

"Partly, I suppose. She never will talk to me about money, and I don't like to ask. She's not looking a bit well, Mollie."

"I know. These headaches," said the young girl anxiously.

"But she's awfully pleased about Lavvy's engagement. And, of course, I suppose that does justify her buying this place. I mean, we didn't know anybody when we lived in London. Lavvy would never have met Sir Miles there."

"No. That's true. But I'd rather Lavvy married into a family that didn't have to swallow hard to get us down."

Mollie did not pretend not to understand him. "I know. One can't help seeing that Lady Lennor isn't very keen on us."

He laughed shortly. "Isn't too keen is a mild way of putting it. But Lennor is. Lavvy's a pretty thing. Queer that you and I should be so plain, Moll."

"Beast!" said his sister vigorously. "Come on. It's getting chilly."

He followed her in through the french window of the drawing-room, stopping to close it after him. She cried out as she saw him in the light. "Tony, you look absolutely done in! What have you been doing to yourself?"

He tried to smile. "Nothing. I told you I've been a long drive."

"Did you get dinner anywhere?"

"No. I hate the tough beef they give one in country pubs—"

"I'll ring. They'll cut you some sandwiches."

"No." He caught her as she was crossing the room and held her, looking down into her troubled face. "I don't want a fuss, Mollie. I can get a drink and some biscuits without bothering the servants. Isn't it time you were in bed, young woman?"

"Never mind me." Her candid eyes searched the dark mobile clever face. Under that clear gaze it began to twitch uncontrollably. The young man uttered a kind of groan and covered it with his hands.

"Tony!" she was really frightened now. "What is it? You've got to tell me."

He sat down abruptly and she stood by waiting, one hand on his shoulder. She knew how sensitive he was under his mask of youthful cynicism, how much he really cared for her and Lavvy, and their mother.

He looked up presently. "I'm an ass," he said bitterly. "I let myself get worked up. I'll tell you—" He picked up Binkie, who, realising that there was something wrong, was standing with his forepaws on the young man's knee and industriously licking the back of his hand. "There was a girl in the train coming down this afternoon, a jolly good sort I thought her. We talked quite a lot. And then just before we got to the station she calmly told me that she was Mrs. Hall's niece, coming to stay with her."

"What did you do?"

"I—it was such a shock. I got up and went into the corridor. And when the train stopped I simply bolted out and jumped into the car and drove away."

"Was Mrs. Hall there to meet her?"

"I don't know. I didn't see her. But I didn't stop to look. There wasn't anyone on the platform, but she must have been in the waiting-room."

"It sounds—rather rude," said Mollie slowly.

He groaned again. "I know. Heaven only knows what she must have thought of me."

"Oh, well—I wouldn't worry," she said consolingly, "if she's anything like her aunt a few snubs more or less won't make any difference. Mrs. Hall must know that you and I and Lavvy simply loathe her, but that doesn't stop her from coming here as often as she chooses and taking advantage of Mother's kindness."

"But she isn't like her aunt," cried Tony with unexpected vehemence. "Do you think I'd have got pally with her if she had been? And that's what makes it so ghastly. That woman will bring her here and push her on to us, and if we're decent to her the old woman will have won all along the line, and if we aren't I shall feel like hell about it. I don't see how she's ever going to forgive me as it is," he added dejectedly.

"Oh Tony!" cried his sister, "is she as nice as that?"

There was a sudden relaxation of tension, and they both laughed.

"Probably not. Didn't I tell you I was an ass? Look out, I heard a car. That will be Lennor bringing Lavvy home. Nip off to bed, Mollie, and I'll get that drink and do a bunk. They'll be at least ten minutes saying good night."

Tony was right. He had time to get himself a whisky and soda, with less soda and twice the usual amount of spirit, and had reached the first floor landing when his elder sister was letting herself into the hall. He heard her high, clear voice addressing her lover.

"Good night, darling. Yes, I'll be ready."

He did not wait for her. Lavvy was exquisite, but she was not the sort of person to whom one tells one's troubles. He walked down the long passage to his room. There was a light under his mother's door. She wasn't asleep then, unless she had gone to sleep with the light on. He felt rather giddy. Too much whisky on an empty stomach. Did he take everything too seriously, make mountains out of molehills? If only his mother would trust him. He wasn't a child. Would it be better to try and get a job in town, any job, instead of going back to Oxford? He fell asleep without coming to any conclusion.

He and Mollie breakfasted together. Lavvy usually had hers in bed. Mrs. Dene, as a rule, was an early riser but Mollie reported that she was still far from well.

"I went in to her, just for a minute. She says she's all right and she's coming down presently, but I'm not very happy about her. Tony, do you think Mrs. Hall will bring her niece round this morning?"

"I shouldn't be surprised," he said gloomily. "Wish you luck."

"What do you mean? You'll be here?"

"No. I'm going up to town again."

Mollie opened her mouth to speak and thought better of it.

Perhaps, after all, if Tony had been rude to this girl he would be better out of the way. Mollie told herself that she ought to be thankful that the girl had seemed nice. She knew that she would have had to be civil to her just the same if she had been as awful as they all felt Mrs. Hall to be. How extraordinary it was that people so dissimilar as her lovely mother and Mrs. Hall could be friends, thought Mollie. It was partly, of course, that her mother was so kind-hearted, so sorry for her old school-mate who had come down in the world. Mollie sighed unconsciously as she rose from the table.

"All right," she said. "I'll take Binkie for his run. Come along, Binks." She stopped at the door. "Tony—does Mother know about the niece?"

"I expect so. Mrs. Hall will have told her."

"I think you ought to say she was in the train, Tony. I've noticed lately that when things happen suddenly Mother's lips go a funny colour."

"Have you? All right. I'll—I'll just mention it."

Tony went on to the terrace to smoke a cigarette. It was a perfect summer morning. Mrs. Dene only kept one gardener and only the small portion of the gardens that could be seen from the windows were in any kind of order, but with the sun gilding mossy paths and overgrown shrubberies the evidences of long standing neglect were hardly noticeable. Nothing could spoil the lovely curves of the ground falling away from the house to the wooded valley below and rising again to the encircling hills. The shadows of the beeches, for which both the Dower House and Lennor Park were famous, lay on the short springy turf cropped by the innumerable rabbits. Binkie was chasing one now. He saw the little dog pounding in pursuit, his young mistress following. Dear little Mollie, what a good sort she was. Worth fifty of Lavvy any day. The difference between flannel and chiffon. Good wearing stuff and a fabric that would tear at a touch.

Several of the ground floor windows were open. He walked down to the south-west corner and entered the room which his mother had made her own. She had come down and was sitting at her bureau writing a letter but she looked up with a smile as he came in. She was a slim, graceful looking woman who looked less than her fifty years. Her fair hair was beginning to turn grey and there was a network of fine lines about her large and rather wistful blue eyes, but her delicate pink and white complexion owed nothing to art. At a time when every other woman is painted she rarely even used powder.

"Tony darling—I'm just writing to the Stores. There are several things cook wants. But afterwards couldn't you take me for a run in the car—to blow the cobwebs away—"

"Of course, darling, if you like." He sat on a stool beside her and taking her left hand rubbed it gently to and fro against his cheek. She looked down at his dark head and her lips quivered a little. He used to do that when he was quite a little boy when he knew, or guessed, that she was worried about something.

"And Tony—didn't you say something about wanting to join a friend at Oxford whose father is a publisher?"

"Lambourne. Yes. I could learn the ropes with them, and after a bit become a partner. But it would mean putting down some capital, and I thought you said it was impossible."

"I've thought it over. I believe I shall be able to manage it. There's no hurry, is there?"

"No. Lambourne will be at Worcester another year at least. Thanks awfully, Mummie."

"I've got to concentrate on Lavvy and her affairs now," she said. "I don't believe in long engagements."

He could not help saying, "I don't know if Lady Lennor will agree with you."

His mother answered quickly. "That's natural. She wouldn't think any girl good enough for her son. But Lavvy will make him a good wife quite apart from her looks."

"Oh, Lavvy's equal to most occasions," he agreed.

"Just be quiet, darling, while I finish this letter."

"All right." He sat on the stool, his long legs sprawling across the bear-skin rug, his head resting against her knee, listening as her pen scratched away over the paper.

"There. That will go by the next post. Ring the bell, Tony. Parsons can bring down my hat. I still feel rather shaky."

"Was your head very bad?"

"It was rather. I was out in the sun yesterday. It was the heat." He remembered what he had to say to her.

"By the way, Mother, there was a girl in the train coming down yesterday afternoon. We talked a bit. She told me she was on her way to stay with an aunt, and—and after a while it turned out that her aunt was Mrs. Hall."

She said nothing and something in the quality of her silence startled him. He looked up at her quickly. "Mother—what's the matter?"

"I felt a twinge. I—I'm not quite right yet—"

"You ought to have a doctor."

"No. Please, Tony. Please don't fuss, dear. You were saying—something about Mrs. Hall's niece—"

"Yes. She seemed"—he hesitated—"not a bad sort of girl. Did you know she was coming?"

"No."

"Well, Mrs. Hall will be bringing her up here, I suppose," he said, trying to speak easily. He usually avoided mentioning Mrs. Hall to his mother.

"Tony—you don't mean that the girl is here, that she came yesterday afternoon to North Lodge?"

"Yes. Why not? She was met, I suppose. I—I was in a hurry. I got into the car and came away."

"I see. What time was it?"

"The 2.50 from Victoria. We got in punctually, I think. 4.27."

"But you weren't in until quite late, Tony, Parsons told me you didn't get back for dinner."

"I went for a run. Do you still want me to take you? It won't be too much for you?" he said solicitously. "You look rather white."

But she shook her head. "It will do me good. Never mind ringing. Run up yourself, dear, and get me a hat. Anything you can find."

She sat quite still while he was gone, leaning back in her chair with closed eyes. He looked at her critically when he returned.

"Better?"

She smiled up at him. "Yes—you old fuss pot."

"I'm not. You may not have known it but for a moment you looked ghastly. I don't want to frighten you, darling, but you've got to take care of yourself."

"I'll try," she said meekly.

"Then I'll fetch the car round."

CHAPTER IV

TONY MAKES AMENDS

LADY LENNOR was lunching with an old friend, now the wife of one of the Canons of Ranchester Cathedral. Lady Lennor herself was the daughter of a former Dean. She was a short, stout woman, very upright, with a weather-beaten complexion and a long upper lip. She was devoted to her only son but it was rumoured that she kept him in subjection, and her friend, who knew her views on newcomers and social climbers, ventured to express some surprise at Sir Miles' engagement. "They tell me she's a beautiful girl—but no one seems to know where they spring from—"

"It was a great shock to me," said Lady Lennor. "Six months ago we had never heard of these Denes. My dear husband sold the Dower House to Colonel Humphries thirty years ago. It has been standing empty ever since the Colonel died. I wish now that we had bought it back. These people aren't keeping it up properly. The park is a waste. They have not taken on any gamekeepers or woodmen, just one gardener to cut the grass and prune the roses, and four maids in that great house. I hear half the rooms are shut up. I believe a few people have called on them. The vicar was anxious that they should. Mrs. Dene gave him fifty pounds towards his church restoration fund. She took a stall at my bazaar for the G.F.S. I must say that the woman pays her way, and she's quite presentable, looks like a lady and speaks like a lady. And the eldest girl, Lavvy as they call her, is exceedingly pretty. Young men can be very foolish, and Miles is no exception. He did not say a word to me until he had actually asked her to marry him. He was dining there that evening, and they must have rung up a news agency within half an hour of his leaving the house, for the engagement was announced in all the principal papers the next morning. I read it myself in the *Morning Post* at breakfast. It hurt me, I must confess. I disapprove and Miles knows it, but what can I do?"

"My dear," cried the friend, "I'm so sorry for you. Will you live with them? Your lovely garden at Lennor Park. How could you bear to leave it?"

Lady Lennor answered sharply. "My dear Augusta, I shouldn't dream of leaving Lennor Park. Miles has always said he expects me to remain. In any case, if he does marry this girl it will not be for some time. He is young. And now I must be getting back. I want to do some weeding. I never let Wilson touch my new herbaceous border. There'll be no peace after this week," she added irritably. "The men will be coming to put up the stands for the pageant."

"Oh, Louisa," cried the Canon's wife. "Don't say you aren't looking forward to the pageant."

"I can't say I am. I was doubtful about it from the first, and I have the pageant to thank for Miles' entanglement. He was going to Norway with friends and stayed at home to take part in it. And the rehearsals were an excuse for the Denes. You know our episode is founded on the tradition that Charles II spent a night in the barn of Borlase's farm just before he escaped to France after Worcester. Miles is taking the part of Charles and Lavinia Dene is Nan Borlase. Well, the mischief is done. Good-bye, Augusta." She pecked her friend's cheek. "Remember me to the Canon."

Her chauffeur with her car was waiting and she drove straight home. She asked the butler who opened the door for her where Sir Miles was.

"Playing tennis, I believe, my lady, with Miss Dene. Sir Miles brought Miss Dene back to lunch here, my lady."

"I see. Very well."

Avoiding the tennis court she went out to her herbaceous border. Her son saw her there when he and Lavvy were returning to the house an hour later.

"Hallo, Mother."

Lady Lennor straightened herself with an effort. She surveyed the two white clad figures with dis-approving eyes, noting that Lavvy's long slim legs were as bare as her rounded arms. They both looked cool. Lady Lennor, who was anything but cool herself, pushed a lock of grey hair back with an earthy hand. Her face was red from stooping. "She looks like pictures of Queen Victoria," thought her future daughter-in-law, trying to suppress a smile as she noticed a smear of mud across the aristocratic high bridged nose.

"I am coming in now," said Lady Lennor. "I've just remembered that the Paiges will be here for tea."

"Will they?" said her son. "We shan't be here. I promised to take Lavvy back to the Dower House."

"Very well," said his mother coldly.

The boy and girl passed on. The stumpy little woman, standing with the basket full of weeds at her feet, looked after them and saw the two, walking hand in hand and swinging their rackets, through a mist of tears. Was she losing Miles?

The young man, meanwhile, turned half apologetically to his companion. "I hope you don't mind my planting myself on you for tea. I simply can't stick the old General and his wife."

"I don't mind a bit, of course. Mother'll be charmed to have you."

"Right. Then we'll buzz off."

Lavinia would have agreed to almost any suggestion he cared to make. She was still very much on her best behaviour with the Lennors. Sir Miles was a sandy-haired young man, not unlike his formidable old mother in appearance, but taller and better looking. He was, Lavvy knew, conventional and perhaps rather narrow in his ideas. He was inclined to lay down the law to her on more than one subject, and she listened with a docility that would have amused her brother Tony if he had been there to hear. Sir Miles was very much in love, but Lavvy did not feel quite sure of him yet. He was far less servile in his adoration than any of her former admirers, perhaps because his position was so much more assured. He must, of course, realise that he was an exceedingly good match for her. Lavvy, who was far from slow where her own interests were concerned, understood that though he had ignored his mother's wishes in becoming engaged to her he would expect her to treat Lady Lennor with the utmost respect. Lavvy, knowing that in the older woman she had an un-sparing critic, not of her looks for they were above criticism, but of her every word and gesture, would have felt it rather a relief to get away from her and back to the less exacting atmosphere of the Dower House if it had not been for one thing.

Sir Miles touched on that one thing as she settled herself beside him in his sports car.

"I say, every time I've been to your house that Mrs. Hall's been there. Is she a relation, or what?"

"No relation," said Lavvy quickly.

Sir Miles was glad to hear it. He had not been favourably impressed by Mrs. Hall.

"I see. I noticed she called you Lavvy."

The girl winced. "Yes. But I haven't really known her long. She and Mother were girls together. Mother lost sight of her for years and years, and then she suddenly turned up again. She—she's had a lot of trouble, I believe, and Mother's awfully kind-hearted."

"Mrs. Hall takes advantage of her kindness?"

"We think so. Yes. But we daren't say so to Mummie. But it's really rather spoilt things at home for all of us lately. We have to take her for drives and play bridge with her, and if she wins we have to pay her and if she loses she says I'll owe it you—" Lavvy stopped, wondering if she had said too much, but Miles, when he answered, sounded quite sympathetic. "Rotten for you, but of course one can't help admiring Mrs. Dene for being loyal to an old friend."

The village, with its thatched cottages clustered around a green and its old flint-walled church, lay between Lennor Park and the smaller estate of the Dower House. Sir Miles drove more slowly with a watchful eye on a small child swinging on a gate and some fowls rooting in the ditch. An avenue of limes led from the south lodge gate to the house. They were half way up it when Lavvy said "There's Tony." Miles saw young Dene a hundred yards away. He was carrying a golf club and his sister's Cairn terrier was trotting at his heels. Lavvy had waved to him and he waved back but he did not stop. "What's he doing?"

"Practising shots apparently," said Lavvy. "He often does. Poor darling, he's the world's worst golfer. He can't see very well."

"Rotten luck," said Miles perfunctorily. He was not really interested.

Tony, meanwhile, walked on rejoicing that he had seen them in time to avoid them. Lavvy would not need him to help entertain her young man. Mollie had gone down to the vicarage to help make cardboard armour for Cromwell's soldiers, and his mother was lying down. Though she said she had enjoyed her drive she had looked very tired at lunch. Lavvy and her baronet could have tea together. They certainly would not want him. He put his golf ball in his pocket and walked on briskly, swinging his club. Binkie, though he lingered now and then to inspect a rabbit hole, always caught up with him sooner or later. Tony had walked round the foot of the curious cone shaped hill that rose between the house and the wilder and more overgrown part of the park on the edge of the heath. It was because of the hill that one could not see the north gate and lodge even from the upper windows of the Dower House. During the craze for landscape gardening in the middle of the eighteenth century, Capability Brown had come to Lennor Park, and, acting on his advice, a grove of trees had been planted on the summit of the hill around a small circular summer house like a pagan temple. It looked dank and forlorn from a distance and Tony had never troubled to climb the hill to get a closer view of it.

He was not thinking of the temple now. He was thinking of the girl in the train. To be quite accurate, he was thinking of what she might be thinking about him and that sudden impulsive rush of his into the corridor. He had not realised at the time how it must seem to her. After all, it was not her fault that her aunt had got on his nerves. When, at a sudden turn in the path he was following, he came face to face with the girl herself he turned scarlet but he held his ground. Hadn't he come this way hoping for just such an accidental encounter that would give him a chance to put himself right with her?

She gave a little gasp. "Oh—"

"I say," he began, "I'm most awfully glad to find you again. I—I had to rush off yesterday. I—I can't explain why. I hope you didn't think—I mean—" He gazed at her imploringly.

Amy was not inclined to be hard on him. There was something that she did not understand, but apparently he had decided that it need not prevent them from being friends, and that was all that mattered at the moment.

"That's all right," she said. "You can't think how nice it is to have somebody to speak to. I've quite decided that I wouldn't care to be a hermit or an anchorite."

"You don't care for the country?"

"It isn't that. Aunt Harriet didn't meet me at the station. I had to walk and have my luggage brought along by the baker. I didn't mind that, but when I got to the Lodge there was nobody there. I supposed my aunt had gone out. I waited and waited—" her voice shook slightly. "She hasn't come back."

He stared at her. "Mrs. Hall? How extraordinary. She expected you?"

"Yes. She told me to come on Monday."

"You are sure there's no mistake? It wasn't next Monday?"

She shook her head. "I don't know what to do." She had turned with him and they were walking in the direction from which she had come.

"If I were you," he said, "I should carry on until she comes back. Unless you'd rather go home, of course. I'd run you to the station if you like, but I do hope you'll stay."

"I haven't got a home," she said. "I think the idea is that I'm to live with Aunt Harriet if we get on. I don't know her really. I suppose you are the friends she spoke of."

"I suppose so," he said in rather an odd voice, she thought. She glanced up at him uncertainly. "You live at the big house? I caught a glimpse of it through the trees when I walked round that hill just now."

"Yes."

"Then my aunt is your tenant?"

"Not exactly. My mother is letting her have the use of the North Lodge. They—they are old friends, I believe. There's no question of rent."

He could not quite keep the bitterness out of his voice when he referred to Mrs. Hall. The girl noticed it but she only said: "It's a dear little place, and I should love it if I wasn't alone in it." They had reached the little gate in the toy palings. "Would you come in and have a cup of tea with me?" Tony hesitated. Mrs. Hall had often asked him and his sisters to tea with her when she first came to the lodge, but they had always made some excuse. Now—he realised that if he was to go on seeing this girl he would have to modify his attitude to her aunt. After all, he thought, there was no question of putting himself under any obligation. He knew Mrs. Hall's habit of bringing an empty basket when she came to see his mother and filling it from their store cupboard. And so, after a pause that was hardly perceptible, he said:

"Thanks awfully," and followed Amy up the path to the door.

She left him in the sitting-room while she ran into the kitchen to put the kettle on the oil stove and set the tray. Tony's face hardened as he looked about him. What a grabber the woman was! Not satisfied with having the place repainted and papered at his mother's expense she had calmly picked out some of their best bits of furniture for her use.

The little bureau had stood in his uncle's study in the house in Chelsea. He had given his mother that lustre bowl for a birthday present three years ago, and he and Mollie had bought her that brass Buddha at a shop in the King's Road. It was strange, he thought, that his mother, who could be so firm with her own children, was so foolishly yielding and compliant with this friend of her girlhood. She had let Uncle Edward bully her, of course, but that was different. They all understood that.

Uncle Edward had paid for their education. It was for their sake, and especially for the sake of Lavvy, her golden girl, that she had lived a joyless life year after year in that gloomy house, the unpaid housekeeper and domestic drudge of that harsh old man. But he had left her all his money. She was free now—

Amy broke in upon his thoughts, coming in with her laden tray. Soon they were talking as volubly as they had talked in the train.

"Aunt Harriet's got quite a lot of books," she said presently, "but they aren't all hers. Some are yours. I saw your name in them."

"Very likely," he said. He wondered what Amy would think of her aunt's methods when she got to know her better. It must be awful to be ashamed of one's relations. Amy, he felt certain, was not in the least like that.

He turned to call Binkie to order. The little dog was sniffing earnestly in the farther corner of the room.

Amy asked if she might give him a biscuit.

"He'll be charmed. By the way, have you food enough until your aunt returns?"

"Oh yes."

Did she expect him to ask her to come back with him to make the acquaintance of his mother and sisters? To her, no doubt, that would seem only natural. But what would Lavvy and Mollie say if he did that? They felt even more strongly than he did about Mrs. Hall. In becoming friendly with this girl he was being disloyal to them. He got up abruptly.

"Thanks for the tea. I'm afraid I must be going—"

Amy's face fell. She had been in the middle of a sentence. Evidently he had not been listening. She was beginning to realise that this young man was as difficult as he was attractive. He seemed to be subject to sudden changes of mood.

"I've enjoyed having someone to talk to," she said rather plaintively.

"Poor kid," he thought again, and then, hardening his heart, told himself that he must stick to his own side. He might talk Mollie over—he was not so sure of Lavvy—but he could not spring her on them without some preparation.

He moved towards the door. "Binkie—where's Binkie?"

Amy looked round and saw that the door leading into the kitchen was open a few inches. "He must have slipped out."

Tony followed her into the kitchen. The back door was open too and there was no sign of the dog.

"He must have run into the garden. I left it open because the kitchen gets so hot when the oil stove is on."

The long narrow strip of ground, enclosed on one side by the park wall and on the other by a straggling hedge, was already in shadow. A few gnarled apple trees struggled to survive in a wilderness of briars, and dead gooseberry bushes choked with bindweed sprawled across what had once been a path. Binkie was barking excitedly somewhere at the farther end. Tony called him, but he did not come.

"He's found a hedgehog, I expect," he said. "I'll have to fetch the little beast."

He started down the path. What a wilderness it was. Probably before long, he reflected, Mrs. Hall would be asking his mother to send a man to dig it up. He wondered she had not done so already. Damn these gooseberry bushes. He had torn his trousers and scratched his leg. He felt warm drops trickling down his ankle. He got another scratch on the back of his hand as one of the branches he had thrust aside swung back on him. He swore again. "Binkie. Come here, you little devil."

He could see Binkie now. The dog was scraping away vigorously at what looked like boards laid on the ground in the midst of a bed of nettles. As he drew nearer he saw that it was the cover of a well.

CHAPTER V
THE WELL

TONY WAS some time gone. At last Amy, waiting at the back door, saw him coming back, forcing his way through the tangle of bushes. He was carrying Binkie under his arm and the little dog was wriggling and trying to lick his master's hand.

"Well?" she said, trying to sound cheerful. "Was it a hedge-hog?"

"No."

Her smile faded as he came nearer and she saw how white he looked. "What's the matter?" she asked anxiously. "Have you hurt yourself?"

"No. Come inside."

She followed him into the kitchen. "What is it?"

Tony's lips felt stiff. He found it difficult to speak.

"Something pretty awful has happened, I'm afraid. You can't stay here. Just chuck what you need for the night into a bag. You're coming home with me now."

"Why?" she persisted. "Anyway, I can't do that."

"You must. Can't you trust me?"

They faced one another in the narrow space between the table and her bedroom door. "I do trust you, Tony"—neither of them noticed at the time that she had used his name, but he remembered it afterwards. "I do. But I've got to know what's the matter before I leave. After all, I'm responsible to Aunt Harriet."

"All right," he said. "There's a disused well at the end of the garden. Binkie was scraping at the cover. I lifted it and looked in. There was somebody there—a face—"

"Are—are you sure it wasn't the reflection of your own?"

"Of course I'm sure," he said roughly. "Try to have some sense." It was a relief to his overstrained nerves to scold her. "We've got to do something about it. How much more time are you going to waste? Why the hell can't you do what you're told?"

"I'm sorry," she said faintly.

He thought she was going to fall. His face changed. "I'm a brute." He put out his left arm and held her rather tightly.

"Oh!" she gasped, and hid her face on his shoulder.

He was greatly embarrassed and more touched than he would have cared to admit. "This is pretty ghastly for you," he mumbled.

She drew away. "I'm all right now. I'll get my things together—"

He took her suitcase from her and followed her down the path. They had walked some way when she spoke.

"Are there any lodgings I could go to in the village?"

"There may be," he said, "but you must see my mother first. The village is farther off, in any case. I must go home first and telephone."

"To the police?"

To his relief she asked no more questions. He shifted the suitcase from one hand to the other. Evidently she had put in a good deal more than she would need for one night. Just as well, he thought. They had skirted the hill with its pseudo-classic grove and temple and were crossing the stretch of turf before the house. Anyone could see them now from the front windows or the terrace.

"It's a large place," said Amy, breaking another silence.

"Yes. Absurdly too big for us. As a matter of fact half the rooms are shut up." He muttered something about eyewash.

Amy said nothing. She felt that in the last few minutes they had drawn apart. He was thinking of his own people now, of his mother and sisters. It had not escaped her notice that he had not asked her up to the house until this had happened. She was not at all sure that she would be welcome. She lagged a little as they crossed the gravel sweep to the front door.

The parlourmaid was crossing the hall with a tray of silver. Tony spoke to her.

"Where is Mrs. Dene, Parsons?"

"She's been resting, Mr. Anthony, but she said she would be down for dinner."

"Either of my sisters about?"

"They are both dressing. I heard Miss Lavinia drawing the bath water just now."

"Oh damn," said Tony. He rumpled his hair. "Let me think. Come in here and wait, Miss Steer. Do you mind?" He took her into the drawing-room. "Just wait here while I get on with it. You'll be all right here, won't you?" he said anxiously.

He looked so young with his hair standing up on end, and so worried that she felt a queer little pang.

"I shall be perfectly all right," she assured him.

"You will? Good. I'll come back as soon as I can." He left her and a moment later she heard him speaking over the telephone. He had closed the door and she could not catch what he was saying. She leaned back in her chair and closed her eyes. She felt very tired.

Tony had rung up the police station at Ranchester and had been told that Sergeant Lindo would come over immediately. He hung up the receiver and went upstairs. He met Mollie on the landing.

"Tony," the began accusingly, "I saw you out of my window walking with that girl and carrying her suitcase—"

"Shut up," he said brusquely. "I left her in the drawing-room. If you shout like that she'll hear you."

"I don't care if she does. You might have waited for her aunt to shove her on to us"—she broke off as he turned and she saw his face. "Tony! What is it—"

He answered wearily. "I'm just going to tell mother. You'd better come with me."

They found their mother seated at her dressing-table. She had changed into a black velvet gown and was just fastening her pearl necklace. Her mirror reflected her silvery hair and worn but still lovely face. She spoke without turning her head.

"Come in. Is that you, Tony? You're late. Be quick and change. Sir Miles is coming back to dinner with us and afterwards he is going to run us over to Ranchester to see some film."

"Hell—" mumbled Tony. He turned to his sister. "Mollie, run down and ring up Lennor Park. Tell him there's been an accident. Anything you like to stop him from coming."

He pushed her out of the room and came back himself. Mrs. Dene was transferring the odds and ends she always carried about with her from a day to an evening bag.

"What are you two whispering about? Come round here, Tony. Don't stand behind me."

"Mother—I'm afraid I'm going to upset you. Something very unpleasant has happened. It—it was like this. I met Mrs. Hall's niece in the park. She told me she was alone at North Lodge. Her aunt wasn't there when she arrived yesterday evening. I walked back with her and we talked a bit. Then Binkie ran down the garden and wouldn't come back. I had to fetch him. Mother, can I get you anything?"

She said in a low voice: "That bottle and that little glass on the shelf. Thank you, dear. Pour out as far as the line. Thanks."

She took the glass from him and sipped the pale milky fluid.

"Shall I go on, Mother?"

"Yes, dear. You don't imagine I am taking this to fortify me against your story, do you? It is time for my dose, that's all."

"I see," he said, "but it's bound to upset you. It's pretty damned awful."

The door opened again and Mollie came in.

"I couldn't stop him, Tony," she said breathlessly. "He'd already started."

The young man groaned. "He would—"

"Tony," said his mother sharply, "I wish you would come to the point."

"All right," said Tony loudly. "The reason why Mrs. Hall wasn't at the Lodge when her niece arrived is that she's drowned herself in the well at the end of the garden."

Mollie uttered a smothered shriek. "Tony, how horrible."

Mrs. Dene said nothing at all. Tony went on talking like a machine that has been wound up and has to go on.

"I saw her face and one arm and her black dress like a sort of balloon floating on the top of the water. It was Binkie who found her really. He kept on barking and wouldn't come back. I should never have gone down there otherwise. I had to get through a lot of thorny stuff. Tore my trousers and scratched my hands. I think I'll change into another suit before Sergeant what's-his-name comes. I brought the girl along here, Mother. I thought that would be what you'd want. I haven't actually told her. At least, not who it is. She may have guessed. You'll be decent to her, Mollie?"

"Oh, Mummie," Mollie knelt down impulsively by her mother and threw her arms round her waist. "This is awful for you, I know. You were fond of her. I'm so sorry I wasn't nicer to her, Mummie. I didn't know she was unhappy."

"She must have been to do a thing like that. But you can't blame yourself, darling. You were kindness itself to her. I did my best," said her mother in a far-away voice.

"She may have gone mad," said Mollie. "People do sometimes, quite suddenly—"

Tony left them together. He went to his room and washed his hands and face. The scratch on his leg had bled a good deal and he wiped it with a sponge. He had just changed into another suit of grey flannels when Parsons came to his door.

"Sergeant Lindo to see you, sir. He said you had sent for him so I showed him into the breakfast room."

"Quite right. I'll come down."

Perhaps he had been foolish to try to stop Lennor from coming to dinner. But of course they could not go to the Pictures and it would be rather awkward. Still—Tony knew he was apt to get worked up over things. Life had to go on. He was relieved to find that Sergeant Lindo was a plain clothes officer, but there was another policeman in uniform standing by the window. The sergeant, a tall, soldierly-looking man with a small toothbrush moustache, had taken up his position on the hearthrug with his back to the fireless grate.

Lindo gave him a quick measuring glance as he entered.

"Mr. Dene? Mrs. Dene's son? I see. I gather that a body has been found in a well on your estate?"

"Yes. In the garden of the North Lodge."

"Can we get there by car?"

"Oh yes. The road is grass grown. That gate is never used now. But if your car has good springs—"

"Then we'll go there at once. It's past eight. It will be dark soon."

Tony saw Sir Miles Lennor's Bentley outside as he went out with the two policemen to their car. He supposed Sir Miles must here arrived while he was upstairs and gone to find Lavvy on the terrace. He hoped Mollie would look after the girl he had left in the drawing-room. He had not been able to fulfil his promise to go back to her. The sergeant was asking questions. He answered them as best he could, describing how the gruesome discovery had been made. He heard himself saying "It was Binkie—" and wondered how often he would have to repeat the story. He was sick of it already. They had reached the Lodge. Lindo stopped the car and they got out.

The sergeant glanced appreciatively at the little one-storied building with its lattice windows, thatched roof and creeper covered porch. "Very pretty. Nice little garden."

"Yes. Mrs. Hall must have worked at it, weeding and planting seeds to get all those flowers in a few months."

"She hadn't been here long?"

"Since the early spring. She hadn't touched the back garden. You'll see."

"Can we get to it without passing through the cottage? Yes, I see there's a path round one side." Tony hung back. "Could I wait in the car? You can't miss it—"

Lindo looked at him. "You had a bit of a shock, eh?" he said, not unkindly. "I'm sorry, but I'm afraid I shall have to ask you to go with us."

He stood aside and Tony saw that he was expected to lead the way.

"One really needs a billhook," he said, "to clear the path. Mind that branch!"

They came to a well cover on the patch of comparatively clear ground close to the ditch and hedge at the bottom of the garden. The marks of the Cairn's sharp teeth and claws were plain on the edge of one of the rotting cross pieces.

"One moment," said Lindo. "Tell me exactly what you did."

"My dog was barking and scratching away just here. I pulled him away and lifted the cover. It isn't so heavy. I hadn't expected to find a well, and they always rather fascinate me. I mean, they're sort of creepy. I looked in. I saw—a face floating in the dark water and something like a huge black bubble that I think must have been part of her skirt filled with air. But you can see for yourselves."

"You replaced the well cover before you left. Why was that?"

"I don't know. I suppose I did it mechanically. I was feeling rather sick as a matter of fact."

"Just so. Very natural," said Lindo. "I shall be getting you to make a statement later on, Mr. Dene. That will do for the present. You can lift the cover now, Collins."

The constable obeyed. The hinges creaked but the cover came up, as Tony had said, quite easily. The well was lined with brick and a few ferns and plants grew near the top. The two policemen stared down into the pit. Tony stepped back and turned his head away.

There was rather a long pause. Tony was just beginning to wonder if he could possibly have been mistaken when Lindo spoke.

"Yes. And you say it's a woman named Hall, the tenant of this cottage, Mr. Dene?"

"I thought it was. I can't be certain—"

"Quite. I can just distinguish a head and a mass of dark clothing."

"How are you going to get her out?" asked Tony, hoping that he would not be asked to assist in the process. Lindo did not answer at once. He seemed to be thinking hard. Finally he said, "You can replace that cover, Collins. Can we use your telephone, Mr. Dene?"

"Of course."

"Good." He wrote something in his notebook, tore out the page and handed it to his subordinate. "Go back to the Dower House. Give that message to the Superintendent, and come back to me. You can take the car; it will save a few minutes. You'll find me in the Lodge. You'll remain with me, Mr. Dene."

Collins saluted and turned smartly on his heel. The sergeant walked slowly up the path to the back door. He had grown noticeably more silent but he spoke to Tony as he crossed the threshold. "The deceased—I am assuming that the body in the well is that of Mrs. Hall—the deceased lived quite alone here?"

"Yes. At least—a niece was going to stay with her, but she only arrived yesterday."

"Where is she now?"

"At the Dower House. She's quite young. I couldn't leave her here under the circumstances."

"Oh—well, I'll be seeing her later. You stay here, Mr. Dene, while I have a look round the other rooms. Please don't touch anything."

"History repeats itself," thought Tony as he stood by the kitchen table and heard the sergeant moving from room to room, opening and shutting drawers. It seemed a long time since he had waited there for Amy. He took a cigarette from his case and lit it. The sergeant seemed to be making a very thorough search. What did he expect to find? He was still in Mrs. Hall's bedroom when Collins returned, but he came out when he heard him.

"Did you get through?"

"Yes, sergeant. The Superintendent says he's leaving you in charge of the case. The others will be along under the hour. Doctor Pearson was out, but he'll get him."

"Good. Then you'll go back to the well now, Collins, and stay there until you are relieved. Keep off all unauthorised persons. It'll be an all night job, I'm afraid. Don't tramp about more than you can help. I want to make a much more thorough examination of the spot and get some photographs as soon as it's light. You can go."

He turned to Tony as Collins went out.

"Nice little place this," he said appreciatively, "and perfectly kept. Spit and polish. Reminds one of the army."

"Yea. You haven't found a farewell letter or anything, I suppose? They do leave one sometimes, don't they, addressed to the coroner?"

Lindo looked hard at the young man.

"Are you suggesting that this was a case of suicide?"

Tony stared back at him. His heart seemed to miss a beat.

"Well—wasn't it?"

"By your own showing it couldn't have been," said Lindo. "Think, man, think. You told us yourself the well was covered."

Tony tried to speak and failed.

Lindo uttered the word he shrank from.

"It's murder," said the sergeant. "Murder. And you've started the machinery whose wheels will only cease running when the culprit has been brought to justice. You've been a bit slow, if you'll excuse my saying so, to see all the implications, but the fact remains that you set the law in motion, Mr. Dene. You put the penny in the slot, in a manner of speaking. It'll be something for you to remember."

"Don't!" said Tony.

Chapter VI

TROUBLE AT THE DOWER HOUSE

When Tony had left them Mrs. Dene turned to Mollie. She was very pale, but she was less prostrated by the shock than Mollie had expected.

"Go at once and tell Lavvy. We don't want Sir Miles here. She had better ask him to take her to dine in Ranchester before going to the Pictures. Well—perhaps not the Pictures. He can take her for a run in the car afterwards. The point is we can't have him here. Lavvy will understand. Tell her Harriet has drowned herself. That's all we know at present. She can tell Miles. He'll keep away then for his own sake."

"All right, Mummie."

Mollie went to her sister's room.

Lavvy had just left the bathroom and was sitting on the end of her bed drawing on a stocking like a cobweb. She went on dressing while Mollie explained. When she had done she said "Hell!"

"I know."

"Miles will hate it, and so will his beastly mother. Whatever made her do it? A well. Like a mouse in a bucket of water. Ghastly. She must have gone mad. I always thought her queer. Get my blue coat out of the wardrobe, Mollie. I'll lie in wait for Miles on the terrace. Expect me when you see me."

Mollie went back to her mother's room.

During her absence Mrs. Dene had rung for Parsons and given her orders.

"The police have come, Mollie. I'm going to have something to eat here. You'll have to cope with that girl Tony brought here. I've told Parsons to get the room next to yours ready for her at once and to bring you both up some food to your room. You can be quiet there. You can bring her to me presently."

"Yes, Mummie."

But when Mollie very reluctantly entered the drawing-room, to cope, as her mother put it, with the stranger, there was no one there. She had waited, listening on the landing, until her brother and the two policemen had left the house, and after that she had run back to her room to fetch a coat.

She rang. The bell was answered this time by Duncan, the housemaid. "Parsons is just getting the trays ready, miss."

"All right. I only wanted to know what had happened to the young lady Mr. Anthony brought in here."

Duncan looked about her rather as if she expected to see the young person in question hiding under one of the chairs.

"I can't say, miss, I'm sure," she said defensively. "I've been upstairs getting the spare room ready."

Duncan, who had been in service in a titled family, had an unconcealed contempt for her present employers and was leaving at the end of the month. Mollie looked at her for a moment. Then she said, "Very well, Duncan. Ask Parsons to leave the trays and come to me here."

Parsons was older than the housemaid and kinder hearted. Her tone, when she came in, was quite respectful. She even permitted herself to betray a little human sympathy for the harassed Mollie.

"She was in here, miss, when I was looking for Mr. Anthony to tell him the police had arrived. Sitting in that chair, she was—"

"Did you speak to her?"

"Only to say 'I beg your pardon.' I think she was crying, miss, or perhaps she just had a cold."

"Oh dear!" said Mollie. "I promised I'd look after her. What can have become of her?"

"She had a suitcase with her," said Parsons. "If you ask me, miss, I think she got tired of waiting. Or perhaps—"

"Yes, what? Go on, Parsons."

"I was going to say, miss, that policeman's got a loud voice. When he said 'I'm Sergeant Lindo'—well, you could have heard him half a mile off. I just thought—some people are afraid of the police, miss."

"That's rather far-fetched, Parsons," said Mollie repressively. "But she was upset. She's Mrs. Hall's niece come down to stay with her, and—I'll tell you now though perhaps you've heard it already—we're afraid poor Mrs. Hall has committed suicide."

"Indeed, miss," said Parsons. She waited a minute, "What am I to do about the trays, miss?"

"Oh, bother food!" said Mollie. "I'll have mine with Mother."

"Very good, miss."

Parsons retired in good order to the kitchen where the cook and the between maid were waiting to hear the latest bulletin.

"Old Mother Hall has done herself in," announced Parsons in the loud uncontrolled voice she reserved for conversation with her fellows.

"Did you ever!" the cook was agreeably thrilled. "Well, I shan't cry my eyes out. I'm sick of making cakes for her to take away with her. Talk about a locust. Done herself in. What did I tell you, Gladys, when I told your fortune last night? The Queen of Spades three times running. Trouble, I said. The cards can't lie. But whatever did she do it for? She was in clover here, free to help herself and no questions asked."

"Ah," said Parsons mysteriously, "that remains to be seen. Young Tony brought a girl along who's supposed to be the old woman's niece, parked her in the drawing-room and forgot her. Now she's hopped it. Poor Miss Mollie's in a taking about it. I'm sorry for that child, cook. Now what about that soup and the cold cherry tart? She and Mrs. Dene are going to eat off a tray in Mrs. Dene's room."

"Silly, I call it," grumbled the cook, giving the soup a final stir. "What's to stop them having their meals?"

Parsons knew. "Sir Miles was coming. Might have been awkward having him there with Mrs. Hall's niece, if she's anything like her aunt. Lavvy was lying in wait for him. They were off together within five minutes."

Gladys had been listening, open-mouthed. "Coo! Will there be an inquest, Miss Parsons?"

"There's the front door bell," said Parsons. "I'll go. You can slip up with the tray, Ruby. Use the back stairs."

"Shan't," said Duncan flatly. "It isn't my work."

"Thank you, dear. You are kind and helpful, aren't you. Here, Glad, you take it. Mrs. Dene's room. Mind you knock before you go barging in."

Gladys, nothing loth, seized the tray, and Parsons went upstairs to answer the door.

Tony Dene came into the hall, closely followed by Sergeant Lindo. The sergeant spoke to Parsons.

"Any telephone calls since my man was here?"

"No, sir."

"Right. Wait a minute." He crossed the hall and took up the receiver, giving the number of the Ranchester police station.

"Sergeant Lindo speaking . . . yes . . . the doctor hasn't started? Good. Tell him early in the morning will do. It's light by five . . . what did you say? Too early? Well, six, then. . . . What? . . . I don't want anything touched while it's too dark to see marks of a possible struggle. . . . Yes. Beyond a doubt. Good-bye."

He hung up the receiver and came back to where Parsons stood demurely by the door. Tony had lit another cigarette and was wandering aimlessly about the hall with his hands in his pockets.

"Can I have the room I was shown into when I arrived, Mr. Dene?"

"The breakfast-room? Certainly."

Lindo turned to the parlourmaid. "Will you ask the young lady Mr. Dene brought here a couple of hours ago to see me."

"She isn't here, sir."

"What?" shouted Lindo.

Tony, who had been looking at them rather vacantly, suddenly came to life. "What do you mean? What's become of her? I asked Mollie—"

"She wasn't there when Miss Mollie went into the drawing-room, sir. I think myself she got tired of waiting and has gone down to the village."

"I see," said the young man gloomily, "she did say something about getting lodgings there. She was afraid she mightn't be welcome. And of course if no one went near her. Oh damn—"

The bell rang again. Parsons opened the door and disclosed a saloon car at the foot of the steps and two stalwart policemen on the mat. Lindo beckoned to them to follow him into the breakfast-room. All three went in, dosing the door after them.

Tony looked at Parsons. "I suppose you'll all be giving notice?" he said unwisely.

Parsons replied in a voice that was as wooden as her face, "Am I to wait now, sir?"

"No. He'll ring if he wants anything, I suppose. Where's everybody?"

"Miss Lavinia has gone out in Sir Miles Lennor's car. Miss Mollie is upstairs with Mrs. Dene." Parsons went back to the kitchen. Tony had reached the foot of the stairs when the breakfast-room door was opened and he was called back.

"Will you ask Mrs. Dene if she can spare me a few moments, Mr. Dene. I can't get much further to-night, but I must ask a few questions, just as a matter of form."

"Oh—very well."

Lindo watched the young man thoughtfully as he went slowly up the broad shallow flight of stairs to the first landing. No doubt he usually took those stairs two at a time. He went back to his two subordinates. "You'll spend the night in the Lodge, Gibbs. Don't touch more than you can help. Parlow will be going over it to-morrow for finger prints and he won't want to find too many of yours." Gibbs grinned and departed.

"You go back to the car and wait, Smith. I'll call you back presently. You'll remain here, in the house. I shall be going down to the village presently and I shall get a room at the Lennor Arms or the King's Head. I shall be up at the Lodge round about half-past five."

The sergeant went back to the telephone. The village constable had been out on his beat when he rang up before and his wife had answered for him. He was at home now, and Lindo gave him some instructions. He was back in the breakfast-room when Mrs. Dene entered. Her son came with her.

"Look here, Sergeant, I'm going down to the village to look for Miss Steer. She's absolutely alone here—"

Lindo interrupted. "That's all right, Mr. Dene. I'll see to that. I'd rather you didn't go out again to-night if you don't mind." He spoke civilly but the note of authority was unmistakable. Tony reddened, but feeling the warning pressure of his mother's hand on his arm, said no more.

Lindo drew forward a chair. "Will you sit here, Mrs. Dene? I'm so sorry to bother you. It will soon be over. Will you switch on the light as you go out, Mr. Dene?"

Tony looked at his mother. "Would you rather I stayed?"

"No, dear."

When the young man had left them Lindo sat down. "I'm sorry to trouble you," he said again. His keen eyes had grown kinder since they rested on Mrs. Dene's worn but still lovely face. Lindo was by way of being a woman hater, he disliked the hardness of the modern type, but there was nothing of the metallic brilliance he found so repulsive about Mrs. Dene. She had wrapped a shawl of silver lamé over her shoulders that matched the shining waves of hair that framed her clear-cut face. She was very pale.

"I want to do anything I can to help, naturally," she said. "I suppose you are quite certain that the body you have found is that of Mrs. Hall?"

"No. We can't be certain until we have got it out of the well." He frowned as he spoke. He was not sure if his superiors would approve of his having left the body where it was. He had his reasons, but would they be regarded as sufficient? "When did you last see Mrs. Hall, madam?"

"She had tea with us here in the garden on Sunday and left about six o'clock to walk back across the park to the Lodge."

"Did she seem to be in her usual spirits?"

"Oh quite. In unusually good spirits, in fact."

"Did she mention the fact that a niece was coming to stay with her?"

"No, she didn't. But there is nothing surprising in that. She did not talk about herself or her plans."

"Not even to you, Mrs. Dene? You were old friends, were you not?"

"Yes."

"She was not a nervous woman, not afraid of tramps, for instance?"

"I don't think she would get tramps at the Lodge. It's such a long way from the main road. But in any case she would not have minded. She was very self-reliant."

"She came up here practically every day to see you?"

"Nearly every day. Yes."

"In the morning?"

"Sometimes. Any time she felt like it."

"Did she come yesterday morning?"

"Yes, she did. I was out. She wanted a cake, and cook let her have one she had just baked. She left a note for me—"

"What about?"

"It was of no importance. Just to say she was sorry she had missed me, and that she had asked for the cake and hoped I didn't mind—"

"So she wrote it here?"

"Yes. I suppose she must have done. I found it on the hall table when I came in."

"Could I see it?"

She looked rather surprised. "I'm sorry. I'm afraid I destroyed it."

"That's a pity. You see, Mrs. Dene, a hand-writing expert might have learned from comparing it with another specimen of her writing whether she was agitated or in any way not her normal self."

"I see," said Mrs. Dene faintly. "Poor Harriet. I can't imagine why she should take her own life."

"Very sad," said Lindo rather mechanically, as if his thoughts were elsewhere. He stood up. "I am much obliged to you, Mrs. Dene. By the way, I gathered from your son that Mrs. Hall was living at the Lodge rent free?"

"Yes. She had had losses—"

"Just so. She was in straitened circumstances?"

"Yes—"

"She wouldn't be likely to have much money in the house?"

"I should not think so."

"I won't keep you any longer now, Mrs. Dene. Thank you." He opened the door for her and gave her a little bow as she passed out. Her son was waiting for her in the hall. She took his arm and they went up the stairs together. She was a tall woman and the black head and the silver head were nearly on a level.

"Good looking family," thought Lindo. "Not the boy, though there's something pleasant about him." He felt sorry for them. He had deliberately left Mrs. Dene under the impression that her friend had committed suicide. She looked so frail that he was reluctant to give her a further shock. She would learn the truth soon enough. Meanwhile, and until the body was taken out of the well and identified, he did not see that he could do very much more. There was the girl, described as Mrs. Hall's niece, who had arrived at the North Lodge the previous day and spent the night alone there. Her story might throw some light on the mystery of Mrs. Hall's disappearance.

Lindo drove down to the village and stopped at the King's Head. The village constable, who had been instructed to look out for Miss Steer, was standing in the doorway and came forward to speak to the sergeant.

"She come in ten minutes ago and asked if she could have a room. Luckily I got here first, in time to give Potter an 'int. So he said she might. She's upstairs now."

"Did you see her? What sort of young woman is she?"

The constable answered promptly. "Nothing like the aunt. Nicely dressed and pleasant spoken."

"One of the capable, efficient type, ready for anything?"

"I wouldn't say that either. You could see she'd been upset. Her voice shook a bit. She seemed timid-like. Now the aunt—not that she often came down the village—"

"How did she strike you?"

"I'd rather not say. But how a real lady like Mrs. Dene could make a friend of such a one—though times are changed as my old father always says, and the way the gentry dress and undress, and them bare backs and all—"

Lindo grinned "Just so. Well, I shall probably spend the night here myself. You can go home now, Dutton. I'll look after Miss Steer."

"Very good, Sergeant." The constable saluted, got on his bicycle and rode away.

CHAPTER VII

DING DONG BELL

AN HOUR LATER Sergeant Lindo sat over a belated supper in the sitting-room of the King's Head. Mrs. Potter had exerted herself to cook a savoury dish of sausages and mashed, and the sergeant, who had missed his tea, was doing it full justice. Afterwards he would smoke a pipe and retire to bed with an alarum clock, borrowed from the barman, and set at four thirty. There was no doubt in his mind that the body in the well would prove to be that of Mrs. Hall. He had heard all Amy Steer had to tell him. It threw no light on the tragedy beyond proving, if she was to be believed, that the murder had been committed before six o'clock on Monday evening. Some time between noon when Mrs. Hall left the Dower House with the newly-baked cake, and six. Well, that didn't help much. No use theorising at this stage. A tramp, or one of these fellows hawking odds and ends about the country. These chaps who had been through the War, shell-shocked and what not, might lose control and hit out. Yes, but how would a man like that know about the disused well? If it had not been for the dog running down the garden she might not have been found for weeks. What had the girl said exactly? She was crying. He had not cared to press her overmuch. Her story seemed right enough, but it was queer that the aunt should be done in just as the niece arrived. Was there some connection? Was the girl as simple as she seemed? She had said she was out of a job, but even to the sergeant's masculine eyes her clothes looked not only good but new. Her suitcase, too, was a new one, and it was not one of those cheap affairs of imitation leather, and she had left some expensive looking garments behind in the drawers and the hanging cupboard of her bedroom at the Lodge. That did not seem to tally with her account of herself. A pretty girl and well spoken, but lots of them could play that part when they liked. He remembered one he had helped to put in the dock at the last Assizes. Butter wouldn't have melted in her mouth until she heard the verdict, and then—

He knocked out his pipe. Time for a quick one in the public bar before the house closed. He might pick up something. No doubt the village was full of rumours by this time. He had heard voices but there was a silence as he entered. He said good evening and gave his order.

"Warm to-night."

Of the five men present, not counting the landlord behind the counter, four were farm labourers who remained prudently silent. The fifth was a thin, sandy-haired youth in the dusty overalls of a motor-cyclist, and he responded with such enthusiasm that Lindo looked at him more closely. He had seen that impudent freckled face before. He recognised one of the most enterprising reporters of the *Manchester Herald*, and, seizing his glass, beat a hasty retreat.

He seemed to have hardly got into bed when the alarm clock shrilled its reveille. He got up with a groan and began to dress. While he was shaving he heard the landlord's heavy step on the stairs. There was a cup of tea waiting for him when he went down.

"That's good of you, Mr. Potter. I'm glad of it."

The valley was full of thick white mist that would clear away later when the sun gained more power. Lindo had to drive slowly, but once he had entered the Dower House Park there was no fear of meeting other traffic.

Reaching the Lodge, he found Gibbs standing in the doorway waiting for him, and Collins, looking heavy-eyed and pinched with cold, at his post among the briars by the well in the back garden.

"Anything to report?"

"No, sir. There was an owl hooting most of the night. No other sounds."

"Good. Cut away to the King's Head and get a good breakfast, and then get back to the station and turn in. Report for duty at six to-night."

"Thank you, Sergeant."

Collins was young, and he had not enjoyed his job. The night had been dark and once or twice he had fancied he heard the wooden cover of the well creak as if—as if someone was trying to lift it from below. It wasn't a nice idea, and not the sort of thing to report to one's superiors. A too vivid imagination was not likely to lead to promotion. He had tried standing on the cover, but that was worse. He would not have cared to live through that night again. He said as much to Gibbs as they walked down to the village together, leaving the sergeant to wait for the others who were coming with ropes and ladders and the police ambulance.

Gibbs grunted. "It wasn't no picnic in the cottage," he said. "All so neat and pretty but I got a feeling that somebody was creeping up behind me. I won't say I didn't doze off one time, but I tried not to. This is my first murder case."

"Same here," said Collins. "It's a queer one, too."

"They'll never find the chap who did it," prophesied Gibbs. "It's like these shop murders. Might be anybody in a manner of speaking."

"I don't know so much about that," argued Collins, "in a sparsely populated countryside a stranger is bound to be noticed. Why I don't suppose three people in a day cross that bit of moorland to the north of the park."

"You know these parts?"

"Yes. I've got an aunt in the village and I used to stay with her when I was a nipper and go blackberrying up that lane that leads to the north gate. There used to be a carriage way from the gate across the common to the cross-road, but it's all grown over with heath and gorse now. They say a Lady Lennor that lived over a hundred years ago at the Dower House had it made so that she needn't pass through the village when she drove out in her coach. She was one of those proud ones that couldn't stick the common people. Said they smelt."

"This place doesn't belong to the Lennors now?"

"No. Sir Miles' father sold it. After the chap who bought it died, it stood empty until these people came in a few months ago. It was the son found the body and rang up the police. A nervy kind of chap, I should say," added young Collins sapiently, "he seemed all on edge. Bit slow in the uptake, too. He didn't see that she must have been shoved into the well by somebody until the sergeant pointed out to him that she couldn't have pulled the cover over herself after jumping in. I never saw a man more taken aback. He turned grey. I thought he was going right off for a minute."

Gibbs grunted again.

The sun had not yet risen, but in spite of the mist there was light enough for Lindo to carry out his plan. He had determined to make a thorough examination of the ground between the well and the cottage before any traces that might remain of the murderer had been trodden down by the heavy feet of the men who were coming to get the body out of the well.

His results were, on the whole, disappointingly negative. Briars and branches of the gooseberry bushes were broken and bruised all along the path between the back door and the well, and there were two gaps in the straggling hedge that divided the garden from the park that were wide enough for the passage of an intruder. Mrs. Hall's assailant might have come and gone that way, slipping out of the park unnoticed by the north gate. On the other hand, Mr. Dene's dog seemed to have picked up a scent in the cottage and followed it to the well. Rather reluctantly he lifted the well cover and laid it back. He avoided looking into the bottom of the well and merely examined the slimy brickwork for two or three feet down. He moved away a few paces and looked at his watch. He had not long to wait. A group of men appeared coming towards him from the direction of the cottage, making their way slowly through the tangled undergrowth. Dr. Mackintosh, the police surgeon, shook hands with him.

"Well, you've got us out of bed early," he said jovially. He was a middle-aged man, with a curt manner. Lindo turned to give instructions to the four men who were carrying two ladders and some coils of rope.

"How deep is it, Lindo?"

"I've no idea, doctor. The Lodge has been unoccupied until recently. The present water supply is from a tank. There's a pump in the scullery. This was evidently disused. The cover is rotting, as you see." He raised his voice. "What does the plummet say, Dunning?"

"Forty feet in all, Sergeant. About ten of water."

"Not as wide as a church door or as deep as a well, but 'twill serve," murmured Mackintosh. "Quite enough to drown in."

The men were fastening the two ladders together. It was not easy to get them into the well. The photographer, at a sign from Lindo, put down his camera and went to help them.

"How did it happen?" asked Mackintosh. "Not an accident?"

Lindo looked at him. "The cover was on."

The doctor whistled. "A case of murder, then. And you're in charge. Congratulations. This gives you a chance to distinguish yourself, my boy. Any signs of a struggle? I'm afraid we've made a mess of the ground."

"That's all right. I've been over it. Nothing definite." He took off his coat and rolled up his shirt sleeves.

"Going down yourself?"

"Yes." He slipped a noose of rope under his arms.

"Hold on to that, Dunning. I'm not sure about the air down there. You may have to pull me up. You've got the other rope. Haul on that when I give the word."

Two men held the top of the ladder steady. Mackintosh, kneeling on the edge of the well, watched Lindo descending slowly and cautiously into those black and slimy depths. His broad shoulders blocked the view of what lay beneath. There was a pause and then some splashing and the ladder creaked as some additional weight was put on it. Then Lindo's voice, reverberating in that narrow space, called to them.

"Pull her up slowly. I'll come up on the ladder to ease her away from the wall."

A gruelling five minutes followed. At the end of it, all concerned were hot and breathless. Lindo, rather white about the lips, and very wet and muddy, was leaning against the trunk of an apple tree and lighting a cigarette. He seldom smoked when on duty but he felt the need of it just then.

Mackintosh had superintended the placing of the body on the canvas stretcher that had been brought for that purpose, and was stooping over the shapeless heap of sodden clothing and clammy ice-cold flesh. Lindo joined him presently.

"The air down there was pretty foul," he said, as if to excuse a weakness he was ashamed of. "And—between you and me, doctor—I don't like touching dead people. Was she drowned?"

Mackintosh covered the body with a piece of tarpaulin and wiped his hands on his handkerchief before he answered.

"No. The back of the skull has been fractured by some blunt instrument. I won't say more until I've made a closer examination at the mortuary. There's something else, Lindo." He looked hard at the sergeant. "There's nobody here can identify the remains, I suppose?"

"No. We've been assuming it's Mrs. Hall. She's been living at the lodge, and she hasn't been seen since Sunday. I thought of asking young Dene to come down to the mortuary some time this morning. I'd like you to carry out the p.m. as soon as possible."

The doctor looked at his watch. "I'll nip back now and have my breakfast and be round before nine. Young Dene, eh?"

"Mrs. Hall is an old friend of the family, I understand. She's in reduced circumstances and they've let her have the lodge rent free and lent her furniture."

"The elder daughter has just got engaged to Sir Miles Lennor, hasn't she?"

"Yes."

Lindo observed his companion with some curiosity. It was not like Mackintosh to ask so many questions, but his interest had evidently been aroused to an unusual degree.

"Man," he said, "I'm telling you—or rather I'm no telling you yet. It'll keep. See you later. And mind you, Lindo, this case'll be the making of you. It'll cause a stir, I'm thinking. Aye—"

Lindo looked after him as he hurried off. He had purposely not asked young Dene to be present when the body was taken out of the well. The boy was highly strung and had obviously had about as much as he could stand on the previous day. It was still very early by ordinary standards and he was not surprised to see that the blinds at the Dower House were not yet drawn when the police lorry and the ambulance crossed the park on their way back to Ranchester.

Tony, however, was awake. He had slept heavily during the first part of the night but had been roused by the first twittering of the birds under the eaves.

He woke with the feeling that he had something definitely disagreeable, something like a long deferred visit to the dentist, before him.

"Oh, damn!" he said as he remembered, and pulled the sheet over his head. Bed was a refuge. Couldn't he sham sick and stay there? No. He was the man of the family. His mother would have to be shielded.

Someone came into his room and pulled up the blind. He uncovered his head and saw his sister Lavvy in green silk pyjamas, her golden hair tousled.

"Lav, you look like an angel peeping out of a burning bush. Some bush. You can use my comb if you like."

"No, thanks." She came to perch herself on the foot of his bed.

"I want to know what's really happened to Mrs. Hall. Mollie said she'd met with a fatal accident and Mother was fearfully upset, and would I make Miles take me out to dinner. I passed that on to Miles and he took it very well. Of course, apart from its being terribly sudden and very sad and all that, I don't suppose he's exactly sorry. And if we're honest we'll have to admit that we aren't, either. I mean, it was awful having her here day after day, listening to everything we said and grabbing everything she could lay hands on, and how Mother could stick it as she did, I can't imagine. Because, you know, Tony, though they may have been tremendous pals when they were girls they obviously hadn't a thing in common now."

Tony sat up and arranged his pillows to support his back.

"Lavvy," he said solemnly, "I've sometimes wondered—" he broke off, "No. I won't say it."

She glanced at his troubled face. He looked pathetically vague and helpless without his horn-rimmed glasses, but Lavvy was more irritated than touched by this aspect of him.

"Tony, I wish you wouldn't blink. It looks so silly. What was the accident?"

"You didn't see a policeman in the hall when you came in?"

"No. It was past twelve. We drove as far as Brighton. Why a policeman?"

"They'll let you off lightly, Lavvy, they'll coo to you. Even the police are human and there's no denying that your face would sink a liner. But they bellow at me. And they creak. God! How they creak to and fro on their lawful occasions."

"Tony, don't dither. I want to know."

Tony dropped his rather laboured facetiousness. "All right, if you will have it. They—they seem to think she was murdered."

She gazed at him. "Tony, how horrible. When? How?"

"We shall know," he said gloomily, "soon enough. Buzz off now, old girl. I want to get up. At least I don't want to—but I've got to."

Mrs. Dene did not come down for breakfast. It was an uncomfortable meal. The two girls looked worried and said little. Tony ate nothing but a piece of dry toast, but he drank three cups of tea. He was going through the newspapers, of which the Denes took three.

"Nothing about it yet," he said as he threw down the last. "Were you two thinking of going anywhere? Not? Good. That sergeant chap said he'd like us all to be on hand to-day in case we were wanted. I'll meet you on the tennis court in half an hour, Mollie. Your service is rotten. You need practice. I'll take you on, too, Lavvy, if you like."

Lavvy shook her head. "No, thanks. I'll look on."

She was thinking that Sir Miles would almost certainly come to take her for another drive. He had made love to her last night with more ardour than he had shown hitherto. Lavvy, who knew in her heart that she had caught a normally rather coldblooded and prudent young man in a weak moment, had always feared his mother's influence. It was no use saying angrily that Lady

Lennor was a snob. She was. But her son admired and respected her, and Lavvy felt that her cold disapproval of the girl to whom he had engaged himself made him more critical than he would have been otherwise. Lavvy, when she had lunched or dined at Lennor Park, had listened carefully to the conversation of mother and son. Her heart had sunk a little as she realised how many people were outside their pale. You had to be Church of England. There were, she gathered, opposing factions in that body, but they were tolerated. The fatal thing was to be Nonconformist. Then in politics one must be Conservative. That was all right. The Denes had been brought up on the most modern lines. Lavvy had never thought about religion. God was a useful expletive. One didn't, of course, believe in those old superstitions. Tony and his friends, all the young people who came to her uncle's house in Chelsea had been funny at the expense of the pictures of the old gentleman with a beard sitting on a cloud like a feather bed. But Miles was different. Of course, his grandfather had been the Dean of Ranchester, and farther back, in the eighteenth century, there had been a bishop whose portrait hung in the dining-room at Lennor Park.

It was in this matter of a family tree that Lavvy knew that she must always fail to reach the standard required of her. Both Lady Lennor and her son were morally entrenched in a fortress built up on solid and socially satisfactory connections from an ancestor of theirs who was Court chaplain to Queen Anne, to Colonel Boult, the Chief Constable, who was related to Lady Lennor through her mother's family. They talked a great deal about their relations.

Not boastfully, but with a kind of unconscious arrogance. This did not annoy Lavvy as it would have done Tony. She envied them. She was ashamed to have to always make vague and unsatisfactory answers to Lady Lennor's questions.

"Are you related to the Worcestershire Denes?"

"I don't know."

"Have you any cousins?"

"I never heard of any. We lived with my uncle until last year. He was an invalid. He wasn't married—"

"You have lost all your grandparents?"

"Yes."

"What was your mother's maiden name?"

"I don't know."

These trials were only temporary. Once she was married Lavvy felt that all would be well. She would see to it that Lady Lennor did not live on at the Park. She could go back to Ranchester where she had spent her girlhood and where she still had many old friends among the wives and daughters of her father's Chapter. When she was gone Lavvy would not mind the family tree. She would herself be grafted on it and could afford to be complacent about its ramifications.

"You'll have the sun in your eyes if you sit there," shouted Tony, when she came down to the tennis court, slim and exquisite as a Lalique figure in her pale blue muslin.

"I don't mind the sun," she answered. In fact she had chosen the only corner from which she could see a car coming up the avenue. But the hours passed and the luncheon gong sounded, and Sir Miles had not come. Lavvy and her sister went in to lunch together silently. Tony had been called away some time before.

CHAPTER VIII

THE MORNING AFTER

TONY HAD GONE UP to his mother's room before he went down to the tennis court. He found Mrs. Dene sitting up in bed with her breakfast tray on her knees. To his relief she seemed much more like her usual self.

"I want you to go up to Town to-day, Tony, and see your friend and his father about taking a share in that publishing business when you come down from Oxford."

"Mother, you said the other day that you couldn't afford it."

"I felt worried just then. I've had a good many expenses. But when Lavvy's married we can retrench. Don't argue, Tony. You know I detest argument," she said rather sharply.

Tony could be very tiresome, she thought. Why did he stand there poking when he ought to throw back his shoulders. Being short-sighted was no excuse. "You heard me, Tony."

"Yes, Mother, but I can't go. I promised the sergeant we'd be on hand if we were wanted. It'll only be me actually. He's going to ring me up when they're ready for me to—to identify the body."

She stiffened. "I see. That's unfortunate. I wish you hadn't got mixed up in this. If only you hadn't gone back to the lodge with that girl. The whole thing—" she added half to herself. "I can't understand it." He saw that she shivered.

"I'd like you to meet her, Mother. She's not a bit like—" he checked himself. "I mean—she's nice."

"She's pretty, I suppose," she said contemptuously.

"Yes. But I'd be just as sorry for her if she was plain."

His mother looked at him with her faint smile. "Really? Well, since you can't carry out my wishes you had better leave me, hadn't you?"

Tony bit his lip. He knew that he had been a fool to mention Amy to his mother. Mollie was the only member of his family who was likely to be kind to her, and Mollie had failed him, too, though not intentionally. His mother, with all her gentleness and the quiet yielding manners that impressed people who did not know her very well, never allowed her children to question her authority. She was devoted to them, or, at any rate, to Lavvy, and she had made many sacrifices for them, but she had never yet consulted them before she took action. The move into Sussex, the purchase of the Dower House, had been planned and carried out by her alone. They were much more under her thumb than outsiders realised.

"All right," he said. "I'm glad to see you looking a little less like a ghost, anyway."

He went down to the telephone and rang up the King's Head. The landlord, answering, said that Miss Steer had taken a room. She had had her breakfast.

"Ask her to speak to me, will you?"

After an interval he heard her voice.

"It's you," he said unnecessarily. He looked round to make sure that the baize-covered door that led to the servants' quarters was closed. "I say, I'm awfully sick about yesterday, keeping you waiting so long, I mean. I had to go off with the police, and my sister Mollie was detained. My mother was upset, naturally. I do hope you'll forgive us. The sergeant left a bobby on duty here and he told me you were staying at the King's Head. I hope they're making you comfortable—"

"Quite, thank you."

"You're not going away just yet, are you?"

"They say I've got to stop until after the inquest."

"Good. I mean—you won't go without my seeing you again? Promise," he said earnestly.

"Very well."

"Splendid. I mean—everything's ghastly, but that's fine all the same. Good-bye."

He picked up his racket and went down the garden to where Mollie waited for him on the hard court Mrs. Dene had had laid down when they moved in. They had begun their second set when Parsons came out with a message. The sergeant had rung up from Ranchester to ask Mr. Dene to come over at once. Tony fetched out the car. Half an hour later he was in the yard of the police station being introduced to a stout, red-faced man with an abrupt manner.

"This is Mr. Dene who found the body, Colonel Boult. I expect you know that the Colonel is the Chief Constable, Mr. Dene."

The Colonel nodded and did not offer his hand. There was another man with braid on his dark blue coat who was addressed as Superintendent and whose name Tony did not catch, and Sergeant Lindo completed the party. The sergeant led the way to an outhouse, unlocked the door and stood aside to allow the others to pass in. Tony noticed a trickling sound of water running from a tap, and a strong smell of disinfectants. The building was lit by a large skylight and a long table stood immediately under it. Something lay on the table draped with a sheet. The sergeant stepped forward and turned back the covering a little way.

"Now, Mr. Dene. Is this the person you knew as Mrs. Hall?"

Tony came forward reluctantly. He had turned rather pale. He stared hard at the dead face and said nothing. His three elders were watching him more closely than he realised. The Colonel and the Superintendent exchanged glances.

"Well?" said Lindo at last.

"I suppose it is," Tony said uncertainly.

"Have you any doubt at all?"

He moved a little to get a better view of the profile. The jutting nose and the heavy lines of the cheeks and chin were unmistakable. And yet she looked different. Was it only the difference between life and death?

"It must be Mrs. Hall," he said at last. "Of course she always used a good deal of make-up, powder and lipstick—"

"You can't recollect any distinguishing mark that would clinch the matter?" suggested Lindo.

"No. I—I never looked at her particularly. Not closely, I mean. One doesn't—not to notice scars or moles or anything, I mean. But it could hardly be anyone else, could it?" He glanced round at the circle of grave faces. "Was she drowned or what?"

The tall man with the grey moustache answered, but without meeting his eye. "I'm afraid we can't give any information at present, Mr. Dene. Excuse me one moment. Superintendent, a word with you outside—" He went out, followed by one of the other men. Lindo led Tony over to a shelf on which the dead woman's clothes lay neatly folded.

"Yes. That looks like her dress. She always wore black. I say, Sergeant, this is just a formality, isn't it? After all, it's pretty obvious—"

"How do you mean, obvious, sir?" asked Lindo.

He attached no importance to the young man's babblings, but he had guessed that Colonel Boult wanted him to be kept out of the way while he and the Superintendent decided on the next step in a case that might have more far reaching consequences than had at first appeared. Incidentally he felt very sorry for Tony.

"Well, I mean, I've been thinking about it, naturally. Some tramp or pedlar must have called at the lodge. I can't imagine

Mrs. Hall giving him anything. He got abusive and she told him off, and then he saw red and bashed her on the head. Then, of course, when he saw what he'd done, he got the wind up. He found the old well and shoved her down it, and there you are—"

Lindo had listened with increasing attention.

"A lonely house and a woman to deal with. Such cases are not uncommon," he agreed. "But what makes you think her head was bashed in, Mr. Dene?"

He looked curiously at Tony. Was this young man, after all, as innocent as he seemed?

Tony, resenting his hard scrutiny, fidgeted. "Oh—I don't know. Was it?"

"Yes, Mr. Dene. The base of her skull was fractured by a heavy blow from some blunt instrument. A very good guess on your part. Ah, here is the Superintendent."

The Superintendent only put his head in at the door.

"You can come now," he said briefly. "Bring Mr. Dene into my office, Lindo. Sorry I must detain you a few minutes, Mr. Dene. Perhaps you'd like to look at this morning's paper."

"Nothing in it about this case?" said Tony.

"No. We've managed to head off the Press men so far. But that won't last. We can't escape publicity, Mr. Dene, and the reading public enjoys murders."

Tony was left alone for what seemed like an hour but was actually twenty minutes. He heard the telephone bell ringing in another part of the building.

He jumped up as Lindo came in. "Can I go now?"

"Yes, sir. And here's your paper relating to the inquest. It will be opened to-morrow at the Town Hall here. Very short and not much to it. At least—not many witnesses called. Just you, sir, and me, and the doctor. Our coroner here is a sensible man. He knows inquests are apt to mess up our enquiries. I'd like you to remain at home until then, if you don't mind."

"All right."

When Tony reached home it was past one. He went straight to the dining-room and found his sisters at lunch.

"Where's Mother?"

"The police sent a car to fetch her to Ranchester. Didn't they tell you they were going to?" said Lavvy. "They want her to identify the—the body."

Tony glanced at Parsons, standing primly by the sideboard, and restrained himself until she had left the room to fetch the next course. Then he burst out. "That's why they kept me. What a filthy trick. What did I go for if it wasn't to spare Mother?"

"You must have made a mess of it," said Lavvy unsympathetically. "Shut up now," she added.

Parsons, her pale face expressionless, came back and began to hand round the stewed fruit.

Tony waited until she had left the room again. "You would blame me," he said then.

Lavvy's nerves were on edge. She had been watching for Sir Miles all the morning and he had not come. It was a relief to have somebody on whom she could vent her irritation.

"I do. If you hadn't been hanging about after that girl the body wouldn't have been found. People would have thought she'd gone away, and we should have been spared all this hateful business."

"Rot. There would have to have been an enquiry sooner or later."

"Not for months probably. Not until after I'd married. Then it wouldn't have mattered so much."

Tony laughed, not pleasantly. "Lavvy, you are priceless. You only think of yourself."

"Oh, what's the use of having a row about it?" cried Mollie. "It only makes it worse."

They were all three on the terrace when Mrs. Dene returned. Tony jumped up and went to meet her.

"Mother—I'll never forgive the sergeant for this."

Mrs. Dene was pale but self-possessed. "Don't get excited, dear. He was quite right not to rely entirely on your identification." She sank into the chair Mollie drew forward. "It was a trying ordeal, of course, but they were all very nice to me."

"What about lunch, Mother?"

"I didn't feel like eating much, but I had a cup of coffee at Merritt's in the High Street, and I got a small black hat that will do to wear with my black and white spotted muslin."

"Mother, you aren't going into mourning?" Mrs. Dene glanced at Lavvy. "My dear, Harriet will be buried in the church-yard here, and I must go to the funeral. I know you all disliked her, but she was an old friend of mine, and I must do what I feel is right. It would look very strange if I didn't."

Lavvy nodded. "Yes, I see. I hadn't really thought—"

Mrs. Dene leaned back in her chair and closed her eyes. Tony looked at her anxiously. She looked so ill, but he knew that nothing would move her once she had determined on her course.

"Why couldn't you leave all that to me, Mother? I mean, making arrangements for the funeral and all that. You'll tire yourself out."

"My dear, I simply gave Merritt's the order. They will do everything. It was quite easy while I was on the spot. I ordered two wreaths, too, at Wyndham's. One from me, and one from you three. Everything we do—or leave undone—will be commented on. We can't be too careful for Lavvy's sake. I half thought Sir Miles would have come over this morning—"

"Well, he didn't," said Lavvy shortly.

Her mother suppressed a sigh.

"Mother—" said Tony.

"Yes, darling?"

"I suppose they didn't tell you more than they did me? I mean—I got the impression that they'd found out something rather important since I last saw Lindo yesterday evening. They were very hush hush with me, but really, I thought, bursting with excitement. In fact it wouldn't surprise me to hear that they've got the chap who did it shut up in one of those cells at the police station and waiting to be charged."

"My dear boy," said his mother quietly, "you are always im-agining things. They may or may not have made an arrest. They didn't tell me anything. There was a rather nice man, I think he was the Superintendent. I said to him that I hoped they would get the murderer. He said, 'Madam, we are doing our best.' They offered to drive me back but I told them I had some shopping to do in the town and would hire a taxi."

"Did you see a stout man with a grey moustache?"

"No." She thought a moment. "I believe there was somebody in the next room. The door wasn't quite closed. Don't let's talk about it any more. How lovely it is out here."

Mrs. Dene gazed down the long slope of sunlit sward to the beech woods and the hills beyond. "I've done all I can," she said.

Tony was looking towards the house. "Oh, hell," he said, "here's Lindo."

Mrs. Dene glanced round with her faint ironic smile. "So it is. Is there a chair for him? Do sit down, Sergeant."

She spoke exactly as she would have done to any ordinary visitor.

Lindo thanked her and took the seat indicated.

"I'm sorry to keep on bothering you like this," he began, "but this is my job and I've got to get on with it. I didn't see either of the young ladies yesterday evening and there are just one or two questions I've got to ask."

"All right," said Lavvy, "go on." Her tone was negligent to the point of insolence.

Lindo stood up. "Indoors, if you don't mind, Miss Dene. We've got to be a bit more formal now. I have my man there ready to take down statements—"

"Very well," she said, "though you'll be wasting your time. I don't know a thing about it."

She went in, followed by the sergeant. Mrs. Dene closed her eyes again. Tony lit another cigarette. Mollie, who had Binkie on her lap, sat stroking him absently. Her turn would come next.

The round faced young constable who was awaiting his sergeant's return in the morning-room was so overcome when he saw Lavvy that he dropped his pencil. Lindo was less susceptible but even he unconsciously varied his manner a little when he spoke to her.

"Sit here, please, Miss Dene," he leaned against the table, looking down at her golden head. "Now—when did you last see Mrs. Hall?"

"She had tea with us in the garden on Sunday. Sir Miles came in his car about half-past five. He was taking me in to Ranchester for the evening service at the Cathedral. She had not left then. I did not see her again."

"Not at all on Monday?"

"No."

"Can you tell me what you did?"

"On Monday? It seems ages ago. We were rehearsing in Lennor Park all the morning. For the pageant, you know. Sir Miles walked home with me across the park, but he didn't come in to lunch. I had rather a rotten afternoon, at least the early part—"

"How was that, Miss Dene?"

"I found I had lost a brooch. I knew I still had it when I left Lennor Park and that it must have dropped off some time as we were walking back. Sir Miles had given it to me and I was very keen to find it again because I knew he would be upset about it. He thinks I'm careless."

"I understand. So you went back along the path you had come to look for it?"

"Yes."

"You told no one of your loss?"

"No. I didn't want to bother my mother. My sister was going down to the vicarage to help make the dresses for the pageant. My brother had gone up to London for the day or I might have asked him to help me hunt for it."

"You found it?"

"Yes. Luckily, but it took hours. Sir Miles was going to fetch me in his car about half-past four. I just had time to get back and change before he arrived."

"I see. You were in the park looking for the lost brooch from about—"

"I didn't look at the time but I should say about half-past two to four."

"Thank you. Did you meet anybody, or see anyone in the distance during that time?"

"Not a soul."

"I see. Were you at any time near the North Lodge?"

"No. I could show you the path if you like. It leads from this house to a little door in the park wall opening on the main road beyond the village. There's another door facing it in the wall of Lennor Park. Sir Miles told me they were made years ago when the Dowager Lady Lennor lived in the Dower House after her son's marriage; but after the Dower House was sold the doors were locked. The keys were lost. Sir Miles has just had new ones made since we became engaged."

"Thank you," said Lindo again. "That is quite clear. Now about Mrs. Hall. You had known her ever since you can remember?"

"Oh no. Mother used to know her, but she'd lost sight of her for years and years. She turned up soon after we came here in March. She had had a lot of trouble. Mother offered her the lodge rent free and lent her some furniture."

"Hadn't Mrs. Hall any money at all?"

"I wasn't in her confidence," said Lavvy. "I shouldn't think she had. Mother helped her a lot."

"You saw a good deal of her?"

"Yes. My mother was very kind to her. She came to tea practically every day, and we took her for drives."

"And I suppose you sometimes had tea with her at the lodge?"

"No. She asked me several times at the beginning, but I never went."

"You and Mrs. Hall didn't hit it off?"

"You can put it that way if you like. I never cared for her, and I'm not very good at hiding my feelings."

"Did she give you any definite cause to dislike her, Miss Dene?"

Lavvy hesitated. "I don't want to speak against the poor thing now that she's dead, but she wasn't very attractive. And I thought—we all thought she took advantage of my mother's generosity. She was grabbing all the time."

"I see. Thank you very much. Would you mind asking your sister to come now?"

"I'll tell her."

Lavvy called to Mollie as she crossed the terrace. "He wants you now."

"All right. Where are you off to?"

"Back to the tennis court. I left my book there." Mollie kissed the top of Binkie's rough beige coloured head with unusual fervour and gave him to her brother.

"Don't let him follow me, Tony." She spoke in a low voice for Mrs. Dene's eyes were still closed and she seemed to be asleep.

The young man nodded and replied in a gruff whisper, "Keep your end up."

"I'll try. Oh, Tony, I'm so frightened—"

The spit of her brother, thought Lindo, with a quick appraising glance at the dark piquant face with its wide humorous mouth and quick glancing eager brown eyes. More sensitive, more highly strung than the beauty, and would need more careful handling.

"Sit down here, miss. Now, when did you see Mrs. Hall last?"

"Sunday afternoon. She had tea with us on the lawn. She walked back to the lodge about six o'clock."

"You were with her during that time?"

"Not all the time. I took my dog for a run after tea. It was very hot. She sat with Mother in the shade of the cedar."

"You didn't see her on Monday?"

"No. We were rehearsing at Lennor Park all the morning. My sister and I, I mean. My brother had gone up to London. I heard afterwards that she'd been here and got a cake from the cook and some groceries."

"Was that usual?"

"Oh, yes. The village grocer only called at the lodge once a week, and she sometimes forgot to order what she wanted."

"You rehearsed all the morning. What did you do after that?"

"My sister was walking back across the park with Sir Miles. They're engaged, you know. I borrowed Mrs. Barrow's bicycle and rode home."

"The vicar's wife?"

"Yes. I was going to the vicarage directly after lunch to help make the dresses."

"Yes. Go on, please. Tell me everything you did."

"Mrs. Barrow kept all the workers to tea. I left about a quarter to seven and walked home. Mother had a bad headache. I had dinner alone—"

"What about your brother? I understood from Miss Steer that he came down from London on the same train in the afternoon."

"Yes. But he didn't come straight home. He had parked his car in the station yard when he went up in the morning. He just went for a long drive and didn't come home until after nine."

"Did he seem at all upset when he came in?"

"Yes, he did rather. At least—why? What do you mean?"

"Just answer my questions. He was upset—"

Mollie tried to think. She had let that out and she would only make matters worse by denying it now.

"Things upset Tony that other people would take calmly," she explained. "He hates hurting anyone's feelings. He talked to Miss Steer in the train, and then, when he found out who she was, he jibbed. And afterwards he realised it wasn't the girl's fault and felt he'd been a beast, so he jumped into the car and drove as hard as he could to get away from himself."

"He jibbed. What does that mean exactly?"

"Well, he told me he got up and left the compartment. It does sound rude—"

"He was on bad terms with Mrs. Hall?" suggested Lindo.

"She got on his nerves. He avoided her as much as possible."

"Had they quarrelled?"

"Oh, no. He always tried to be civil for my mother's sake."

"Why for Mrs. Dene's sake?"

"She was an old friend. Mother asked us to be nice to her."

"Well, he was upset. How did he show it?"

"He didn't say much until I asked him and then he told me what had happened and how rotten he felt about it."

"Was he pale? I'm sorry to press you, but the word upset does not convey any definite impression to my mind."

"He looked tired. Yes, he was rather white—"

Mollie started. "What are you hinting at? You don't imagine—"

Lindo checked her with an uplifted hand. "Routine questions," he said smoothly. "It's like painting a picture. You have to get every detail in the background. We're painting a picture of last Monday afternoon. Or making a mosaic if you like, setting every piece in its place."

Mollie was reassured by these metaphors, as he meant her to be. She smiled up at him gratefully. "I see. Thank you very much."

"Not at all. Thank you. I'm through now for the present."

He opened the door for her, shut it after her, and turned to the young constable who had been industriously taking notes.

"Better find out when she arrived at the vicarage. It's probably okay, but we mustn't leave any gaps."

CHAPTER IX

LADY LENNOR IS WARNED

SIR MILES LENNOR, who was a conscientious landlord, had spent the early part of the forenoon with his agent at one of his farms where he had agreed to erect new cowsheds. His presence was required, but perhaps he was not altogether sorry to have a valid excuse to keep away from the Dower House. Lavvy's rather confused account of a fatal accident had been amplified by Wood, the agent, whose first words had been, "A bad business about this murder at the North Lodge, Sir Miles. They say the police are combing the neighbourhood, looking for the man who did it."

"Let's hope they find him," he had said repressively, and changed the subject. Wood was a capable fellow and as popular as any agent could expect to be with the tenants, but Sir Miles, who was not a good mixer, was always rather stiff with him.

When he got home the butler waylaid him in the hall.

"Lady Lennor wishes to speak to you, Sir Miles. She is in the drawing-room."

"Very well."

Lady Lennor came to the point at once.

"Why didn't I hear about this horrible affair from you, Miles?"

"That woman being killed, you mean? I didn't think you'd be interested."

"How can you say that!"

"You always say you dislike gossip. I understood it was an accident. Wood, just now, said something about murder."

"James Boult rang up from Ranchester. He asked if he might come over to lunch. He seemed very worried."

"Well, as Chief Constable he's responsible—"

"I don't mean that. Worried on our account."

Her son did not affect to misunderstand her. "You mean because of this happening at the Denes' place? It's unfortunate, certainly. One tries to avoid that sort of notoriety. Here is Boult, I think."

The butler announced Colonel Boult. The luncheon gong sounded while the Colonel was shaking hands with Lady Lennor, whom he called Cousin Jane.

"I want a few words with you both afterwards," he said. "Mustn't talk before the servants."

Meals at Lennor Park were never amusing, but they were perfectly cooked and served, and Sir Miles' father had been a good judge of wine and had left a well stocked cellar. The silver on the long table of gleaming mahogany included seventeenth-century salt cellars that would have fetched large sums at Christie's. Lady Lennor was unaware of their artistic merits but saw to it that they were kept bright. She talked to her guest about her garden. He was not interested but he listened dutifully. Sir Miles said nothing.

Lady Lennor led the way into the library. "Please smoke, James," she said graciously. "I don't mind."

"Thank you. I must not stay long. I have to get back to Ranchester. This case"—he cleared his throat—"you've heard something?" He took a cigar from the box Sir Miles held out to him.

Lady Lennor answered. "Hopkins, my maid, told me that a woman who has been living at North Lodge was dead, that her body was found in a well yesterday evening, and that there was a great deal of talk already in the village."

"Yes, yes. Just so." The Colonel drew at his cigar. "Did you ever meet her, Lennor? I understand she was on friendly terms with the Dene family."

Sir Miles answered reluctantly. "Lavvy told me she was an old friend of her mother's. She was often there, certainly, but she remained in the background. She was introduced to me by Mrs. Dene, but we never exchanged a word. She seemed an odd sort of person, but I shouldn't call her pushing."

Colonel Boult said nothing for a moment. Lady Lennor looked at him sharply.

"James, you are keeping something from us. What is it?"

"I can't tell you, Cousin Jane. But—what about a cruise to Norway, Lennor? It's the right time of year for it. Or—or Canada—"

"My dear James," said Lady Lennor, "you forget the pageant. Miles is taking a leading part in one episode. He can hardly go away until that is over. It would be thought very strange." After a moment she added sourly, "No one can regret the association of our name with all this more than I do. If Miles had listened to me—but he is of age, and the advice of older people is seldom welcomed."

"You can't blame Lavvy, Mother, because somebody she knows has been murdered," said the young man irritably, "it's a thing that might happen to anyone."

"It has never happened to me," said Lady Lennor, "but I am not blaming her."

"In your place," said the Colonel, "I'd go away for a bit. I can't say more than that. I'm stretching a point as it is. And yet—perhaps you're right, Cousin Jane. God knows. It's a choice of evils."

He looked so worried that Lady Lennor began to be really alarmed. "James," she said vigorously, "I hate people who drop hints. I insist upon your speaking out. Are you trying to tell me something I ought to know about Miles? He may have been fool-ish—he often is—but I can hardly believe—"

The Colonel stood up. "No, no. I was so shocked, so horri-fied—I hoped to keep you out of it. But the engagement has been published everywhere. Very difficult. Very painful and distress-ing—"

"James," said Lady Lennor, and her voice, usually so loud and confident, trembled. "You are frightening me—"

"I'm sorry," he said, "you'll understand soon enough." He looked at his watch. "I must be off," he said with relief. "Look here, Lennor, take my tip. If you can't go away altogether, at least keep away from the Dower House for a day or two. You'll see why soon enough."

Sir Miles went out with him to his car.

"I wish you hadn't said all that in front of my mother," he said.

"My dear boy," said the Colonel, "you'll need all the help she can give you. Good-bye." He settled himself in the driving seat.

"It's something about this case?" said Sir Miles.

"Yes. It's—it's beyond us, Lennor. I'm going to call in the Yard." He let in his clutch.

Sir Miles turned and went slowly back into the house. His mother was waiting for him in the library.

"Did he tell you anything more?"

"Nothing."

"You'll take his advice?"

He had gone over to his writing-table and was taking some papers from a drawer. He answered without turning his head in her direction. "His advice? Of course not. Boult's an interfering old busybody. As Chief Constable he's a bad joke. As a matter of fact I've a lot of letters to write, and I wasn't going over to the Dower House to-day in any case."

The morning had passed very slowly for Amy Steer. She had been given the sole use of a small and rather mouldy sit-ting-room at the back of the King's Head, and she had only left it when called to the telephone to speak to Tony Dene. She had been a good deal cheered by his evident anxiety on her behalf.

It was nice, she thought, to feel that she had one friend in the world. But she did not regret having come away from the Dower House as she did. She had waited in that drawing-room for over an hour, and no one had come near her. It was evident that neither Mrs. Dene nor her daughters wanted her. She could not blame them. No one cares to have a perfect stranger thrust upon them.

How glad she was that she had not spent all the hundred pounds her aunt had given her now that she was once more thrown on her own resources. The landlady had brought in her breakfast herself and had taken that opportunity to remind her that Sergeant Lindo hoped she would stay on at the King's Head until after the inquest. Mrs. Potter had made it clear that the sergeant's hope was equivalent to a command.

"He wants to have another talk with you, miss, some time to-day. That's why you've got the use of the little back room. My husband said I was to tell you we're making no extra charge for that."

Mrs. Potter had been civil but not exactly cordial and had answered Amy's questions in a non-committal manner. Amy had seen nothing more of her, and, after the telephone call, the morning had seemed interminable. There was only one novel among the tattered books on a shelf in the sitting-room, an aged and well thumbed copy of *East Lynne*. Amy tried to read but she was too worried and unhappy to be able to concentrate her attention. Her troubled mind was constantly occupied with the events of the past few days, going over the ground again and again from the moment at the Free Library when she had seen Mrs. Hall's advertisement. Only one thing was certain. The promised respite from the struggle to earn her livelihood was not to be hers. After the inquest and the funeral she must go back to London and begin again, waiting in queues, haunting agencies. She had added considerably to her wardrobe and that was one bright spot. On the other hand at least half the clothes she had bought only a few days ago in such a glow of happy anticipation would be of very little use to her in any job she was likely to get. At one o'clock Mrs. Potter brought in her dinner.

"And Sergeant Lindo's just rung up, miss. He'll be along somewhen this afternoon, and he's having the rest of your luggage sent here from the North Lodge."

Amy made a valiant but not very successful effort to eat the hard beef and boiled potatoes followed by tinned pineapple. Her trunk arrived soon after the meal was cleared away and she went up to her room to get out another and more comfortable pair of shoes. She saw at once that everything in the trunk must have been taken out and replaced. The clothes were neatly folded but not as she had folded them. What had the police expected to find among her jumpers and slips and rolled-up stockings? They must suspect her, she thought uneasily—of what? She changed from her cotton frock into a knitted jumper and tweed skirt. She had begun to feel chilly sitting hour after hour in the sunless back sitting-room. She was just going down when Mrs. Potter called up the stairs.

"The sergeant's here, miss."

Lindo had come straight to the King's Head from the Dower House. He smiled at Amy as she came in and drew forward a chair.

"Sit down here, Miss Steer," he boomed, "I hope you're rested? The Potters making you comfortable? That's right. Now I just want to run through what I asked you last night and get a little more information if I can."

"Please," she said, "I want to know first—the—the body in the well—was it my aunt?"

"The body is now at the mortuary, Miss Steer. It has been identified by Mr. Anthony Dene and by his mother as that of Mrs. Hall."

"Poor thing," said Amy. "How dreadful." He expected her to ask if the deceased had drowned herself, but she said nothing more. He waited a moment and then resumed.

"I made notes of what you told me last night. I have it here that you replied to an advertisement, I may say that we've verified that, Miss Steer. The advertisement, I mean. We found it in the back files of the paper you mentioned. It had been appearing for three weeks past."

"Yes."

"Have you the letter you received in answer to yours?"

"No. I'm afraid I didn't keep it."

"Ah. A pity. You see, Miss Steer, that would have been proof that you were a relative, or that she accepted you as such. She arranged to meet you in the ladies' waiting-room at Victoria last Thursday at eleven?"

"Yes."

"What passed at that meeting?"

"She told me she was my father's sister and asked me to come and stay with her. She said she had good friends and I should enjoy myself. She gave me some money to buy clothes and pay my fare, and told me to come on Monday and she would meet me."

"How much money?"

"One hundred pounds."

"A tidy sum. In notes?"

"Yes. She took them from her handbag. Twelve fives and the rest in one pound and ten-shilling notes. I—it quite took my breath away. But she said I should need nice clothes. Evening frocks—"

"Have you any of this money left?"

"A little. Eleven pounds and some silver."

"Will you let me see the notes?"

He was amused to see that she clutched the little bag on her lap more tightly. "You—you aren't going to take them from me? It's all I've got."

"We may want to trace those notes, Miss Steer. That's why I'm afraid I must have them. But I'm prepared to give you perfectly good one-pound notes in exchange."

She looked relieved. "Oh—that's all right, then."

The exchange was made. He placed the notes she had given him carefully in an envelope and stuck it down.

"And now, Miss Steer, I want you to cast your thoughts back and recall all you ever heard at home about your Aunt."

"I never heard anything. I didn't know of her existence until last week."

"How is that?"

"My father died when I was a baby. I don't know if my mother had quarrelled with his family, or what. Anyway she never spoke of them. She was an only child herself and her parents were dead, so I haven't any relations on her side either."

Lindo made no attempt to conceal his disappointment. "I was relying on you to help us there, Miss Steer. Of course if Mrs. Dene is a life-long friend we may get the necessary information from her, but it's useful to have two sources and check one by the other. What's that?"

Mrs. Potter had opened the door and put her head in.

"You're wanted on the phone, Sergeant."

"Oh, very well. I'll come."

He was not gone long. When he came back his manner was more hurried.

"I'm expecting a colleague to join me here, Miss Steer. He'll want a word with you, so kindly wait. Meanwhile I have a bit of routine work I can get through."

The vicarage was a hundred yards farther down the village street. His ring at the bell was answered by a neat little maid. He asked for Mrs. Barrow and was shown into a shabby dining-room. The vicar's wife had seen him coming up the drive and she did not keep him waiting.

"Sorry to trouble you," he said, "but I am Sergeant Lindo, and I am making some enquiries in connection with the death of the tenant of North Lodge."

Mrs. Barrow looked flustered, "I'm afraid I can't help you at all. My husband did call twice, but each time she was out. And she never came to church."

"Well, I was thinking more about Monday," said Lindo. "Miss Mollie Dene tells me she was here during the afternoon."

"Oh, yes. We had our weekly working party for the pageant. Mollie was here—but she came very late, only just in time for tea, and we had that at four."

"You are sure of that, Mrs. Barrow?"

"Oh, yes. But surely—it's of no importance?"

"None whatever. These are routine questions," said Lindo breezily. "Working out a time table." Lindo was thinking hard as he walked back to the inn. Mollie Dene had told him that she went to the vicarage directly after lunch, but Mrs. Barrow said she did not arrive until nearly four. The sergeant had been favourably impressed by Mollie's youthful candour. He wondered if he had let her off too easily.

"I'll have to be a bit sharper with that young lady next time," he reflected. She would have to account to him for that lost hour.

The landlord was waiting for him at the door of the inn. "They've rung up again, Sergeant." He took the message before he went into the sitting-room where Amy was waiting for him.

"I've got to go back to Ranchester, Miss Steer. A car will be sent to fetch you to-morrow for the inquest. I'm not sure if you're going to be called to give evidence but you'll have to be there in case."

"Very well," she said faintly. "May I go for a walk now? I'm so tired of sitting here."

"Most certainly," said Lindo in his most fatherly tone. "A little stroll will do you good."

The landlord, who had been lingering in the passage, followed him out to his car.

"I think I ought to tell you that your call wasn't the only one. There was one for her just now. Young Mr. Dene up at the Dower House. I heard all she said. I fancy she's going to meet him down the road—"

"I'm glad to hear it," said Lindo unexpectedly. "It's dull work going for walks by oneself." He disliked Mr. Potter, who was not, as he happened to know, quite so law-abiding as he appeared to be. He let in the clutch and drove away, leaving the landlord staring after him.

CHAPTER X
INSPECTOR COLLIER TAKES CHARGE

AMY WALKED as quickly as she could through the village. Though there was nobody about she had a feeling that she was being watched from behind the lace curtains and the geraniums in the cottage windows. She was a stranger and therefore an object of interest, and probably they all knew about her aunt. After passing the last house the road made a sudden turn to the right up a short but steep hill and then descended with another abrupt turn, into a hollow. From the top of the hill she had a view across the Dower House Park. As she looked that way she saw Tony Dene. He was standing talking to a girl in a light coloured dress and a red beret. They were on the edge of a copse and while Amy watched them they turned and entered it together.

She walked on more slowly, feeling a little nervous now. She supposed that Tony was bringing one of his sisters to meet her. "I hope she's nice," she thought anxiously. After a while she stopped, and, taking a little mirror from her handbag, examined her face critically and powdered her nose. This bit of the road was very secluded, with the grounds of the Dower House on one side and Lennor Park on the other. Amy was walking very slowly now for the stile at which Tony had said he would meet her was in sight and there was no sign of him. She had been standing on the grass by the roadside for some minutes when he came hurrying along the path, vaulted the stile, and came eagerly up to her. He was alone.

"Have I kept you waiting? I'm frightfully sorry. Let's walk on."

"Was that your sister with you just now?"

He had fallen into step beside her. "Just now? What do you mean?"

The warmth had gone out of his voice. Her own had grown colder when she answered. "I saw you in the distance from the top of the hill."

"I see," he said. "No. Are you all right at the King's Head? I mean—all this is pretty rotten for you."

"Yes, it is," she said dully, adding, "I hope to get away to-morrow."

"Back to London?"

"Yes."

"And wipe us all off the slate? Well, I don't blame you."

"Not you," she said impulsively.

He had been staring straight in front of him but at that he turned his head to look at her. "Do you mean that?"

"Of course I do. You've been very kind. I'll always remember that."

They walked on for a minute or two in silence. Then he said, "Amy—there are lots of things I want to say to you, but it wouldn't be fair to you."

"Why not?"

"Because—we're in a mess—and I'm beginning to think it's even worse than it seemed at first. I had to go in to Ranchester this morning to—to view the body."

"It was my aunt?"

"Oh, yes."

"The sergeant was at the King's Head just now," she said. "He seemed disappointed that I couldn't tell him anything about her."

"Did he tell you that she had been killed by a heavy blow on the back of her head?"

"No," she said faintly.

"Well, I suppose it ought to have been obvious to me that she was murdered from the moment that I found the cover on the well," he said. "It was very dense of me not to grasp that. I'm afraid I shouldn't shine as a sleuth. Are you going to be at the inquest?"

"The sergeant said I'd better."

They had retraced their steps to the stile. They were both disappointed. They had got on so well together before, but the tragedy in which they were involved seemed to have put an end to that. Tony seemed stiff and self-conscious. Amy thought he might walk on with her towards the village, but he stopped at the stile and held out his hand.

"Good-bye."

"He doesn't trust me," she thought sadly as she made her way back to the King's Head. "But why was he so anxious to meet me if he had nothing to say to me?" She sat in the dreary little parlour at the back of the inn, trying to read *East Lynne*, until Mrs. Potter brought in her supper.

Amy looked with distaste at the slices of underdone cold beef and the lumps of crimson beetroot swimming in vinegar.

"I'm not hungry and my head aches. I think I'll go to bed."

"Pity you didn't say so before and save me a bit of trouble," said the landlady sourly. "You had a nice walk, too," she glanced curiously at the girl's flushed face. She had sent her young nephew out to spy on her lodger and he had reported that she had met young Mr. Dene along the road. "A bit of news for you, miss, that I heard just now in the bar. They say the Chief Constable's not satisfied with Sergeant Lindo's goings on, and has called in the Yard. The sergeant was rung up from headquarters while he was here. I said at the time he looked like a man who's had a knock. Thought he was going to make his name over this job, I daresay."

Mrs. Potter was right. Lindo had heard from his Superintendent that the Colonel had come back to the station after lunch and had got into touch with Scotland Yard.

"They're sending somebody down at once. He'll be here about five and you'd better be on hand to show him the ropes. I'm sorry, Lindo—"

"It's all right, sir."

The sergeant felt rather bitter nevertheless as he drove back to Ranchester. He had not been twenty-four hours on the case yet, and he thought he had done pretty well. It was his first murder and he had been very keen. But he was a sensible man and he had no intention of venting any chagrin he might feel on the man who was coming to take his place.

He found the newcomer in the Superintendents room when he got to the station. The Superintendent introduced him.

"This is Sergeant Lindo who has been in charge of the investigation until now. Lindo, this is Inspector Hugh Collier, of Scotland Yard."

Lindo brightened. He had heard of Inspector Collier. He was reported to be easy to work with and always ready to give credit where credit was due. He was a youngish man with a slim active figure and a lean pleasant face. He smiled as he held out his hand.

"I've booked a bedroom and a sitting-room at the Station Hotel. Perhaps you'll come along now and have a spot of dinner with me and we can talk things over in a friendly way," he suggested. Lindo accepted gratefully. He had had a heavy day and had eaten when and where he could. The Station Hotel catered for the better class of commercial travellers and the cooking, though plain, was good. Lindo, inclined to be shy at first, was quite at his ease before they reached the end of their meal. The duck had been tender and the peas were marrowfats.

"That's done me a lot of good," he acknowledged when the waiter had finally left them to sit over their coffee and cigarettes. "I was up before five. . . . I've done my best, Inspector."

"I don't doubt it," said Collier heartily, "I'll see you get your share of the bouquets—if any—but it's early to talk of those. Now let's get down to brass tacks."

Lindo produced his notebook and embarked on his narrative.

"That's as far as I've got," he concluded. "You see how it looks. One can guess at a motive, and feel certain suspicions of certain persons, but there isn't, so far, any evidence to justify an arrest."

"I've seen the body," Collier said, "and I know all about the big surprise. It throws an odd sort of light on this Mrs. Dene. How does she strike you?"

"A handsome woman, very quiet and well mannered. Quite the lady. Several people have expressed their surprise that she could be a friend of such a vulgar person as the deceased."

"Yes," said Collier. "It does seem curious. Well, we shall see. That contused wound at the back of the head must have bled freely. You found no bloodstains?"

"None."

"Evidently the murderer wasn't pressed for time. If it was young Dene he'd have had—how long?—nearly two hours from the moment he left the station and drove off in his car until the niece arrived at the lodge. Yes, the time factor isn't going to help him much."

"His story is that he went for a long drive and came home about nine. He seemed hot and bothered when his sister saw him between nine and ten o'clock. He says he was upset because he'd been rude to this girl on the train."

"Why was he rude to her?"

"He couldn't stick the aunt. One can hardly blame him for that if he thought his mother—"

"Hamlet and Gertrude," murmured Collier.

He lit another cigarette. "Can you tell me why your Chief Constable was in such a hurry to call in the Yard? You had the case well in hand, and they generally wait a bit longer."

Lindo cleared his throat. "I think he wanted to shift the responsibility. You see he's a cousin of the Lennors, and Sir Miles is engaged to the elder Miss Dene."

"I see. Very trying for everybody being mixed up in such a scandal. What sort of impression has young Dene made on you?"

"One can't help liking him," said Lindo, "and it's in his favour that he called the police. Why should he do that if he'd done the job?"

"Quite. Has he put forward any theory?"

"He suggested an attack by a tramp or a hawker."

"That's a possibility. Will you find out what casuals were in the neighbourhood on Monday or Tuesday, Sergeant? See if you can get on the track of anyone of that sort sleeping in a doss house Monday night who seemed at all flush of money or was anxious to wash his clothes."

"Nothing was taken from the lodge, Inspector. There was nearly a pound in silver and coppers in the handbag I found in the bedroom."

"That suggests that the motive was not robbery, but we can't rule out the hawker theory at this stage. Was any weapon found?"

"Not yet, sir. The murderer cleaned up pretty thoroughly. It makes it hard for us."

"We'll have to work on the time factor," said Collier. "Where is the inquest being held?"

"At the Town Hall. Two o'clock. Well, good night, Inspector, and thank you for having me, as the kids say." Lindo spoke cheerfully. This man from the Yard seemed a good sort. He would be pleasant to work with.

After he was gone Collier went for a stroll through the steep winding streets to the green bird-haunted space shaded with aged elms that divided the busy haunts of men from the House of God. The great gate leading to the precincts was closed but he stood for a while looking through the bars at the clustering spires that pierced the night sky. On his way back to his hotel he noticed the Town Hall, an eighteenth-century building with a portico and a steep flight of steps leading to the main entrance, with a bust of George I in a periwig, looking down from a niche above. He walked round the building, down a side street and another that ran parallel with the Market Square, and was glad to see that there were several exits from the back of the hall. He did not anticipate a big crowd on the first day of the inquest, but arrangements had been made with the coroner to take only formal evidence of identification before an adjournment. Later, if they made an arrest, they would have to deal with crowds. Collier did not fancy the idea of bringing a prisoner down those steps. Well, time enough to worry about that.

He was being lent a car by the local authorities and he found it waiting for him in the yard when he came down the next morning. He was studying a local ordnance map while he ate his breakfast. He had said he would drive himself. He liked to work alone if possible. He was coldly received by Parsons.

"It's very early. The mistress is not down yet. I doubt if she can see anyone. She hasn't been well."

"I'm sorry," said Collier, "but I've come on business. This is my card. I am prepared to wait."

Parsons showed him into the morning-room and went to tell Tony, who was at breakfast with his sisters. Lavvy was sipping orange juice. Mollie, who was quite indifferent to her figure, was helping herself to bacon and eggs.

Tony groaned. "What another of them? Did you tell him my mother wasn't up yet?"

"Yes, sir. I said the mistress was resting."

"I'll see him myself."

"I showed him into the morning-room, sir. And I think I ought to tell you—the cook and I both thought so—"

"What, in heaven's name? Has the kitchen boiler burst?"

"It's about Duncan, sir. She never came in last night."

"Never came in?"

"No, sir. It was her afternoon and evening out, but she should have been in by ten."

"You mean she just walked out on us," said Lavvy. "It's just the sort of thing she would do. She was under notice anyway."

"She didn't pack her box or anything, miss. Cook and me don't know what to think."

"Didn't she go to the Pictures at Ranchester once before and miss the last bus and come back the next morning?" said Lavvy.

"Yes, miss. But she ought to be here by now if that's what happened."

"She'll turn up presently," said Tony. "Quite right to tell us, Parsons."

He left his sisters to finish their interrupted breakfast and went to the morning-room. Collier, who was standing by the window, was struck by his youth.

He introduced himself. "I've come down from Scotland Yard. Colonel Boult asked us to take over."

"But surely it's a fairly simple case. Can't the local people handle it?"

"I'm afraid I mustn't discuss that, Mr. Dene. It involves my going over some of the ground again which may be boring for you. I'm sorry—"

"Oh, that's all right. So long as you don't harry my mother. She's not strong, and this has been a great shock."

"Naturally," murmured Collier. "But I rather hoped to see her—"

"She won't be getting up until lunch time," said Tony definitely. "And after that I shall drive her in to Ranchester for the inquest."

Collier, after a moment's reflection, decided not to press the point.

"Very well," he said easily, "later on will do. The inquest won't last long."

"Won't it? How can you tell? I thought juries sometimes took ages over the verdict."

"The inquest will be opened and the medical evidence given that will allow the funeral to take place, and then it will be adjourned to give us the opportunity to get on with our investigation."

"I see," said Tony. "I say, Inspector, is my mother's presence really necessary?"

"I'm afraid it is, Mr. Dene. Very unpleasant, I know, but inevitable. If I may make a suggestion—"

"Please do."

"In your place, Mr. Dene, I would arrive early and park my car not in the square itself, but in the street at the back of the Town Hall, and go in by one of the side doors. You don't want to push your way through a crowd."

"Good God! Is there any chance of our having to do that?"

"I'm afraid you must be prepared for something of the sort," said Collier.

He was conscious of a slight sense of nausea. The boy looked so defenceless.

CHAPTER XI

SENSATION IN COURT

"THIS WAY, SIR."

Tony took his mother's arm. "Look out, darling. There's a step." They emerged without warning from a dark passage smelling of disinfectants into a large room lit from above. There was a platform at the far end with some chairs and a table covered with a faded red cloth, and another table close to the wall on the left at which three young men sat whispering together. They all stared very hard at the Denes as they passed, and Tony realised that theirs must be the Press table. From that corner a rivulet of ink would flow that might become a sea to-morrow.

A young constable was shepherding the witnesses into the seats reserved for them. Tony saw Amy Steer, but she did not look at him. She had not gone into mourning as his mother had but was wearing a beige skirt and jumper and a brown beret. A middle-aged man with sandy hair going grey was sitting next to her. He betrayed impatience as the jury were being called and sworn in and looked several times at his watch. The coroner, on the other hand, was obviously in no hurry. He was a member of a local firm of solicitors who in his younger days had frequently taken part in private theatricals. He had a leading role now and was evidently determined to make the most of it in spite of the repressive efforts of the police.

"There is no longer any legal obligation to view the body, members of the jury, and you have decided to waive your right to do so. Very sensible. You have spared yourselves a painful and an unnecessary ordeal. Unnecessary because we are to hear the sworn evidence of the doctor who was present when the deceased was taken out of the well and who subsequently made a post-mortem examination of the remains. I shall call Sergeant Lindo as my first witness. Sergeant Lindo."

The sergeant appeared from the back of the hall and stood on the right of the coroner. He had been on duty at the police station on Tuesday evening at twenty minutes to eight. Mr. Dene had telephoned from the Dower House that there was a body in a well in the garden of the North Lodge. He had gone immediately to the Dower House, taking two men with him. Mr. Dene, who was very agitated, had accompanied him to the lodge which was situated at some distance from the Dower House near a gate which for many years had not been used for vehicular traffic.

The coroner looked up from his writing. "Why do you say that, sergeant?"

"Well, it struck me that it was a lonely, unfrequented part, sir. On the other hand the gate was not locked. One could get in or out that way and strike across the moor to the main road without passing through the village. I hadn't at that time heard anything to suggest that there had been foul play, but the cover was on the well, and I learned from Mr. Dene that he had had to lift it to look in. He was attracted to the spot by his dog scratching at the boards. I saw the body partially submerged and arranged to have it brought to the surface as soon as it was light next morning."

One of the jurymen asked a question. "Why not at once?"

"It was growing dark and I needed help and tackle. I made arrangements for an early start and we were on the ground before six. We got the body out. Dr. Mackintosh was present and he showed me a contused wound at the back of the head. The body was placed in the ambulance and brought to the mortuary."

"Were there any signs of a struggle?"

"No."

"Was Mr. Dene present in the morning?"

"No. He was asked to come to the mortuary later in the day. After some hesitation he identified the deceased as the tenant of the North Lodge."

"Thank you. That will do for the present, Sergeant Lindo."

The coroner held a whispered conversation with the superintendent.

"I understand that Mr. Dene is not legally represented?"

Tony, catching Lindo's eye, interpreted its message and stood up. "No, sir. I didn't think it would be necessary."

"I certainly think it would be advisable. Is there anyone here you would care to brief? Perhaps not. You want more time for consideration. I shall call you, Mr. Dene, as the ends of justice require but I shall not take advantage of your inexperience. Come here, please, and stand by the table."

"Pompous ass," thought Tony ungratefully, as he made his way across the court. The black binding of the Bible was cold and clammy. It felt like a toad. He repeated the usual formula. The coroner shook out his pen and tried the nib on a bit of blotting-paper.

"Now, Mr. Dene, all we are trying to do to-day is to establish as far as we can the identity of the deceased. You saw the body in the mortuary on Wednesday morning."

"Yes."

"The whole body?"

"No. It was covered with a sheet. They turned that back and showed me the head."

"You recognised the deceased from that?"

"Yes. Of course she looked very changed. I mean—she always used a lot of make-up and long earrings that were very characteristic. But she was a woman with large and rather pronounced features. There could not be any mistake."

"You are quite sure, Mr. Dene?"

"Absolutely."

"Just so," said the coroner. He sat pinching his underlip and gazing reflectively at the young man. "I don't think I'll ask you anything further at this stage."

Tony was relieved but a little puzzled, too. He went back to his seat beside his mother. "It wasn't so bad after all," he whispered.

She made no reply.

The coroner was holding another consultation with the Superintendent. They seemed to come to some agreement for he nodded.

"I shall now call Dr. Mackintosh."

The doctor was on his feet instantly. The sergeant had taken the Bible woodenly as part of an accustomed routine, and Tony had fumbled and hesitated and nearly dropped the greasy little volume in his nervous anxiety to do the right thing. The doctor snatched it as he might have snatched an instrument from the slow-witted assistant during an operation.

"Now then—" he began, but the coroner was not to be hurried.

"One moment, doctor," he said blandly. "You were present in the orchard at the back of the premises known locally as the North Lodge on the Lennor Dower House estate on Wednesday morning while the police were getting a body out of the well?"

"I was."

"You made a cursory examination of the remains on the spot, and a more detailed one later at the mortuary?"

"Yes."

"Will you inform the jury as to the result of these examinations." There had been some shuffling and whispering at the back of the court during the earlier part of the proceedings, but the silence was now profound.

"I found a large contused wound at the back of the head. I should say a blow had been delivered with great force by some heavy, blunt instrument, such as a metal paper weight or doorstop, or a hammer, or a flat iron might have done it. The water in the well had washed away the blood but I found some splinters of bone entangled in the hair."

"Would this injury be the cause of death?"

"Undoubtedly."

"Can you tell us anything further, doctor?"

"Yes. When I examined the body in the mortuary I found it to be that of a man."

Tony gasped. That was impossible, of course.

His mother's old friend. His mother—

Inspector Collier, sitting unnoticed in his dark corner under the gallery, had kept his eyes fixed on Mrs. Dene, and he was puzzled by what he saw. Had she or had she not been prepared for a statement that had taken most of those present completely by surprise? There had been a quick lift of the head and nothing more. She sat as she had sat throughout, quietly attentive, her ungloved hands folded in her lap, with nothing but her extreme pallor to show that she was in any way affected by the ordeal she was undergoing. There had been no change in her attitude when her son was giving evidence, and there was none now. A remarkable woman, he thought, with a will of iron and an extraordinary control over her emotions. Did she feel what had seemed to be solid earth sliding away under her feet? There was nothing to show it.

The buzz of excitement at the back of the court had been quelled. There was an expectant hush. The journalists at the Press table were scribbling feverishly. This was going to be front page stuff. A scoop. What luck, they were thinking, what heavenly luck!

The coroner was speaking. "Have you anything to add to that, Dr. Mackintosh?"

"Only that the body was that of a healthy and well nourished individual of about fifty. The approximate height was five feet eight inches, and the weight ten stone seven. Three teeth in the upper jaw had been stopped. There were no scars or distinguishing marks, nothing in any way abnormal." The foreman of the jury intervened. "Excuse me, sir. The jury are a bit confused. I mean to say—what about Mrs. Hall?"

"The evidence before us indicates that the deceased passed under that name. How was this person dressed, doctor?"

"The underclothing was of pink silk trimmed with lace. The dress was of black silk. Everything, naturally, was stained and sodden with water, but all appeared to be of good quality."

"I must warn the jury that we are here to determine the cause of death," remarked the coroner, "the sex of the deceased may not be relevant. I have one further question to ask this witness. Is it possible that this person died as the result of an accident? Could the injury to the head have been caused by a fall, by striking the sharp edge of a fender for instance?"

"Only if he fell from a considerable height, and in that event I should expect to find other injuries, including extensive bruises."

"I see. Thank you. That will be all."

A constable opened a door near the platform and the doctor hurried away.

"I shall not call any further witnesses—" began the coroner. He broke off as Mrs. Dene stood up.

"May I speak?"

The coroner adjusted his glasses. "I would advise you to wait until you have had legal advice, madam."

"I only want to speak the truth. I don't need a lawyer to help me to do that. I want to say that the evidence of the last witness came as a terrible shock. I never dreamed of such a thing. Even now I can hardly believe it."

"Your evidence will be heard in due course, Mrs. Dene." He raised his voice. "This court is now adjourned until a date which will be decided later."

The big doors were opened, letting in a current of fresh air. There was a scraping of chairs and a shuffling of feet.

A policeman came up to the Denes. "This way, sir." Tony took his mother's arm and they followed their guide by way of a lobby filled with ladders and pails and brooms through a back door into the street where Tony, remembering the Inspectors hint, had left his car.

Tony only spoke once on the way home and that was to ask his mother if he was going too fast for her. She was usually nervous when he was driving. But this time she only shook her head. The weather had changed while they were in the court, the sky was overcast and a fine rain was falling. Lavvy and Mollie had come in from the garden and were awaiting their return in the drawing-room. Lavvy was telling her fortune with a pack of cards and she only turned her head without moving as her mother came in, followed by Tony, but Mollie threw down her book and ran to Mrs. Dene.

"Darling, you look terribly tired. Was it too awful?"

Mrs. Dene sank into a chair. "Ring for tea, Mollie."

Mollie glanced anxiously at her brother. "What was the verdict?"

"They haven't got to that. The inquest was adjourned. Shut up now. Let's have tea first."

Parsons was wheeling in the tea wagon. Nobody spoke until she had left them. Then Mrs. Dene said, "You pour out, Lavvy. No. I don't want anything to eat. Tony, we must tell them now. We may not have much time. That man from Scotland Yard will be coming and I shall have to see him this time."

"Yes," said Tony drearily, "I suppose so." He knew she was right.

Mrs. Dene drank her tea and set down the cup.

"The police doctor says Harriet Hall was a man."

The two girls stared at her, uncomprehending. "A man? But—you mean the body found in the well? Then it wasn't Mrs. Hall after all—"

"Tony identified her, and so did I."

"Mother!" cried Lavvy, and then got up abruptly and walked over to the window where she stood with her back to them. The other two were silent.

Mrs. Dene looked from one to the other. "I didn't know," she said passionately. "You've got to believe that or—or everything will fall to pieces. Good God! Do you think I should have had the courage to sit there if I had dreamed what was coming."

Tony moistened his lips. "You never suspected? But, of course, if you say so—all the same—years ago, when you were young—I mean—was this a life-long imposture?"

He saw her hesitate and his heart sank. He longed to be able to trust her, but it was not easy.

"I suppose so," she said at last. "One hears of such cases. It's no use discussing it. We've just got to accept the fact. I'm terribly sorry for all your sakes—" her voice broke.

Mollie came at once and knelt by her, rubbing her face against her shoulder. "Mummie, darling, don't cry. Don't—"

Lavvy, who all this time had been staring out of the window at the rain-swept terrace with angry eyes, whirled round.

"Easy to say that when you've involved us all in the most ghastly scandal. You knew we all loathed the creature, but you would have him here. You lent him the lodge and furniture. Nothing was too good for poor Mrs. Hall. One would almost think he had some hold over you—" her voice changed. "Mother! He hadn't?"

"Shut up, Lavvy," said her brother fiercely. "You're mad—"

He stopped. Mrs. Dene was speaking. "Get up, Mollie dear. Lavvy, pull yourself together. We needn't make bad worse."

They had all heard the front door bell.

CHAPTER XII
TEA LEAVES

AFTER THE INQUEST Collier waited to speak to the Superintendent. The Chief Constable had hurried away, betraying an evident desire to avoid any discussion of the case, and the coroner, too, was gone.

"She took it very well," he remarked. "I felt sorry for the boy."

"So was I," said the Superintendent. "The poor devil cringed. I suppose there's no doubt Hall, or whatever his name was, was her lover?"

"Most people will assume that," said Collier, "but I'm not sure. It's plausible, and yet it's far fetched. But we must be prepared for the unusual in this case. I'm off to the Dower House now."

"Cruel!" he thought as he drove along the road the Denes had taken some twenty minutes earlier. He thought of the hunted fox, panting, mudstained, dragging his brush, with the pack at his heels. He disliked working on cases where there were what are called extenuating circumstances. It was painful to have to strive to get a term of penal servitude for a man you rather liked, worse still when you might bring him to the gallows. Who had killed Hall? Was it young Dene? He had no real alibi apparently from the moment he had left the train on Monday afternoon until he returned to the Dower House after nine o'clock. But a jury would need something more positive. Hall had not been seen alive since about noon on Monday. And who was Hall anyway? It was too early to form theories. Collier stopped at the King's Head. The police had arranged to have Amy Steer sent back from court in a taxi. It was not yet opening time but the landlord came out to him after he had sounded his horn twice.

"Will you tell Miss Steer I'm coming to see her presently. In about an hour's time."

"I hear the inquest was adjourned," said the landlord. "Excuse me, Inspector, but is it a fact that—"

"You'll see it all in the morning papers," said Collier brusquely, and drove on.

He passed up the avenue of limes to the Dower House, saw the Denes' car at the foot of the steps, and brought his own to a standstill beside it.

The door was opened by the parlourmaid. He stepped into the hall. "I want to see Mrs. Dene."

"I'll tell her. Will you wait in here, please." She opened the door of the morning room. Then, as he was passing in, she said, "There is something fresh we think you ought to know." He glanced quickly at her face, the impassive face of the well trained servant. He judged her to be about thirty-five and of the type that has no use for men.

"Is there? What is it?"

"It's about the housemaid, Ruby Duncan. It was her half day off yesterday, and she hasn't come back. She wasn't meaning to go for good. Her clothes are all lying about in her room, and a letter to her married sister half written on her chest of drawers and the pen left in the ink—"

"Have you spoken to Mrs. Dene?"

"Yes. I did this morning. She said Duncan must have gone to Ranchester to the Pictures and missed the last bus. But she should be back now."

"All right," said Collier. "I'll make enquiries. Is she a local girl?"

"No. Her home's in Streatham."

"About this half written letter you saw in her room. Did you read it?"

Parsons looked down her nose. "I am not in the habit of reading other people's letters."

Collier suppressed a smile. "Of course not. I'm afraid I am though. It's sometimes a part of my job. I'll have a look at the young woman's room before I go. But first I'll see Mrs. Dene if you'll ask her to be so good."

Mrs. Dene did not keep him waiting.

"You wanted to see me, Inspector? Please sit down. I'm sorry I couldn't talk to you yesterday, but I am not well. This terrible affair has been a great shock."

"Naturally," Collier agreed. His tone was sympathetic. "I am so sorry to have to trouble you, but you can be of great assistance to us if you will. You see—I'll be quite frank with you, Mrs. Dene. We have two theories regarding this crime. This may be one of those cases where a tramp or a hawker attacks someone who has declined to give him money. But we have no evidence of that, so far. Or the attack may have been made by some former associate of the deceased. Now—please forgive me, Mrs. Dene—I heard you say in court that you were not aware that the so called Mrs. Hall was a man."

"I was not."

"How long had you known this person?"

"About sixteen years."

"No more than that? I understood from your son that you were girls together."

"No. I was about thirty. My children were quite small. I lost sight of her after that."

"She was married then?"

"She—he—was known as Mrs. Hall. I thought she was a widow."

"She was extremely kind to you?"

"Yes."

"She was a neighbour of yours?"

"Yes."

"Where were you living then?"

"I—I'm not sure. We moved about a lot."

"Can't you give me some idea?"

"I'm afraid not."

"But if this person lived near you. Doesn't that help you to fix it? She didn't move about with you, did she?"

"No."

"Was it in or near London?"

He was watching her closely and he saw that little beads of sweat were standing on her upper lip. He was not blind to the beauty of that white strained face or to its mute appeal for mercy, but he had his work to do.

"Were you a widow then?"

"My husband died about that time."

"You left this place and went to another?"

"Yes. We moved about."

"Of course, Mrs. Dene, if this worries you I can apply to your son for information."

"He knew nothing whatever about Mrs. Hall before she came here in March."

"She had done you a kindness in the past?"

"Yes."

"Do you mind telling me what it was exactly?"

"She—she lent me some money."

"But you are a wealthy woman, Mrs. Dene."

"I wasn't then. I had nothing. After my husband's death I kept house for a relative, and he paid for my children to be educated. When he died last year he left me everything he had."

"Thank you. That is very clear. So when this person whom you had known as Mrs. Hall turned up here and recalled your former friendship you offered her the use of the North Lodge?"

"Yes."

"You lent her furniture and gave her money at various times?"

"Yes."

"She had one hundred pounds from you last week?"

"Yes."

"Did you know that she gave it to the niece who was coming to stay with her to spend on clothes?"

"No. She said nothing about the niece. The girl's arrival took us all by surprise."

"You would not have approved?"

"It was no business of mine."

"But you were paying the piper. About how much money has the deceased had from you since March, Mrs. Dene?"

"I really have no idea."

"You could tell by looking at your pass book, couldn't you?"

"No. I never made out cheques for her. She had no banking account. I just gave her a little money in pound notes or ten shilling notes."

"One hundred pounds at a time?"

"Not as a rule. Never before last week."

"Are you overdrawn at the bank, Mrs. Dene?"

"I don't think so. I've had a good many expenses. This place costs more to run than I realised when I bought it. We all love it, but I thought of trying to sell after my daughter's marriage. Of course, now—" her lips trembled. "I don't know what will happen." She was remembering Lavvy's hard voice and angry eyes.

Collier was turning over the pages of his notebook. He had there a precis of all the information he had had from Lindo. "It's such a pity that you can't remember where you and the deceased were living at the time that he lent you that sum of money. How much was it, by the way?"

She hesitated. "Five hundred pounds."

"I see. He wasn't so badly off then. Had he private means, or some kind of employment?"

"I don't know."

"You see, Mrs. Dene, if we knew the place and the time we could take up the enquiry from there."

"I'm sorry. I can't remember."

"Where was your husband buried, Mrs. Dene?"

He saw a pulse beating in her throat. "Somewhere in London—I mean—he was cremated."

"I see. At Woking?"

"Yes."

"Then your mind is not a complete blank, Mrs. Dene. You do remember that."

"It will be if you harry me much more."

"I am sorry," he said again, and meant it.

He had learnt a good deal from the interview and there were other aspects of the case to be considered. He stood up.

"I won't trouble you any further to-day. Just one point, Mrs. Dene. Your parlourmaid told me just now that one of the other servants is missing."

"Oh—that would be Duncan, the housemaid—she may have simply walked out. She was leaving at the end of the month. She was very unsatisfactory. I shall probably get an impudent letter from her in a day or two asking that her things may be sent on to her."

"Very likely," said Collier, "but perhaps while I am here I had better have a look at her room."

"Oh certainly. I'll take you up," she said at once. Parsons had been lingering in the hall but she vanished when she saw that Mrs. Dene was accompanying the detective. The servants' bedrooms were on the top floor.

"I think this is Duncan's room," said Mrs. Dene, turning a handle. "It does look as if she had meant to come back," she admitted.

Ruby's brown uniform frock and muslin cap and apron lay across a chair. One of the drawers had been left open and a crumpled silk blouse and a stocking were hanging out. A paper-backed novelette lay on another chair by the bed with a candle-stick whose candle was half burnt out.

"That's the cause of half the fires in country houses," remarked Collier, "they always blame the electricity system." A twopenny bottle of ink stood on the broad window sill with a pen in it and near it on a bit of blotting paper a sheet of pink note paper on which a letter had been begun. He read the few scrawled words:

DEAR OLD MAUDIE,

How's you and Perce pretty tollollish I hope same here but oh how dull and I won't half be glad to be back in dear old London. Don't worry about that money. I'll pay it all back and a bit over. There's ways and means. I'm going to have a jolly good try anyway. But first of all

Mrs. Dene had remained in the doorway. He did not wonder at that. The window was shut and the room had a close smell. He looked in the hanging cupboard and lifted the curtain that covered a coat and a mackintosh hanging from hooks behind the door.

"Have you made any discoveries?"

He glanced at her quickly. "None. Except that, as you say, she meant to come back. I will ask you to leave the room just as it is, please. Tell the other maids not to touch it."

"Very well."

"On second thoughts," he said, "I'll see them myself. I must ask a question or two. Are these the back stairs? Good afternoon, Mrs. Dene, and thank you for your help."

He found the three remaining women servants at tea. The cook, who was large and exuberant, greeted him warmly.

"Pleased to meet you, I'm sure. I've heard a lot about you from Miss Parsons. Come to put our country bobbies to rights, haven't you? You could do with a cup of tea, I daresay?"

"Thanks. I should like one."

"Set a chair for the gentleman, Gladys."

The youthful between maid who had been gazing at him with round-eyed curiosity, hastened to obey. The cook filled a cup and cut a large slice of plum cake for the visitor.

"You've got an appetite, I hope. Miss Parsons took their tea up when they got back from the inquest, and not one of them had a bite, and it was one of them almond cakes Mr. Anthony's so fond of too. But when the milkman told us what had come out in the evidence I didn't wonder. Fancy that Mrs. Hall! Mind you, I always felt there was something queer about her, but I never thought of that. Well, I mean to say, one doesn't." The cook sat with her elbows on the table and, holding her cup with both hands, blew thoughtfully on her tea. "If you ask me," she said judicially, "there's a lot at the back of this."

"I'm inclined to agree with you," said Collier.

"I'm sorry for the young ones," said Parsons, "They've always thought the world of their mother, him and Miss Mollie especially, though Lavvy's her favourite."

The cook, whose manners were unrefined, imbibed her tea with loud sucking noises, "Ar," she said. "The gentry round about won't touch them with a barge pole, not after this. They could have got over the murder. I lived in a family once where the married daughter shot a young fellow. She got off. Said she didn't mean it or something. It didn't make no difference to the people who came to the house. But this is different. Their name's mud after this. You'll see."

"You're getting off the point, cook," said Parsons.

"What d'you mean, the point?"

"The point is who murdered him and who shoved him down the well. You haven't got anybody yet, Inspector?"

"Not yet," said Collier.

The cook smacked her lips with gusto. "Then there's still a murderer at large, and maybe he hasn't done with us yet."

The little between maid uttered a smothered shriek. The cook, who was evidently determined to make the most of the dramatic possibilities of their situation, nodded solemnly. "Gladys wouldn't sleep alone last night, Inspector, and I don't blame her. Ruby Duncan's gone. It may be her turn next."

Parsons looked reproachfully from the cook, whose little eyes, sunk in fat, were twinkling with cheerful malice, to the scared face of Gladys.

"You shouldn't tease her, cook. It's just her fun, Glad. There's no danger, is there, Inspector?"

Collier was silent for a moment. He sat facing the window and through it he could see the park land stretching away to the encircling woods, deserted and desolate, through a veil of falling rain.

"I can't say that. There may be. I wouldn't advise you to go out alone at present."

Nobody spoke. Gladys gasped and edged her chair nearer to the parlourmaid's, and even the cook seemed a trifle dashed.

"About Miss Duncan. I wonder if you could tell me what she was wearing when she went out?"

It was Gladys who answered. "Her black and white check dress with a red belt and a red beret, and her red handbag. I know 'cos I met her coming out of her room, and I said 'Aren't you all dolled up. Who is he this time?' and she said 'Never you mind.'"

"Had she a young man?"

"Not a regular one. Picked up a different boy each time," said the cook. "Hot stuff, if you ask me."

"She had a chap in London," said Gladys, "but she's not one to let on. Sort of secret about him, she was."

"Did he ever come down to see her?"

"Not that I know of."

Collier looked at his watch and uttered an exclamation. "Snakes and ladders. I must be getting on. Thanks for the tea. I was jolly glad of it. And I've never tasted better cake, Mrs.—"

"Truby, and my friends call me Mabel," said the cook graciously. "I've always wanted to meet a 'tec from the Yard. I've read about them in books. What's your next step, or is that asking too much?"

He smiled. "Not at all. I'm going on to the lodge now. The scene of the crime."

"Coo!" said Gladys.

"By yourself?"

"Certainly."

"If you'd had time I'd have read your fortune in your cup," said the cook. "There might be a warning in it. You're on the small side for a policeman if you don't mind my saying so. Suppose the murderer's hanging around. They say they always come back. Drawn to it like—" Her voice had dropped to a blood-curdling whisper.

"That would be a bit of luck for me," said Collier.

Mrs. Truby shook her head portentously. "I don't like the look of the leaves in your cup. You be careful, Inspector. Look behind you. I see something stealing along like a shadow—"

"Where?"

"In your cup."

The little eyes were not twinkling now. He saw that she was in earnest. "I'll be careful," he promised.

CHAPTER XIII

A LATE CALL

MOLLIE SAT ALONE in the drawing-room until she could not bear it any longer. Then she went upstairs and knocked at her mother's bedroom door.

"Mummie—may I come in?"

"Is it Lavvy?"

"No—it's me—Mollie."

"I really need a rest, dear."

"All right."

Mollie knew that she came third, and rather a bad third, in her mother's affections. Mrs. Dene was intensely proud of Lavvy's beauty, and she was proud of Tony because he was a boy—but Mollie was just ordinary. "Oh, if she'd only turn to me," the girl thought. "I wouldn't be beastly to her." She walked down the passage and tried her sister's door. It was locked, and an angry voice bade her go away.

"Very well. But you're a rotter, Lav, going on like this. I'll never forgive you for the way you turned on Mother after all she'd been through."

"Shut up. The servants will hear you."

"That's all you care about. Keeping up appearances."

"Appearances? My God! Are there any left?"

Mollie bit her lip hard. After all, perhaps Lavvy was right. It was rather undignified to quarrel through a door. She made her way downstairs, pausing at the landing window to watch the detective from Scotland Yard drive off in his car in the direction of the North Lodge, and found her brother in the boot-room struggling into an old mackintosh. "Where are you going, Tony?"

"I'm going to see Amy Steer. Now the inquest is adjourned she may be going back to London."

"Is that wise, Tony?"

"Probably not. But I've got to see her."

"Why?"

It was dark in the boot-room, but not too dark for him to see that Mollie's round freckled face was swollen and disfigured with crying. Poor kid, he thought, and answered more gently.

"This must be as big a shock to her as it was to us, and she's quite alone, Mollie."

Mollie hesitated. "You're sure she's all right, Tony? I mean—now we know Mrs. Hall was a man one can't help thinking all sorts of things. This niece was very—very sudden. He may have been married. She might be his wife, and he just called her a niece—"

"What a mind you must have!" said Tony indignantly. "If you'd taken some notice of her the other evening when I brought her here instead of leaving her until she got fed up and walked off to the village you'd know better."

Mollie's lips trembled. "I thought you'd forgiven me for that. We were all so upset, and the time slipped by—"

"All right. Don't blub. But it just shows how much sympathy she'd be likely to get here."

"You're—you're awfully keen on her, aren't you?"

"Yes." He settled his beret at a rakish angle and made for the door. "I am."

"Oh, Tony—let me go with you—"

He looked back at her. "Better keep out of it, old girl."

"Mother and Lavvy don't want me. You and I've always been pals, Tony—"

"That's true. All right. But be quick."

"You aren't taking the car?"

"No. It's Mother's car, and I'm pretty sure she wouldn't want me to go. I realise that I've depended too much on Mother, Mollie. I've got to learn to stand alone. Put on your galoshes. We'll take the short cut through the woods and the grass will be sopping with all this rain."

Mollie brightened. That was more like Tony. He was always thoughtful. She took his arm presently as they trudged across the park. "Tony, do you understand what it's all about? I mean—Mother can't have known Mrs. Hall was a man, can she?"

"No. Of course not." But his tone lacked conviction.

They walked some way in silence before she spoke again.

"Mother always stood up for Mrs. Hall. She gave her everything she asked for, but—looking back, I think she was always afraid of her."

"Yes. But don't say that to any of the policemen, Mollie."

"Oh—why not?"

He answered between his teeth. "You've got to be damn careful, what you say. We all have."

They had both dreaded meeting people in the village street, but the rain had driven everybody indoors.

"They've given her the back sitting-room. We'll walk straight through," said Tony as they reached the inn. But the landlord came out of the bar and intercepted them in the passage.

"Good evening, Mr. Dene. Good evening, miss. What can I do for you?" His tone was familiar and he stared at them greedily. Tony, who had never liked the man, answered stiffly.

"Is Miss Steer in?"

"Miss Steer? She's gone. Paid her bill before she went into Ranchester for the inquest, and took her luggage along with her."

"Oh. Did she leave any address?"

"Not with me, she didn't. She'll have to with the police. They won't be losing sight of her yet awhile," said the landlord with a grin.

"I see. Thank you," said Tony, and marched out.

Mollie followed him anxiously, not daring to speak for she saw that he was on the verge of an outburst.

At last, when they had walked about half a mile, she said, "Where are we going?" He stopped short and looked about him vaguely through spectacles misted by the driving rain.

"Home, I suppose. Oh hell, we've come the wrong way. Sorry, Mollie. That leering beast made me see red. And it was a bit of a facer—her going like that." After a pause he added. "She's lucky to be able to get away. We've got to stick it here."

"Couldn't we shut up the Dower House and go back to London?"

"That depends on Mother."

"She'll do whatever seems best for Lavvy," said Mollie. "Lavvy's been waiting all day for Miles to come round, or ring her up."

"Does she really care for that chap?"

"I'm afraid she does."

"Mother was very bucked about their engagement," said Tony moodily, "she bought the Dower House to give Lavvy a background and a chance to get off with somebody like Lennor. The question now is if he's keen enough on her to stick to her through thick and thin. Personally, I doubt it."

"We mustn't give way," said Mollie. "I'm going to change into one of my best frocks for dinner. I won't slink. I won't slink," she added fiercely.

"Right you are," said her brother approvingly, "that's the stuff."

They dined alone, for Mrs. Dene and Lavvy remained in their rooms. Afterwards, at Tony's suggestion, they sat down to a game of chess in the library. He had thought of turning on the loud speaker and dancing, but Mollie was unwilling. She had hardly slept since the discovery of the body in the well, and she was more tired than she cared to admit.

Parsons came in soon after ten to ask if they wanted anything more. The servants were going to bed.

"Time you went up, Mollie," said Tony, "you look all in."

But the girl shook her head. "Not yet."

"All right."

After a while the doorbell rang. Tony glanced at the clock. It was past eleven.

"Who can it be at this hour? Stay there, Mollie. I'll go." But she followed him into the hall.

He opened the door, letting in a gust of cold rain-laden air. There was a big saloon car drawn up outside. Its wet roof reflected the light from the hall lamp. Three men were sheltering under the portico from the downpour. One of them stepped forward. It was Sergeant Lindo. He saw Mollie in the background and removed his hat.

"We've come to fetch you along to Ranchester, Mr. Dene."

Tony had turned rather white. "In the middle of the night? What's the idea?"

"It's my duty to warn you that anything you say may be used in evidence against you."

"Good God!" Tony had to moisten his lips before he could go on. "Does that mean that I'm under arrest?"

"Not exactly, Mr. Dene. You are being detained pending further enquiries. I would advise you to change into another suit and put whatever you may need for a day or two in a bag now. Saunders, you will accompany Mr. Dene to his room and remain with him."

Mollie came forward and slipped her hand into her brothers. He did not turn his head to look at her but he squeezed her fingers hard. She said in a high shaking voice. "It's ridiculous. You must be quite mad, Sergeant."

"I'm sorry, miss. Will you be as quick as you can, Mr. Dene?"

"Very well." He dropped his sister's hand and turned away. Saunders followed him.

"Sergeant—" gasped Mollie.

Lindo looked at the small shaking figure with compassion. He had hoped all the women of the family would have retired for the night. "If I was you, miss, I'd go straight to bed. If your brother's done no wrong he'll clear himself easy enough."

"Can I see him if I come into Ranchester in the morning?"

"That depends," he said cautiously, "but there's no harm in trying."

Tony was running down the stairs. He had changed into a grey flannel suit and was carrying a small suitcase. His guard followed him closely. Mollie ran forward.

"Darling—"

He kissed her hurriedly. "All right, kid. Don't worry. And don't tell Mother and Lavvy until the morning. It's all a mistake, of course."

She watched him go down the steps to the car. Lindo said "Good night," as he passed out. She answered him mechanically. She was alone.

Chapter XIV

FROM INFORMATION RECEIVED

Collier had spent an hour at the North Lodge, going over the ground that had already been covered by Sergeant Lindo and his men. He would have to make time later on to compare his notes with theirs. Meanwhile he had to drive back to Ranchester to meet the colleague who was coming down from the Yard as a result of a telephone conversation he had had with his Chief earlier in the day. He had asked for Sergeant Duffield. They had worked together before and always in harmony. Duffield was slow, dogged, enduring. His honest admiration for his more mercurial friend's methods was tempered by his native caution. He had to have things explained to him and Collier found that the consequent check in the process of deduction was salutary.

He was on the platform when the 7.20 came in.

"Glad you were able to come, Duffield. I've booked a room for you where I'm staying. There'll be a spot of dinner ready for us in my sitting-room. I hope you didn't dine on the train." Collier glanced at the bookstall as they left the station and saw the posters of two evening papers.

SINISTER TURN IN WELL MYSTERY
AMAZING EVIDENCE

SEX OF VICTIM IN WELL CASE
SENSATIONAL DISCLOSURES

"They're making the most of it. I knew they would," he remarked.

"I read about it in the train coming down," said Duffield. "It's a new one on me."

"And me. We've taken his finger-prints and sent them up to the Yard. Who was he, anyway? Called himself Mrs. Hall. We've been through his belongings at the lodge and there isn't a thing to help us. Women's clothing, best quality, but ready made and unmarked. A large supply of cosmetics, including a depilatory, and safety razors. Here we are."

They crossed the road and entered the hotel. A cold meal was laid ready for them in Collier's sitting-room. "I'm afraid we must not allow ourselves more than half an hour," said Collier as he unfolded his napkin. "There's a young woman in the case, an alleged niece of the victim, who arrived on the scene on Monday evening. She wants to go back to London but the police here have induced her to remain until to-morrow. They've found her lodgings where the landlady will keep an eye on her."

"Is she a suspect?"

"The so-called Mrs. Hall was last seen alive about midday on Monday when she left the Dower House after having grabbed a cake and some groceries from the store cupboard. This niece arrived on Monday evening and spent that night and the following day alone at the lodge. According to their story young Dene met her accidentally in the park and went back to the lodge with her. His dog ran out at the back and began to scratch at the cover of the well. Dene lifted the cover and saw the body and communicated with the police. The body was got out the following morning. Had it been in the water thirty-six hours, or twenty-four, or twelve? So far the police surgeon won't commit himself. Lindo says the girl is O.K. This Mrs. Hall had been advertising for the relatives of somebody named Steer. She answered the advertisement and got a letter, which unfortunately she did not keep, from an aunt she had never heard of. A meeting was arranged in the ladies' waiting-room at Victoria, and as a result of that meeting the girl came down to the North Lodge."

Sergeant Duffield grunted his disapproval.

"Some of these young girls have no more sense—"

Collier pushed back his chair. "We won't judge her unheard. She was present at the inquest, but I was too busy watching the Denes to pay much attention to her. Come along."

The sergeant rose obediently, with his mouth full of bread and cheese, and lumbered off in the wake of his more active superior officer.

Amy Steer's landlady showed them into a neat little sitting-room. The girl rose to receive them. She looked pale and worn and was evidently very nervous, but she answered Collier's questions without hesitation, and told them everything from the moment she had seen the advertisement to her arrival at the North Lodge.

"You had expected your aunt to meet you at the station?"

"Yes. She said she would. I waited on the platform and then I decided to walk."

"Didn't young Dene offer you a lift?"

"No. He had gone."

"His manner changed when he learned who your aunt was?"

She hesitated before she answered. "Yes."

"You gathered that he disliked her?"

"I—yes—"

"Miss Steer—you were present in the court room this morning. You heard the medical evidence. Did it surprise you?"

Amy flushed. "Very much. I was horrified."

"You had no suspicions? Think—look back," he urged.

"I—I only saw her that once in the waiting-room at Victoria. She—I wasn't very favourably impressed. She frightened me rather. She was a big woman, heavily built, very much made up. But—she seemed kind. I was out of a job—she said I would have a lovely time with her—she gave me some money to buy clothes—"

"You took her to be your father's sister?"

"Yes."

"Had your father ever mentioned her to you?"

"My father died when I was little. My mother never spoke of his family. I don't think she knew them."

"I see. Not even what part of the country he came from? Think—did she never happen to say your father was a Northumbrian—or a Devonshire man, that might help us, you see, Miss Steer."

She shook her head. "I don't remember. I am hoping now that it wasn't any of it true, and that he was not related to me at all. But if he wasn't, why did he give me money and bring me down here?"

"We hope to clear everything up in time," said Collier. "Now I want you to recall your arrival at the lodge. I've got the statement you made to Sergeant Lindo here, but you may be able to supplement it. You found the door on the latch and went in. There was nobody in the cottage. You looked into every room. Did you notice anything unusual?"

"Wait a minute," she said. "In the sitting-room—there was some beautiful old furniture and bright cushions and chintz—I loved it—but there were no rugs on the floor—and in one corner the bricks looked damp."

"The corner beyond the bureau?"

"Yes. How did you know?" She went on without waiting for an answer. "There was another thing. I thought I'd get myself a cup of tea. When I went to light the oil stove in the kitchen I noticed it was still warm. I thought my aunt must have gone out just before I came in. I expected her back any minute all that evening—" Amy shuddered.

"Now—I don't know what to think—"

The two men exchanged glances. This was important. To Collier the implications were obvious and sinister enough. He was tolerably certain now that the sitting-room of the cottage was the scene of the crime.

If this girl had arrived a few minutes earlier—

He changed the subject abruptly. "I'm afraid you've been given what the Americans call a raw deal, Miss Steer. They tell me you want to go back to London?"

"I've got to try to find a job. I'm living on what is left of the hundred pounds she—he gave me."

"I'd be glad if you'd stay on here a few days longer. After-wards—we have a certain amount of influence, you know—we might be able to find you a post—"

When Collier smiled there was something very attractive about his lean brown face. The girl looked up at him doubtfully.

"Thank you," she said.

They left her then. They had walked a hundred yards down the road on their way to the police station before Duffield spoke.

"What's our next port of call, Inspector?"

"The mortuary. I want you to have a look at the deceased, and you won't have another chance."

A constable on duty unlocked the mortuary for them. They did not stay long.

The constable was waiting for them in the yard. "Did you want to see the Superintendent, sir?"

"I'd be glad of a word with him."

The Superintendent, who was in his office, received them cordially. Collier introduced Duffield, they all sat down, and cigarettes were handed round.

"We've done our best for you, Inspector, rounding up all the tramps, hawkers and vagrants in a thirty-mile radius. They've all got pretty good alibis. It would be easier if we knew within a few hours when the crime was committed."

"I can't tell you that," said Collier, "but the murderer was in the sitting-room of North Lodge wiping up the blood on the floor just before six o'clock on Tuesday evening."

"Great Scot! How did you get that?"

"Indirectly, from Miss Steer. She told me she noticed that the bricks in one corner of the room were damp, and the oil stove in the kitchen was still warm when she put on a kettle. I spent an hour at the lodge myself this evening. I noticed that the bricks in that corner had been washed recently and I got some brownish matter from between the cracks. I'm going to have it analysed, and if it isn't blood I shall be surprised."

"You think Hall was killed in the cottage and his body carried down the back garden to the well?"

"Yes."

"He'd weigh—about what?" asked Duffield thoughtfully.

"Between ten and eleven stone."

"Then that rules out the woman. A woman might have struck the blow, but she couldn't have moved the body."

"Unless she had help."

"It's plain enough who did it," said the Superintendent. "The job is to find evidence to put before a jury. Hall was just a common blackmailer. He knew something about the Denes and was bleeding them white. The eldest girl had just got engaged to Sir Miles Lennor. He pushed them a bit too hard and they decided to get rid of him."

"You think the whole family were in it?"

"I wouldn't say that. It may have been young Dene and his mother. But—Miss Lavinia told Lindo she spent some time in the park hunting for a brooch she had lost, and the younger girl's story's even thinner than hers. She started for the vicarage just after lunch, and according to the vicar's wife she didn't arrive until nearly four o'clock. Not one of the lot can account satisfactorily for Monday afternoon."

"On the other hand," said Collier, "it was young Dene who found the body and rang up the police. If he hadn't, this might well have been one of the undiscovered crimes. You know what the guilty parties do in this sort of case. They explain the disappearance of the victim by telling everyone that he or she has gone abroad. That's what I should have expected here. To my mind young Dene's behaviour on Tuesday when he walked back to the lodge with Miss Steer and had tea with her in the very room where the murder was committed was that of an innocent man."

The Superintendent shook his head. "I can recall a dozen cases where a murderer slept and ate his meals, not only once but for days and weeks, on the scene of his crime. Crippen, Mahon—"

"I grant you that. But they didn't rake up the remains and ring up the nearest police station. That's what is holding me up. But for that I'd be inclined to agree with you that young Dene is our man. But what proof have we? Where's Sergeant Lindo, by the way?"

"He's gone to get a bite of food. He'll be back any minute. That's him now in the outer office talking to somebody—"

He broke off as Lindo entered after a perfunctory knock.

"Is Inspector Collier—Oh, there you are—"

"This is my colleague from the Yard. Sergeant Duffield."

"Pleased to meet you, Sergeant. The landlord of the King's Head at Lennor is outside with a boy. He's got some information. He wouldn't tell me what it was but he says it's important—"

"Bring him in, Lindo. It's that fellow Potter, isn't it? A slippery customer. He nearly lost his licence at the last Brewster Sessions."

The burly sergeant ushered in the landlord and an undersized and white-faced boy who might have been any age between nine and thirteen and whose accent when he spoke was recognised by the two Yard men as that of the New Cut.

"Well, Mr. Potter, any more rabbits been planted in your coat pockets?" enquired the Superintendent.

"You will have your joke, Superintendent. I didn't know about them rabbits no more than a babe unborn, but never mind that now. It's about this case. First of all, was the police offering a reward for finding Miss Duncan, Ruby Duncan what was housemaid up at the Dower House?"

"No."

The landlord seemed a trifle abashed by the coldness with which he was being received. He adopted an injured tone.

"Not even the price of the petrol I wasted bringing the kid along in my car, and leaving my poor wife alone to serve in the bar? It's nothing to you, I s'pose that another murder's been committed—"

He had no cause to complain of the impression he had made now. The Superintendent leaned forward in his chair. Lindo's jaw dropped. Collier made one of the swift darts that were so disconcerting to shifty witnesses unprepared for him.

"Another murder! Whose?"

"Ruby Duncan. Don't look at me like that. I didn't do the poor girl in. You hear young Len. He's my wife's nephew, been staying along with us after measles. London bred, he is, and as sharp as a needle. You tell 'em, Len."

The boy, divided between his excitement at seeing real 'tecs from the Yard and a natural distrust of all policemen, swallowed hard and licked his lips.

"I was in the park playing at clues and footprints, and I found her under the bracken. Her head was bashed in and flies all over it—"

"He ran home and told me and I brought him along here," said his uncle virtuously.

"Quite right, Potter," said the Superintendent.

"You'll be going yourself, Inspector? Ring up the doctor, Lindo. Where exactly did you find her, sonny?"

"In the park, close to the wall, about a hundred yards from the North Lodge."

Collier produced a sketch map of the park and the boy indicated the spot with a grubby forefinger.

"Just there. Did you draw this yourself, mister?"

"No. Somebody here did it for me. Now you tell me something. How did you know who she was?"

"Miss Duncan knows my auntie. She often comes in for a cup of tea at our place before she catches the bus to Ranchester."

"That's right," Potter corroborated.

"But if her head was, as you say, bashed in," Collier persisted.

"She'd got the same dress on she was wearing yesterday afternoon, and the red beret she had on her head then was lying in the grass beside her."

"You saw her yesterday afternoon?"

"Yes."

"When? Where?"

"Walking in the park with Mr. Dene."

The Superintendent smothered an exclamation and Collier's face was very grave. He asked several more questions and the boy answered readily. Miss Steer had gone out and his uncle had told him to follow her. From the top of the hill beyond the village there was a clear view of one comer of the park and he had seen Ruby and young Dene cross an open space and enter a copse together. He was positive that Miss Steer had seen them too. Half a mile farther on Dene had come over a stile from the woods alone and joined her. They had walked on together, but Len had been afraid to follow them.

"I thought if he saw me I might get a hiding," he explained. He had gone home and Miss Steer had come in about half an hour later. "I saw her through a crack in the bar door. She'd been blubbing. Her eyes were red."

Lindo came in to say that the car was ready and the two C.I.D. men hurried out. Potter would have followed but the Superintendent stopped him.

"Better take your nephew home now. It's getting late. How old is he?"

"Eleven. Pretty noticing, ain't he?" said the proud uncle.

"Remarkable," said the Superintendent dryly. "If he gets any sharper he'll cut himself."

The landlord reddened. "What yer mean by that?" he demanded belligerently.

"Well, I wouldn't make a practice of putting him on to spy on your visitors if I were you. It might be bad for business if it became known."

Potter stared. He was genuinely shocked by this ingratitude.

"Well, I'm damned. I put myself out to give the police valuable information and that's all the thanks I get. A lot of stuck-up, useless—a fat lot of crimes you'd find out if you hadn't no help from outsiders. Come on, Len—"

He had nearly reached the door when the Superintendent spoke again.

"Potter!"

It might have been the crack of a whip. The landlord's tone changed. "Yes, sir," he said quite humbly.

"The boy will be called as a witness, as he found the body. Make him understand that he'll have to tell the truth—and nothing but the truth, and the less either of you talk in the meantime, the better. You can go now."

CHAPTER XV

IN THE TRAP

TONY HAD NOT uttered a word during the drive in to Ranchester. He was conscious that he was being closely watched by Sergeant Lindo, who was sitting beside him, and the young constable on the drop seat facing him, who had stood by while he hurriedly pushed a suit of pyjamas and a few necessaries into his bag. He saw them both stiffen to attention when he felt in his pocket for his handkerchief. If he had been a dangerous wild animal, he thought, they could hardly have been more on their guard with him. Queer. What had happened to produce this change of attitude? During their previous encounters Lindo, in spite of his stolid official manner, had seemed quite human. "They're going to spring something on me," thought Tony, and his heart sank.

In Ranchester the street lamps were turned out at eleven. The High Street was dark and silent. The headlights of the car shone for a moment on the old Townhall as they crossed the market square. Was it only that same afternoon that he had sat there numbed with shame and horror? The car stopped and the young constable got out and held the door open. He was taken down a stone-paved corridor with white-washed walls into a room furnished like an office where four men awaited him. One, who was seated behind a desk, he knew to be the local superintendent of police. Of the other two, who were in mufti, one was Inspector Collier. It was he who spoke first.

"Won't you sit down, Mr. Dene? Sorry to bring you here at this time of night, but a discovery has been made which seemed to give us no choice in the matter. We want some information which you may be able to give us. On the other hand it is my duty to tell you that you need not answer any questions. You can refuse to make any statement until you have consulted your lawyer. We don't want to take any unfair advantage of you."

Tony was silent for a moment. He was trying to think. Wouldn't his silence, if he remained silent, make a bad impression? And how could any lawyer help him along the difficult path he had to tread?

"I'm quite in the dark," he said at last. "I wasn't given any choice about coming or not. Am I under arrest, or what?"

"You are being detained pending further enquiries. You can smoke if you like—"

"Thanks," Tony took a cigarette from his case and lighted it. His hands were shaking, but not much.

"Put your questions," he said. "I'll see if I want to answer them."

The others were looking at him strangely, he felt, as if he were separated from them by some barrier, a curious, intent expression on all their faces. For the first time he was conscious of a sick thrill of fear for himself, his own safety. Was he being led into a trap?

"I'm waiting," he said. The man he did not know had a notebook open on his knee ready to take down everything he said. Tony glanced at him and looked away.

"You are on friendly terms with Ruby Duncan?" They were all watching him and they all saw that he was disagreeably surprised.

"Ruby? That's the housemaid. Not particularly. No."

"You were with her in the park yesterday afternoon, weren't you?"

"I met her quite by accident."

"You walked along together."

"We happened to be going the same way."

"I have a map of the park here, Mr. Dene. Will you show me on it where you met and where you left her?"

"Certainly." Tony came over to the table on which Collier had opened the map. "I was here when she came up behind me. She asked me the time. Her wrist watch had stopped. I told her. Then we walked on, as you say, together by the footpath across this open space and through this copse to this point where the path divides. She turned off this way and I went on."

"Thank you. That confirms what we know already. Will you tell us what you did after leaving her, Mr. Dene?"

"I came out on the road by the stile you've got marked on your map. I met Miss Steer along the road and walked a little way with her. She went back to the village and I went into the park again and mooched about for a bit."

"Did you meet Ruby Duncan again while you were, as you say, mooching about?"

"No."

"Did you walk in the direction of the North Lodge?"

"No. I spent some time sitting on a fallen tree trunk, smoking and thinking."

"You saw nobody?"

"Not a soul."

"You have a good memory, Mr. Dene?"

"Pretty good."

"Could you repeat the substance of your conversation with Ruby Duncan yesterday afternoon?"

"I might. But what's the idea?"

"Ruby's body has been found this evening, Mr. Dene, lying hidden in the undergrowth by the park wall about a quarter of a mile from the North Lodge."

Tony heard himself saying "Good God! Do you mean she's been murdered, too?"

"I'm afraid there's no doubt of that."

"How ghastly."

"I think if you could tell us what you and she were discussing, it might throw some light on the case, Mr. Dene."

"It wouldn't." Tony made an obvious, a far too obvious effort to pull himself together. "I—I just asked her if she was going to the Pictures, and she said she thought she might. And I said there was a pretty good film on at the Regent. And we talked a bit about film stars. And that was all."

"She was going to the Pictures here in Ranchester?"

"I understood her to say so."

"She would have to catch the bus in the village?"

"I suppose so."

"But she took the path that led away from the village to the more unfrequented part of the park?"

"Yes."

"How would you account for that?"

"I can't account for it."

"I see. Thank you, Mr. Dene. You're quite sure that was all?"

The cathedral clock was just striking the hour. Tony waited until the last echo of the twelve strokes had died away. Then he replied with another question. "Do you think I committed these murders?"

"We're trying to find out who committed them, Mr. Dene."

"Yes, of course. Well, I didn't. That means that the murderer is at large, and if he was in the park yesterday afternoon he may not be far off. I hope the police are taking precautions. I don't want anything to happen to my mother or my sisters." He stared round at them defiantly as he spoke.

There was an appreciative gleam in Collier's shrewd blue eyes. It was the Superintendent who answered blandly, "We will do our best, Mr. Dene. And now I daresay you are ready for bed. Your breakfast will be brought to you at eight o'clock and you can have writing materials. I should certainly advise you to send for your lawyer the first thing in the morning. Good night."

He had touched a bell on his desk. A constable who had answered it took Tony's bag from him and led the way to the cell that had been got ready for him.

Mollie, at that moment, was lying in her bed in the dark, thinking. She had taken Sergeant Lindo's gruffly proffered advice and had not awakened her mother. Time enough to tell her when the morning came that they had taken Tony away. Tony, who pretended to be hard-boiled but who really minded things so terribly. Why, her earliest recollection was of Tony shutting himself up in the lumber room in their uncle's house for hours and hours after his dog was run over. He had come home, white and tearless, carrying the little shaggy body in his arms. Mollie began to cry as she remembered it and those tears did her good. They resolved the faint doubt that had begun to form at the back of her mind regarding her brother and what he knew and what he might possibly have done. She fell asleep then and woke to find the sun shining and Parsons standing by her bed with her early morning tea.

"Please, Miss Mollie, Mr. Tony's not in his room and his bed hasn't been slept in."

Mollie sat up and reached for her dressing-gown. "That's all right, Parsons. He was sent for late last night. He had to go in to Ranchester in connection with—with this case."

"Very good, miss. Shall I run your bath water?"

"No. I'll do that myself."

She had to see her mother first. She drank her tea in a hurry and went across the landing to Mrs. Dene's room. She found her mother awake and drinking her tea. She looked pale and heavy-eyed but she tried to smile when she saw Mollie.

"Hullo, darling—"

"Mummie—"

"Has the post come in? Was there a letter for Lavvy? I'm hoping Miles may have written—"

"Never mind Lavvy," said her sister impatiently. "The sky won't fall if Miles does let her down."

"But I do mind—Mollie, what the matter?" Mollie had meant to break the news gently, but she couldn't.

"The police—the police fetched Tony away last night."

"What!"

The spoon clattered in the saucer as Mrs. Dene set her cup down. "Now—tell me—"

"There isn't anything else to tell."

"Do you mean that they arrested him for—for the murder?"

"They said he was being detained. A policeman went up to his room with him while he put some things in a bag."

"You were there?"

"Yes."

"When was this?"

"About eleven. We sat up playing chess. The servants had gone to bed."

"You should have called me, Mollie."

"He wouldn't let me. The question is what are we to do for him now?"

Mrs. Dene pushed back her hair from her forehead. "You're right. Get dressed, Mollie, and then bring the car round, will you? I'll be ready in half an hour."

"Yes, Mother."

"We'll start directly after breakfast."

They were finishing breakfast when Lavvy came down.

"Mother, he hasn't written. I'm going to ring him up. I simply can't bear this suspense—"

Her mother looked at her vaguely. For once Lavvy and her affairs were not uppermost in her mind. "You know where he is then?"

"Know where he is? I don't understand. He's at Lennor Park, I suppose."

"Oh—I thought you meant Tony—"

"Tony! Is it likely I'd be worrying about Tony—"

"Not at all likely," said Mollie, bitterly, "all the same it may interest you to know that he's spent the night in a police cell in Ranchester."

"Mollie!" cried her mother. "What's the use of being unkind to Lavvy. We must stick together. And you must be brave, Lavvy dear. I'll be back as soon as possible. Come on, Mollie."

Lavvy stared after them, bewildered and appalled. She heard the car start. It was like a bad dream. Miles. That horrid old mother of his was keeping them apart. "If only I can see him alone it'll be all right," thought Lavvy. She would ask him to take her away at once. They could be married at the registrar's office and go abroad to some place where nobody knew. That her mother and Tony and Mollie would be left behind troubled her not at all. She did not think of them or even of her lover except in relation to herself. In her thoughts she clung to Miles desperately, but only because he represented the fulfilment of her ambition. To be young Lady Lennor of Lennor Park, cherished, looked up to, admired and envied. Was she to lose all this because of—of the way other people behaved? "I'll never forgive Mother or Tony if they've spoilt my chances," she thought.

She tried to eat but the food seemed to turn to sand in her mouth. "I won't wait," she told herself feverishly as she went to the telephone in the hall. She was shaking with nervousness as she took up the receiver and asked for the number. "Lennor Park. Hallo. Can I speak to Sir Miles, please? What? Miss Dene speaking. Miss Lavinia Dene. What? . . . I see . . . thank you. . . ."

She hung up the receiver and stood staring with unseeing eyes at a bowl of roses on the hall table. The Lennors' butler had answered her. Sir Miles was away from home. He had gone abroad with her ladyship. No letters would be forwarded and the date of their return was uncertain.

CHAPTER XVI

MOTHER AND SON

COLONEL BOULT had driven straight to Lennor Park after the adjournment of the inquest. He felt that it was due to his cousin Jane to let her know the worst as soon as possible. He found mother and son together in the library, pretending to read but obviously awaiting his coming.

"Disgusting!" was Lady Lennor's comment when he had done. Sir Miles said nothing. He was standing by one of the windows with his back to them and playing with the tassel of the blind. At any other time his mother would have begged him not to fidget, but now she refrained.

"Thank you, James," she said, "that settles it, of course. I don't know what the country is coming to when estates like the Dower House can be bought and occupied by people of that sort. Revolting. We will leave to-night and remain away until it is all over."

"The best thing you can do," Colonel Boult agreed. "I'm sorry, Cousin Jane. You won't like leaving your garden."

"I try not to think of that," said Lady Lennor with a sigh which was meant to reach the ears of her son standing rigid and silent in the window embrasure. Was he going to defy her and declare his intention of standing by the girl in spite of her scan-

dalous family? For an instant both she and the Chief Constable
waited, but the young man neither moved nor spoke.

"He'll toe the line," thought the Chief Constable. A touch of
contempt was mingled with his relief. Such prudence was admi-
rable no doubt, but he would really rather the boy had shown a
little more spirit.

Two hours later Sir Miles and his mother had left Lennor
Park for London in the Rolls. Hopkins, the maid, was to follow
the next morning by train with the bulk of their luggage. The
servants were being left on board wages. Lady Lennor, brisk and
efficient as ever in this crisis in her son's life, had found time to
write to the secretary of the Pageant Committee. The Rolls was
at the door and her son, coming into the library, found her addressing the envelope.

"I'm just coming, dear. What a mercy I had a letter from your
Aunt Marion only yesterday. This is what I've told the committee. My sister Lady Freke's health is giving rise to anxiety and
as she has expressed a wish to see me I feel it my duty to go
out to India at once. My son will not hear of my undertaking
so long a journey alone. The pageant will, of course, be held in
Lennor Park as arranged. Sir Miles and I regret our unavoidable
absence very much, and that we shall not be able to take part in
the Lennor episode."

"Is Aunt Marion ill?"

"She distinctly said she was feeling very run down."

"I see." He was looking at her with a sort of half smile. Not
a very nice or respectful expression, she thought, but she felt it
wiser to make no comment.

The journey up to Town was a silent one. Lady Lennor had
a letter pad and her fountain pen with her, and wrote numer-
ous notes to friends and to charitable organisations of which she
was the patroness. She used the same formula to them all. She
knew well enough that nobody would believe her, but appearances must be kept up.

"He'll leave everything to me," she thought irritably, "just
like his father."

They had reached the outer suburbs when the young man broke the long silence.

"Where are we going?"

"To Bence's, of course."

Lady Lennor had stayed at Bence's Hotel when she had come up to London with her father, the Dean, to have her teeth stopped and hear Albani sing at the Albert Hall. She had stayed there later with her husband and would never have dreamed of going anywhere else. Bence's was dark and stuffy. There were very few bathrooms and running water in the bedrooms had not been thought of, but it had remained very expensive and very exclusive.

The head waiter had been there forty years and he ushered them to the table they always occupied with just the right amount of unction to soothe Lady Lennor's wounded susceptibilities. No one, seeing him hovering about them could have imagined that he had just been reading an account of the adjourned inquest, headed, "Sex of Victim. Sinister Mystery of Body in Well," which referred to the fact that Miss Dene's engagement to Sir Miles Lennor had been announced only a few days previously. He was so exactly the same as he had always been that he helped to foster Lady Lennor's illusion that they had done with the whole distasteful business. She had not noticed the posters of the newsboys as they drove through the West End. Sir Miles had, but he said nothing. They were going to India by the *Oceanic* sailing the day after to-morrow, if they could get berths. His mother had told him that. The shipping offices were closed, of course, but the manager of Bence's had been most helpful in the matter.

"You can go round in the morning and make the arrangements, Miles, and then you had better do some shopping. You'll need hot weather kit, and guns. Your uncle will arrange a trip up country for you. I daresay you will be able to shoot some tigers."

"Yes, Mother."

Lady Lennor glanced up from her sole au gratin with a shade of uneasiness. The young man's submission was almost too complete. It gave her nothing to work upon. He should, she felt, have offered some opposition which would have enabled her to tell her friends that she had had a great deal of trouble with Miles—the poor boy was so chivalrous. Though she would not admit it even to herself, she was a little puzzled by his stolid compliance. Throughout his life he had often had to yield, always, in fact, when she had exercised her authority, but it had always been under protest. She had always prided herself on understanding him.

"Have you got a headache, dear?"

"No, thank you, Mother."

Lady Lennor pressed her lips together.

"I have engaged a private sitting-room. They are absurdly expensive, but I thought that under the circumstances we had better avoid the public rooms. I told Hopkins to pack the Halma board. I suggest that we play a couple of games and then go to bed. It has been a long day and we have much to do to-morrow."

Several heads were turned as they left the dining-room to watch the stout, middle-aged woman in the dowdy black silk draped with priceless old lace, followed by the rather loutish young man who, to the more observant, seemed so desperately unhappy. None of their fellow diners were aware of their identity, and it would not have occurred to any of the staff to ring up a newsagency. That would have been entirely foreign to the traditions of Bence's.

By ten the next morning Sir Miles was in Pall Mall booking first-class accommodation on the *Oceanic*. He paid by cheque, and went shopping on the lines laid down by his mother. She was not with him. That was one comfort. She was spending the morning at Harrods. He got back to the hotel at ten minutes to one. The porter, who had been at Bence's almost as long as the head waiter, came forward as he entered.

"There's a young lady, Sir Miles—"

The young man turned and saw Lavvy.

His first feeling was one of helpless irritation. More worry, more rows. Then, as he gazed at that flower-like face lifted so appealingly to his, other feelings prevailed.

He spoke to the porter. "Has her ladyship come in?"

"Not yet, sir."

"All right. Come on, Lavvy." He drew her into the lift that was Bence's one concession to modernity. They had hardly reached Lady Lennor's sitting-room when he turned to her again and took her in his arms.

She clung to him desperately and he tasted her tears salt on his lips.

"Darling, how did you get here?"

"I knew you always stayed at Bence's. I rang up a garage at Ranchester—Mother and Mollie had gone out—I just caught an up train. I had to see you, Miles. I can't live without you—"

"Kiss me, Lavvy," he murmured.

He did not want to talk, but she persisted. "We've got to fix things up before your mother comes—"

"What do you mean?" he asked rather sulkily.

"Darling," the soft lips brushed his cheek again, "can't we be married at once by special licence or something—"

"Impossible," he said, "but I mean to stick to you, Lavvy. Only we can't think of marriage now. We'll have to wait until I come back from India."

"You're going to India?" she said faintly.

"Yes. We sail to-morrow. That's fixed absolutely. But I was going to write to you—"

"Oh, Miles—" the big blue eyes filled with tears again, "it's so ghastly at home now. Can't you take me, too? I'll make your mother like me. Do, do—"

He shook his head. "You don't know her as I do. Pull yourself together. You'll have to stick it. After all, it's your family."

"I don't want to see them ever again," she said bitterly.

He was startled in spite of his infatuation. "Gosh, that's pretty callous. But you don't mean it. Come on, Lavvy, I'll take you out to lunch and see you into a train at Victoria later. We'd better go before Mother arrives. She may be here any minute."

Lady Lennor returned to the hotel ten minutes after the porter had closed their taxi door on Sir Miles and his companion. He gave Lady Lennor her son's message. She was not to wait lunch for him. He would be out all the afternoon. She was alarmed, but there was nothing to be done. She rested for an hour after lunch, finished her packing, and wrote some more letters. It was past six when the young man strolled in to their private sitting-room. He looked flushed and his eyes were unusually bright.

"Hallo, Mother," he said easily.

"Where on earth have you been? You have no consideration for me." Her tone was icy but it did not seem to affect him at all.

His smile broadened. "You're hard to please. We're sailing to-morrow. Isn't that enough?"

"That girl followed you here. Young women nowadays—"

He laughed. "Poor Mother," he said and turned on his heel and left her.

CHAPTER XVII

THE DENES AT HOME

YOUNG DENE had been taken to the cell where he was to spend the night. Collier took his leave of the Superintendent.

"I shall be around early to-morrow. We shall have to get in touch with this poor girl's relatives."

"I suppose you want the inquest to follow the same lines as the other? Just enough evidence of identity and so forth to allow of her being buried and then an adjournment while you get on with the job?"

"That's right." He sighed. "I wish we hadn't taken this step, Superintendent. If this lad is innocent—"

"But the evidence—he was seen with her. You suspected him of the first murder. If he'd been arrested earlier Ruby Duncan might be living now."

"You may be right," said Collier, "but I'm not happy about it."

"In my opinion," said the Superintendent, "you had no choice. Not after the story we had from that nephew of Potter's."

"That reminds me, I must see Miss Steer about that and check up on the boy. How long would it take to get from the stile the boy spoke of to the place where we found the body? Duffield, you and I have to do a spot of hiking to-morrow."

"I feel as you do about young Dene," said Lindo.

"He's a nice lad. I can imagine him laying out the so-called Mrs. Hall, but this second murder of a defenceless girl—"

"That's my difficulty—or one of them," Collier admitted. "But we've got to face the fact that both murders were almost certainly committed by the same person, the second to cover up the first."

"You mean the girl Ruby knew something and was threatening to split?"

"Obviously, Lindo, you got her statement. Where was she on Monday afternoon?"

"She got leave to go down to the village to post a parcel. The parcel was posted. I verified that."

"Did she go on foot?"

"No. All the maids have bicycles."

"She probably saw something that put her on the track of the murderer and, instead of telling you, Lindo, thought she saw her way to making a bit by blackmail. A dangerous game to play with a desperate man."

"That's right," said the Superintendent. "It's the likeliest motive. I don't know what you're worrying about, Inspector. It's your case and I'm not butting in, but in your place I'd apply for a warrant to-morrow and bring him before the bench. The evidence may be circumstantial but it's pretty damning in my opinion."

Collier looked at him with a half smile. He was accustomed to a somewhat restrained if not an actually hostile attitude. The local police only too often resented the calling in of the Yard as a reflection on their methods. This was far from being the case at Ranchester. He got on excellently with Lindo and the Superintendent's pose of detached interest suited him well enough, but he could not resist a comment.

"It's all right now that the Colonel has shifted the responsibility on to us, isn't it. Between ourselves, of course. Awkward for the Chief Constable putting his cousin's future brother-in-law in the dock. But for that you'd have tackled this job your-selves, wouldn't you?"

The Superintendent looked slightly taken aback but he answered with equal candour. "Maybe we should."

"Just so. But you didn't and it's my case, and before I apply for a warrant I've got to be certain in my own mind. Come on, Duffield. Good night, Superintendent. Good night, Lindo."

Collier slept soundly. He had trained himself never to lie awake worrying over his cases. He and Duffield had breakfasted and were at the station by nine o'clock. One report had come in from the officer he had detailed to make enquiries about the Dene family through the firm of house agents through whom Mrs. Dene had bought the Dower House. He read it carefully and handed it over to Duffield. The Superintendent was busy with the routine work of his office but Lindo had joined them in the small room that had been assigned to the two detectives from the Yard.

He, too, read the report.

"Seems O.K.," he remarked. "Mrs. Dene kept house for her brother-in-law at Chelsea. He was a rich man and seems to have paid for the education of her children. He died about a year ago leaving everything he possessed to her. She sold the Chelsea house, bought this place in the country and moved in last March. Doesn't help much, does it."

Collier pointed to the last of the neatly typed paragraphs. "The house in Chelsea was bought by the late Mr. Dene sixteen years ago. It is not known where he came from and I have been unable to find anyone who knew him previous to that date."

"That may be significant. How is young Dene this morning?"

"He looks rather hollow-eyed, poor devil."

"I asked him again if he would have a lawyer, but he declined."

"We shall have to let him go," said Collier.

"You still think we made a mistake, Inspector, when we brought him here?"

"I do. I was rattled, I must confess, by this second murder. Who's that? What do you want?"

The constable who had knocked at the door put his head in. "It's Mrs. Dene, sir. She wants to see her son."

"Is she alone?"

"Miss Dene is with her, but she's left her outside in the car."

"All right. Bring her in here."

The three men rose as Mrs. Dene entered. Grief and anxiety had changed the character of her beauty but had scarcely lessened it. She was very pale and there were dark shadows under her eyes but her grace and dignity were unimpaired. She sank into the chair Duffield had brought forward for her and faced them with the same iron self-control she had shown in the court room on the previous day.

"My daughter told me this morning that my son was brought to Ranchester late last night by the police. I did not know such a thing was possible."

"He came of his own free will, madam. I was waiting for a telephone call from London and was unable to leave the station. We thought that under the circumstances Mr. Dene would be willing to suffer a certain amount of inconvenience. We believed him to be in possession of some information—"

"He knows nothing whatever," she said quickly.

"He was seen in the park with Ruby Duncan on the afternoon she disappeared."

For the first time she flinched perceptibly. "That girl—"

"Ruby's body was found last night in some under-growth not far from the North Lodge. She had been killed by a blow with some blunt instrument that fractured the base of her skull."

Collier had kept his eyes fixed on Mrs. Dene's while he spoke. She stared back at him with eyes wide with horror. He could have sworn she was not acting. She looked as if she were going to faint. Lindo fetched a glass of water. She drank some and gave him back the glass. "Please forgive me," she said, "it was a shock."

"Naturally," said Collier. "Now that you are here, Mrs. Dene, perhaps you could help us by telling us all you know about the poor girl."

"I know very little. I got her about three months ago through a London agency. She seemed rather flighty and her work was not satisfactory. She was under notice to leave."

"Did you suspect her of being on—shall we say too familiar terms with your son?"

"Certainly not," she said indignantly, and again Collier reflected that if it was acting it was very good acting. "My son is not that kind of young man. She may have tried to attract him, but I am sure she did not succeed."

It was the most unguarded thing she had said. It betrayed her cold hostility to the poor murdered creature whose body, stripped of its tawdry finery, was lying in the mortuary not a hundred yards away. It did her no good with Collier and his face hardened slightly, but his manner remained suave.

"Mr. Dene does not deny that they were walking together in the park."

"She may have caught up with him and he was unable to shake her off. Tony couldn't be rude to anybody."

Collier said nothing for a moment. Then he turned again to Mrs. Dene.

"I wish you could make up your mind to be quite frank with us," he said.

"I have answered all your questions to the best of my ability, Inspector."

"Precisely," he said grimly.

"I do not understand you."

"I think you do."

She shrugged her shoulders.

"Can I see my son?"

"Certainly. I daresay he is ready by this time to drive back with you to the Dower House."

Lindo gasped but Duffield betrayed no surprise. He was inclined to agree with Collier that more might be learned by leaving young Dene at large. Besides they could not detain him much longer without charging him and there was not enough evidence for that. Collier glanced towards him. "Sergeant Duffield, will you tell Mr. Dene that Mrs. Dene has come to fetch him home? I'm afraid I'll have to ask you all to remain within call at the Dower House for a few days to come, Mrs. Dene."

"I have no intention of leaving the Dower House," she said. "It is my home. Oh, Tony—my dear boy—"

Young Dene had appeared on the threshold of the room. He looked tired and anxious and the smile with which he greeted his mother was strained.

"I'm to come back with you?"

Yes. She took his arm. Duffield, obeying a sign from Collier, saw them to their car.

Mollie was in the driver's seat reading a special edition of a local paper, the *Manchester Echo*, which she had bought to while away the time of waiting. She lifted a shocked face to her brother.

"Tony, they found Ruby's body last night. Did you know? Isn't it awful—"

"It is. And they think I did her in. Can you beat it? Move along, please. I'm going to drive." He glanced over his shoulder. "Are you all right, Mother?" He let in the clutch.

Mollie gasped involuntarily as the car shot forward.

"Tony, do be careful—"

"Don't worry," he said, "we bear a charmed life where road accidents are concerned. We are being reserved for higher things."

Mollie was silenced by the concentrated bitterness of that jeering voice. They had covered the five miles of road and were half-way up the avenue when she spoke again.

"Tony—I'm so terribly glad to have you back."

He flashed a quick glance at her. "Are you? You're a good kid."

Mrs. Dene and Mollie entered the house together while Tony took the car round to the garage. Mrs. Dene had not addressed a word to her daughter. She was not angry with her, she was simply unaware of her presence. She was always apt to forget Mollie. Parsons came out of the butler's pantry where she had been cleaning the silver as they crossed the hall.

"May I speak to you, madam?"

"Certainly, Parsons, what is it?"

"Gladys Binns has left, madam. She was afraid to stay after hearing about Ruby. The baker told us. He gave her a lift to the station on his van. She said she hoped you would excuse her, madam, but she wouldn't spend another night under this roof." Mrs. Dene listened calmly. "She was very young, wasn't she. I really cannot blame her. But I hope you and cook mean to remain with us, Parsons?"

"Yes, madam, so far as I know at present. But we're short handed with two gone."

"I'll try and find somebody to fill the gap. Where is Miss Lavvy?"

"She's gone up to London for the day, madam."

"Oh—I see—"

Mrs. Dene went slowly upstairs. She was hurt by Lavvy's reticence. Lavvy had not been near her since yesterday when she had said such cruel things.

Mary Dene sighed, gripping the banister rail and dragging herself up from stair to stair. She was very tired. Had all her struggles, all her efforts been worth while? It had all been for Lavvy, her beautiful darling—to give Lavvy her chance.

She lay on the sofa at the foot of her bed for the rest of the morning, but went down when the luncheon gong sounded. During the meal everyone made a determined effort to behave normally.

"I'm glad Lavvy is having a day in Town," Mrs. Dene said. "That little woman in Bond Street where she got her rose velvet is selling off. You might go up another day, Mollie."

Just before they left the table Parsons brought in a note for Mollie that had come by hand.

"What is it, dear?" Mrs. Dene could not quite control her painful anxiety.

Mollie had turned very red. "It's nothing. From the vicaress." She stuffed the note into the pocket of her cardigan. "I'm taking Binkie for a run. Will you come, Tony?"

"All right."

"What was it?" he asked when they were safely out of the house. "Something beastly, of course. Your face told me that."

"Did it? I must learn dissimulation. It was from Mrs. Barrow to say that under the circumstances she feels that it would be better if I didn't come to the pageant working parties."

"Of course, my child. What did you expect? We're pariahs since yesterday. I really wonder at Parsons and cook staying on. They both look so respectable. It's darned good of them really," said Tony, making a swipe at a delphinium with his stick.

"Tony, you've broken it, and it was such a lovely one."

"Sorry. I felt like that."

"Let's forget human beings," said Mollie in a small voice and after rather a long silence. They had left the gardens and were walking aimlessly over the rough turf of the park. She was watching Binkie, who was coming back to them after a sally in pursuit of a rabbit. Binkie was enjoying his walk.

"If we murdered every soul in Lennor, Binkie would love us just as much," she said.

Tony laughed for the first time that day. "More, if he's got any sense."

She took his arm. "Turn sharp to the left, Tony."

"Why?"

"There's a man in that bit of wood just ahead, probably a policeman in plain clothes looking for clues."

"Gosh, so there is. I suppose we've got to put up with it. Blast him all the same."

"Tony," she glanced up at the set young face, "you don't know who did it, do you?"

"I do not. Can't we get away from the subject? What's Lavvy up to?"

"I've no idea. Parsons told me the Lennors went away last night. They're going out to India to Lady Lennor's sister who is dangerously ill."

"How nice for them. And has Lavvy started in pursuit? I wouldn't put it past her. Turn about, Mollie, there's a blighter with a camera."

"Let's tell him he's trespassing. He's miles off the right of way."

"And see ourselves on every picture page to-morrow? No fear. There's only one way to deal with Press photographers."

They turned and ran, with Binkie barking joyously at their heels.

"What next?" panted Mollie.

He took her literally. "Tennis. Thank Heaven Mother had the hard court made in the old herb garden. There's a high wall all round it."

They were in the library after dinner when Lavvy arrived.

"I had a taxi from the station. You might pay him, Tony."

Mrs. Dene and Mollie gazed at her expectantly as she came forward into the circle of lamplight. She was looking extraordinarily pretty and seemed quite unembarrassed. "How quiet it seems here after London. I had dinner on the train."

"Did you—" began her mother almost timidly.

She could not forget how angry Lavvy had been with her only yesterday. But Lavvy apparently had forgotten.

"I had lunch with Miles," she said, "and we went to the Pictures. Anything to get away from his awful mother. He's going to India. It's the best thing really while it's so ghastly here, but we're going to be married directly he comes home."

Tony had come back from paying the taxi driver. "Good work, my dear child," he said ironically.

"My darling Lavvy," began her mother, but she turned away impatiently.

"It's been a tiring day. I want a bath more than anything, and then I'm going to bed. Good night, everybody."

After she left the room there was a silence that no one seemed disposed to break. Mrs. Dene was thinking wistfully that Lavvy might have kissed her. Tony was thinking how characteristic it was of Lavvy not to ask how they had been getting on and if anything had happened during her absence.

"Well," he said at last with fictitious cheerfulness, "what about hitting the hay? It's nearly ten."

Chapter XVIII

THE SHOP IN LUKE'S PASSAGE

The inquest on Ruby Duncan was opened at the Fire Station, an arrangement which enabled the police to keep the general public out on the score of lack of space. The London papers, now fully awake to the dramatic possibilities of the case, had sent down special representatives, but the only witnesses called were a young woman from Peckham, the wife of a grocer's assistant, who identified the body as that of her sister, Sergeant Lindo, who deposed to finding the body in a plantation of the Dower House park, and the police surgeon who described the injury to the head, which, he said, must have been caused by a heavy blow from some blunt weapon.

At this point a juror intervened to enquire if he might ask a question. The coroner eyed him coldly. He disliked interruptions.

"If it is relevant."

"The blow was struck from behind when the girl's back was turned?"

The coroner glanced at the doctor who replied, "Yes."

"Like in the other case?"

The coroner frowned. "We have nothing to do here with any other case. The police are pursuing their enquiries. This enquiry is adjourned for a month—"

The reporters, after unsuccessful efforts to get past the stolid policeman on duty at the south gate of the Dower House filled their columns with interviews with the landlord of the King's Head and his wife and nephew. There would be articles in some of the livelier Sunday papers in which the problem of Mrs. Hall would be compared with that of Savelette de Lange and the Chevalier D'Oex and certain theories concerning Queen Elizabeth, but meanwhile the police had very little to say.

Collier was working hard. He was trying to discover the real identity of the man who had called himself Mrs. Hall, and so far without success. Mrs. Dene, he was sure, could have enlightened him, but for reasons of his own he left her alone for the time being. Amy Steer was willing enough to help him. She had offered to stay on in Ranchester if she could find a job. Through her landlady, who was the mother of P.C. Saunders, she was recommended to and engaged by a Miss Fraser who had just opened a tea shop in one of the ancient timbered houses in Luke's Passage, a narrow paved lane leading from the High Street to the Cathedral. Miss Fraser, who was an elderly Scotswoman, silver-haired and apple-cheeked, had taken a fancy to Amy. When Collier called on the girl one evening after supper he found her still hard at work in Mrs. Saunders' front parlour making the frilled muslin cap and apron she was to wear in the shop.

He noticed with satisfaction that she looked better and seemed tolerably cheerful.

"This is better than the King's Head, eh?"

"Oh, much—"

"Did you see anything of the boy when you were there?"

"Young Len? He was a horrid child. I'm sure he went into my room and pried into my things. I found the marks of his sticky paws everywhere."

"You don't surprise me," said Collier drily. "I believe he has some idea of joining the force when he grows up. I shall have retired by then, I hope. Did you know he followed you when you went out?"

"When—" He saw her colour rise.

"You met Mr. Dene on Wednesday afternoon, Miss Steer. He climbed over a stile to join you. Previously you had seen him in the distance."

He seemed to be waiting for an answer so she said, "Yes."

"Was he alone?"

She laid her sewing down on her lap. "He was walking with a girl. I thought it was his younger sister—"

"How was she dressed?"

"Why?"

"Never mind. Answer my question."

"She was wearing a light dress and a red cap."

"Did young Dene seem his usual self that afternoon?"

"I don't know."

"What do you mean—you don't know?"

"I know so little of him really. He asked if I was comfortable at the King's Head, and apologised for his sister not seeing me the day before."

"Quite jolly, in fact."

"Hardly that. He was upset about the murder naturally."

"Naturally," Collier echoed her.

Amy was looking at him. "Why are you asking all these questions? There was no harm in our meeting."

"None. But I'm afraid you may be asked to repeat in the witness box what you have just told me. That girl you saw was Ruby Duncan, who was housemaid to Mrs. Dene. She has been missing since Wednesday. She was found the following night, but you probably know that. You will have read the account of the inquest in the local papers."

Amy was silent. She was seeing again in her imagination those two distant figures crossing the open space and disappearing among the trees. Tony—and the girl who, a few hours later had been found lying face downwards in the bracken with the impudent little cap that had crowned her curls stained with a darker red. Tony, who was already under a cloud because he had hated Mrs. Hall.

"It's—it's wicked," she cried, "wicked and absurd! He isn't that sort."

"Can you prove his innocence?" he asked gravely.

"No. But I'm certain."

"He has one loyal friend. But we have to rely on evidence, Miss Steer. We asked him what passed between him and Ruby that afternoon in the park. He said she asked him the time and they talked about film stars. I'm afraid he was lying. I've been told a good many lies in the last few days."

"Not by me," she said with spirit.

He smiled. "I know. . . . But then you've nothing to hide so your candour can hardly be accounted to you for righteousness. Have you any idea why Hall brought you down here, Miss Steer? Why he advertised as he did?"

"I think he really was related to my father," she said.

"You think he really meant to do you a good turn?"

"Yes. At least—I don't know what to think now," she said doubtfully, "but at the time I was sure of it."

"I suppose it is no wonder you were deceived. He was well made up and seems to have played his part, but you felt no distrust? You were taking a risk—"

"I was out of a job and down to my last few shillings. I didn't like her much, but she seemed kind. You don't know what it means to a girl to be given a hundred pounds to spend on clothes."

"I suppose she would be apt to see the donor through a golden haze."

He wondered if it had ever crossed her mind that she might have some cause to be grateful to Hall's unknown assailant. He was not sure of the use the dead man had meant to make of this girl, but he had not much faith in his good intentions. He recalled that only last night when they were discussing the case Lindo had suggested that Amy Steer should be added to their list of suspects.

Duffield had demurred. "She's a good kid. Anyone can see that."

"Exactly. There you have the motive. She's a good girl. After she arrived at the lodge he—well, you can imagine what might have happened. There was a struggle. Mad with fear she picked up the paperweight. These modern young women can sock you one on the jaw if they want to."

"She said I should have a good time, dinners and dances and—and fun," said Amy.

"Yes, that's quite possible," said Collier thoughtfully. He saw that she did not realise what that meant. The tenant of the North Lodge, sure of his hold over the Denes, had been about to force his newly discovered niece on them. Another turn of the screw. That the girl herself was innocent, unaware, would not affect the issue. She liked young Dene. Collier divined that it was a feeling that might easily ripen to something warmer. And before long she might be standing in the witness box swearing his life away.

"Well, now you've got a job, haven't you?" he said.

She brightened at that as he had hoped she would. "Oh yes. With Miss Fraser."

He got up to go. "I wish you luck."

Amy felt happier the following day than she had done for a long time. For one thing it seemed evident that the new tea-shop was going to be a success. A large number of people, mainly women, came in between half-past ten and twelve for morning coffee.

"They've come to have a peek at you, my dear," said Miss Fraser shrewdly, "between you and me I thought that might happen. But they'll come again because the coffee's good." From half-past three until six when the shop closed they were kept so busy that Miss Fraser said, "If this lasts I'll be needing another assistant. Not one of the scones left."

The shop had been converted from a private house and consisted of three ground floor rooms and a passage thrown into one. A part of the oak panelled partitions had been left to form cosy corners and inglenooks. The ceiling was low pitched and crossed by huge oak rafters and some of the shaded electric lamps had to be kept burning all day. Miss Fraser and Amy were there until eight o'clock washing up and sweeping and dusting. "I've half a mind to put up a notice 'No Smoking,'" said Miss Fraser, mourning over a hole burnt in one of the rugs. "The very first day. But I might as well put up the shutters."

Amy was too tired when she got back to her lodgings to do anything but go straight to bed, but the pocket of her muslin apron was heavy with coppers and small silver, and she slept better than she had done since she left London.

The next day there was some falling off in the number of customers but Miss Fraser took that philosophically.

"We've got to remember yesterday was market day and a lot of folk had come in from the country round."

They kept the shop open until half-past six, having realised that some people wanted a late tea after coming out of the first performance at the Picturedrome in the High Street. On the third day they felt they were settling down. Already some faces were familiar. Wives of cathedral clergy dropped in for morning coffee after matins and on their way to change their novels at the circulating library, and young men parked their sports cars in Paternoster Street and brought their girl passengers through the Passage to the new shop. Amy was kept busy. It was just what she needed to keep her mind from dwelling as it tended to do on Tony's troubles. About four o'clock there was not a vacant table, and Amy, hurrying to and fro from the service hatch with her laden trays, was beginning to wonder if the supply of newly-baked scones would suffice. But later there was a lull, and by six the last party had gone. Amy picked up the sixpence left for her under a plate, heaped the crockery on her tray and carried it into the kitchen where her employer, hot and tired, but triumphant, was indulging in a belated cup of tea.

"Is that the lot?"

"I think so. Shall I wash up?"

"You're tired. Leave it for once. I've got a woman coming in to sweep and clean up to-morrow morning. She'll do that. Was that the door bell?"

"I don't think so. I'll go and see."

Amy returned to the shop but there was nobody there. She opened the door to let in a breath of fresh air and as she did so became aware of a distant clamour that sounded like a crowd at a football match. It grew louder as she listened and was evidently coming nearer. She spoke to a woman who was hurrying down the Passage, dragging a small child by the hand.

"What is that noise? Has anything happened?" The woman, who looked frightened, said something that Amy could not catch about "a rough lot," and passed on.

Amy looked down the Passage towards the High Street. A man and a girl were running towards her. The street behind them was suddenly full of people, a struggling pushing crowd. The burly figure of a policeman with arms outstretched was blocking the narrow entrance, holding them back. The two fugitives were approaching. Impulsively Amy went to meet them.

"Quick—come in here."

When they were inside she closed the heavy oak door and bolted it. Amy's heart was thumping as if she had been running, too. She was looking at Tony Dene who was wiping the yellow mess of a broken egg from his white face.

"Some chap threw one," he explained unnecessarily, "and it wasn't a new laid one either. I'd brought Mollie in to see the Harold Lloyd film. When we came out a crowd was waiting for us and they started hustling us and yelling insults. I believe the manager of the cinema telephoned for the police, but the crowd was too big for them to disperse. We managed to shove through but they followed. A bobby waved to us to bolt down here. I say, it was jolly decent of you to let us in here. Mollie couldn't have run much further."

"I hit one of the beasts," said Mollie. "Hard. I made his nose bleed. I'm glad. I hope he bleeds to death." She burst out crying.

Miss Fraser had come out of her kitchen and was standing by.

"The poor bairn," she said, "what she needs is a nice hot cup of tea and some of my oat cakes. You're quite safe here. They'll think you ran out the other end of the Passage. Sit down and rest yourselves and we'll bring you a real Scotch tea." She drew Amy after her into the kitchen. "It's young Dene and his sister, isn't it?" she whispered, "I thought so. I'll get the tray ready. You go and talk to them. Poor things. They haven't too many friends."

Amy went back to them. She was trembling in sympathy. Tony had taken off his horn-rimmed spectacles and was rubbing them. She saw that he looked much younger without them and that he had very thick dark lashes. His hands were shaking. He turned to Amy quickly, eagerly, as to an old and trusted friend.

"We had planned to come to tea here. That chap from the Yard told me you were here. I like it, don't you, Mollie? That shade of blue," his teeth were chattering, "it's funny I feel cold," he said.

Mollie blew her nose. "That's shock," she said. She blinked at Amy, "I wonder if you've got a compact? I seem to have dropped mine."

"Yes, of course. Sit down here. I expect the tea's ready." She left them and came back with the tea.

"Won't you have some with us?"

"I'll pour out if you like."

"I wish you would," said Mollie, "I should probably drop the teapot. I'm still shaking. I suppose we'll have to keep inside the park gates after this. How jolly!"

Tony said nothing.

"It's so horribly unjust," said Mollie, savagely buttering her oat cake. "What have we done?"

"You heard what they were shouting," growled her brother.

"Who killed Ruby Duncan?"

"I suppose they'll think that until the real murderer is found. Isn't it ghastly to think he's somewhere about? I wish the police would hurry up." She turned to Amy. "They've warned us not to go out alone even into the garden. The between maid's left. She was afraid to stick it. The cook and Parsons have been marvellous. Mother's got a temporary, through an agency in the High Street to take poor Duncan's place, but I don't like her much, do you, Tony?"

"I've hardly seen her." He stood up as Miss Fraser joined them.

"I say, this is awfully good of you, letting us stay here. I expect you want to be closing down really."

She looked at him with kindly eyes. "Dinna fash yourself. It's no inconvenience. Amy and I never leave before eight. I have to count the day's takings and there's clearing up to be done. You can stay as long as you like. You're ower young to be in all this trouble."

"Thank you," he said. "Then you don't think—"

"I do not." She held out a capable work worn hand and he gripped it hard.

"Now I'll get back to my work," she said.

"Can't Mollie and I do something to help?"

Miss Fraser glanced at the two girls who were engrossed in conversation. "You might give Amy a hand with the washing up if you can trust yourselves not to break my crockery."

"Oh, I'm all right now. Come along, you two. Where's the sink?"

Amy looked doubtfully from one to the other. "Do you really mean it?"

"Of course."

"This way then."

Miss Fraser, sitting at her desk and hearing the murmur of voices and even, now and then, laughter mingling with the clatter of pots and pans in the kitchen wondered if she had done right in throwing these young people together. For the moment at least they had forgotten that all the world was against them. All, or nearly all. But though she had known Amy for so short a time she felt responsible for her. So far public feeling had been favourable to her and she was generally regarded as the victim of circumstances. She might lose a good deal by association with the Denes.

"But I doubt if I could prevent it if I tried," she told herself. "She's ower fond of the lad already, and he of her."

She was locking her desk when they came back into the shop. At the same moment there was a knock at the shop door. Miss Fraser went to it.

"Who is it?"

"It's all right, miss. It's me. P.C. Saunders."

She drew the bolts and the policeman standing outside came in.

"I saw you nip in here, sir, out of the tail of my eye like, while I was keeping the crowd back," he explained. "Everything quiet now, and I took the liberty of bringing your car down from where you'd left it to the other end of the Passage."

"Thank you," said Tony, "you personally did your best for us and I'm grateful, but it's pretty rotten, you know, if my sister and I can't go out without being molested."

"That's right," said Saunders, "but if you don't mind my saying so it was a mistake to come out and go to a comic film this afternoon."

"Good Heavens! Why? Aren't we ever to smile again like the chap in the history books?"

The constable cleared his throat. "Well, you see, sir, Ruby Duncan's funeral was at three and a lot of the people here went to it. The procession was nearly a mile long and lots came in from the places round, and a good many of us had to be at the cemetery keeping order. And there was a good deal of talk about her employers not having sent a wreath, and then it got about that you and the young lady were at the cinema seeing a comic—"

Tony had turned rather white again. "I see," he said. "I didn't know about the funeral. It does sound rather a rotten thing to do. Though as to sending a wreath—" he seemed about to say more but checked himself. "Come along, Mollie. Good-bye, Miss Fraser. You've been a brick—"

"Good-bye everybody," said Mollie jauntily, but Miss Fraser saw that her eyes had filled with tears.

"I'll see you to your car, sir," said Saunders. Miss Fraser closed the door after them.

"Have you finished the washing up?"

"Yes. It's all done. Miss Fraser, you were splendid."

"I did as much once for a hunted fox," said Miss Fraser reminiscently, "and the huntsman hammering at my door and all, and the hounds baying and fine ladies and gentlemen with their horses streaked with sweat waiting in the lane. And the language. 'You're no gentleman,' I said out of my bedroom window. They had to go away at last. And when they were all gone I let the puir beastie out of my scullery." She chuckled. "He came back the next night and killed five of my chickens."

"Tony won't do that."

"I'm not saying. I'm sorry for the lad. He's under a cloud."

"It's so unfair," said Amy hotly.

"Unfair or no that'll be the way of it until they've found the one they're after and put him in the dock."

Miss Fraser had switched off all the lights except one. They sat at a table near the door in the little circle of shaded lamplight. They were both tired after being on their feet all day and glad of a little rest. Amy slipped off her shoes and wriggled her toes luxuriously.

"You ought to wear low heels like mine," said the older woman. "I wonder what the police are doing. Nothing fresh in the papers this last three days. Two people have been killed. I'd say there were three alternatives. I'm thinking of the first murder now. Either one of the Denes, or all the Denes did it."

"But why?" cried Amy.

"Blackmail, of course. What a child you are."

"Oh!"

Miss Fraser glanced at her curiously as she sat with her elbows on the table and her chin resting on her clasped hands. "Do you mean to say you never thought of that as the probable motive?"

"Never. Why should—"

"Oh, it wouldn't be the children. Mrs. Dene's the dark horse there. Think it over, Amy. You've got to face the facts. The man may have been your father's brother, but we can't be held responsible for our relations."

"No. But that's only a guess. What are the other alternatives?"

"An unpremeditated attack by a tramp or a hawker. Not very likely, and made less so by the second murder—unless, of course, the two crimes are distinct and unconnected."

"You ought to be a detective, Miss Fraser," said Amy admiringly, "you sound awfully good at it."

Her employer looked pleased. "I've aye been interested," she admitted modestly, "and whiles I've thought I could have done better myself in some cases that I mind. In real life, that is. But I've heard there's a lot of rules they have to keep. In fiction detectives can do almost anything. But we were saying about the alternatives."

"Yes. Do go on, dear Miss Fraser."

"It would be somebody out of Hall's past life. Somebody who knew his secret and wanted a share in his profits. Somebody he quarrelled with and said no to—" Miss Fraser looked at her watch. "I didn't know it was so late. I must run. I've a letter half-written at my lodgings that must go by the last post. I'll leave you to make sure the windows are closed and turn off the light at the meter. Good night, my dear."

Amy saw her out and lingered for a moment at the shop door. The Passage was deserted at that hour. The crowd had dispersed some time ago. She turned quickly, fancying she heard a movement, and saw a young man emerge from the partitioned cosy corner at the far end of the room.

"Sorry I startled you," he said. He was smiling but his eyes were quick and restless and he looked incessantly from her to the door while he spoke. She recognised him as having been in for a cup of tea on several occasions. She had served him earlier in the afternoon but she thought he had left after paying his bill. He was sharp featured, with fair hair, and something about his voice and manner, a touch of deliberate affectation, made her think he might be an actor until he enlightened her.

"I was here when the Denes barged in, and I overheard your conversation just now. You mustn't mind. You see it happens to be a part of my job to keep an eye on you, Miss Steer."

"Oh"—she stared at him—"do you mean that you're a detective?"

"Near enough. But that's got to be between you and me. It must not go further."

"Will you be seeing the Inspector?" she asked.

He darted one of his quick glances at her. "Why?"

"I've thought of something I ought to have told him before, something Mrs. Hall said to me at Victoria. I can't think how I came to forget it—"

"What was it?"

"She said she had a nephew but she had done with him."

He was silent for a minute. Then he said, "And you fancy that may be important?"

"Yes."

"Well, I'll pass it on. And meanwhile the less said the better. Do you understand?"

His manner had changed and become so bullying that she faltered, "I don't think I do."

"You were talking with the Denes, talking with the old Scotch woman who runs this place. Too much talk. See?"

"I—I—"

"All right." His manner changed again and became as genial as before. "I believe I can trust you, Miss Steer. I'll tell you something. There is something very wrong down here and the Yard know it. That's why I've been sent down to work independently of everyone else. You get me? Everyone. I'm responsible only to the Chief, and if I'm to deliver the goods I've got to work fast. Now I believe I can clear young Dene, but I shall need your co-operation. Can I rely on that?"

"Oh yes," she said eagerly.

"Good. Then not a word to anyone about having seen me. And not a word about the nephew. You're right. That may be important. I'll have it followed up, but I don't want the Inspector to touch it at present. You've told me, and that's enough. You get that?"

"Yes."

"I shan't be coming here again but you'll get a note from me. You can call me Mr. Smith. It isn't my name, but it will do for the present. I daresay you don't know much about the Yard?"

"Not really. I've read thrillers."

He laughed. "They tell you a lot of lies. Still, the Big Five do exist."

"Are you—"

His quick dancing blue eyes rested for an instant on her innocent absorbed face. He laughed again. "The British public get quite a thrill out of one of their institutions," he said. "Never mind who I am, Miss Steer. You've got a big surprise coming. Meanwhile, I rely on you to carry out my instructions when you get them. You won't let me down?"

"I'll do my best," she said.

He was at the door now. He opened it a few inches and looked up and down the Passage. "All clear. Good night."

CHAPTER XIX

THE PRICE OF SILENCE

COLLIER HAD HAD to submit to some rather querulous comments on his conduct of the case from the Chief Constable. Colonel Boult, relieved by the prompt departure of the Lennors and his cousin Jane's assurance that her son's unfortunate engagement would be broken off, saw no further need for tact in handling the Denes, and was beginning to regret that he had called in the Yard. He had called on Collier for a report of his progress, if any. He had always had his doubts about young Dene, and the fact that he had been the last person to be seen with Ruby Duncan seemed to him to clinch the matter. He was inclined to bluster. Collier kept his temper and answered civilly, but he was firm.

"I'm not ready to make an arrest yet, Colonel, and I'd be glad if you'd wait another day or two for my report. I'm going up to Town and I may not be back before to-morrow."

"Leaving the case to stew in its own juice?" said the Colonel sarcastically.

The interview was taking place in the superintendent's room at the station. The superintendent, who had effaced himself as far as possible, looked very uncomfortable. He thought the Chief Constable was being unfair, but he dared not intervene. He tried to make amends when the Colonel, growling something about incompetence, had gone back to his car, by the extra warmth of his manner. Collier understood. "It's all right," he said with a shrug, "I'm often in hot water. I'm used to it."

"He's worried about the expense," the superintendent explained. "He told me he thought we ought to be able to carry on with fewer men. He's thinking of the county rate and all that."

"I see. Well, I don't want to antagonise him unnecessarily. But you know the position, Superintendent. There's a murderer at large. We can't rule out the possibility of homicidal mania, though I think myself that both crimes were the work of a sane man. Still, I may be mistaken. That's why I'm having the park of the Dower House patrolled. I've warned the women not to stir out alone. There's one man keeping near the house and another on duty at the south gate—the north gate, of course, has been kept locked since the discovery of the first body. I don't see how we can reduce our forces. Any trouble at the funeral?"

"Oh, I forgot you hadn't heard. There was a big crowd but fairly orderly. Coming back to the town from the cemetery it got about that young Dene and his sister had been seen going into the Electric Palace at the top of the High Street where they are showing the latest Harold Lloyd. For about twenty minutes it looked nasty. The Denes had to bolt with about two hundred people after them. Fortunately Saunders, who happened to be about, made them run down Luke's Passage and prevented the crowd from following. It's a narrow entrance and he's a hefty chap, and they got away."

Collier frowned. "The young fool. He ought to have known better. Well, it will teach him a lesson. Perhaps he'll stay put now until this is cleared up. Is that clock of yours right, Superintendent? I want to catch the 7.15 up. I may not be back until the day after to-morrow."

He dashed out, leaving the superintendent to get on with the arrears of his routine work. Lindo was away. He had been given the job of making a few enquiries about the antecedents of Potter and his wife. The landlord of the King's Head was not a local man and since his coming there had been more poaching than before and a perceptible increase in drunkenness. "I'm afraid," Lindo had said reluctantly, "we can't rely on his evidence. We'd better find out a little more about him before we use it at all."

And Collier had agreed.

"Why did he bring the boy to us with that story? It's true. Miss Steer corroborates it. But what was his motive? Self-importance? It looked like malice to me. Again, why? What has young Dene done to them?"

The question was so far unanswered.

Colonel Boult had left unsatisfied and he did not lack persistence. He did not come in to Ranchester but he rang up the superintendent soon after nine the following morning. He was worried, as the latter had suspected, about what he called the damned extravagance of that fellow from the Yard.

"He's working on the case, or supposed to be, and that pudding-faced sergeant of his"—the superintendent cleared his throat—"yes, Superintendent, I will say it. Pudding-faced. And he's got Lindo and the Lord knows how many besides. Speak up, can't you."

"I beg your pardon, sir—"

"How many?" barked the Chief Constable so loudly that his interlocutor started.

"Three at Lennor, patrolling the Dower House—"

"I thought as much. Rubbish. Leave the one at the gate to stop them if they try to get away. The others are quite unnecessary. Call them off at once—"

The superintendent hesitated. "Inspector Collier said—"

He was not allowed to finish his sentence. "Never mind him. The chaps there are our men, aren't they?"

"Yes, sir."

"Very good. That's my order. Carry it out."

Tony Dene and his sister had reached home safely, after being shepherded from the shop in Luke's Passage to their car by P.C. Saunders. Neither had really got over the shock of the hostile demonstration.

"I wish we didn't have to go back. I wish we could drive on and on to some place where nobody knows us," she said drearily.

"I know." He did not turn his head. He kept his eyes on the road. "It's queer. The Dower House is beautiful, but I feel now I'd rather be living in a slum. It can't be much longer though," he added half to himself.

"Are we going to tell Mother about this afternoon, Tony?"

"No. Unless she talks of going into Ranchester for shopping or anything. Then we'll have to. She'd have to be warned. The same with Lavvy."

"We ought not to have gone, I suppose, but I felt I should go mad if I stayed shut up in the house any longer."

"Rough luck on you, Mollie, being howled at and hissed, when you've done absolutely nothing."

She shuddered. "Let's try to forget it. That old Scotch woman at the tea shop was kind, anyway, and Tony—"

"Yes."

"I like Amy. I think she's a dear."

She had her reward in seeing the tragic young face relax for a moment. "I thought you would. I'm glad."

It was raining again, a fine rain like mist that blotted out the hills. Tony drove the car round to the garage while Mollie went into the house. Her mother and Lavvy were both in the library, reading. A fire had been lit and the room looked cosier and more cheerful than usual with the flickering flame reflected on the oak panelled walls and the ceiling. Mrs. Dene looked up from her book. "You're late. Was it a good film?"

"Not bad. I'll take Binkie for his run before dinner. Come on, Binkie."

Binkie, hearing his name, jumped out of his basket.

"Not alone, Mollie," said her mother quickly, "Tony must go with you."

"Oh, bother, I'm always forgetting. All right. Do you really think he's out there somewhere, prowling? The place is stiff with police."

Nobody answered her. Mollie picked up Binkie, who wriggled under her arm, trying to reach up to lick her face, and went to find her brother. Glancing up as she crossed the hall she saw the temporary housemaid peering down at her from the landing. It crossed Mollie's mind that she might have been put in by the police to spy on them. Would they do a thing like that? Mollie did not know.

She met Tony coming in and they put on raincoats and went down the miry garden paths through the dripping shrubberies where the patter of rain drops sounded like light following feet. Binkie rushed on in front, barking joyously.

"He's happy, bless him," said Mollie.

"Not quite," said Tony, "he knows there's something wrong." They had reached the little wicket gate that divided the garden from the park. "Better turn back here. It will be quite dark in a few minutes."

Mollie took his arm. "Tony, Mother's always been so wonderful. I've admired her tremendously ever since I've been old enough to see what a lot she put up with for our sakes. Uncle Edward was very trying but she bore everything so that we could go to good schools. It must be ghastly to be dependent on someone like that, bad-tempered and tyrannical. She was so terribly pleased with this place when she bought it, poor darling. She could do what she liked at last. She was so delighted to be able to give Lavvy her chance."

"I know."

"Tony—that man—Mrs. Hall—must have had some kind of hold over Mother—"

"Of course."

"Do you know what?"

He set his teeth. "I do not."

"She only cares for Lavvy," said poor Mollie, sighing.

"Have you only just realised that?"

"No. I always knew it, but she didn't let one see it quite so plainly. She's too tired now to go on pretending."

"Was she unkind to you just now?"

"Oh no. Only completely indifferent."

They trudged back together in the falling rain with Binkie now close at their heels. The darkness was pressing about them. Mollie started violently when a twig cracked under her feet.

"He creeps up behind," she said suddenly. "Oh, Tony, let's run, I'm frightened."

"Rot," he said, but he began to walk faster. His own nerves had been shaken by their recent experience. He breathed more freely when they were back in the lighted hall.

Inspector Collier and his colleague dined in the restaurant car on their way up to Town. Collier was unusually silent. He was plainly dissatisfied with the progress he had made and dreading the criticism of his superiors.

"If we were allowed to use third degree methods we might get the truth out of Mrs. Dene. But we can't and that's that."

"And if you do find out why he was blackmailing her it'll supply a motive but no direct evidence that she killed him," Duffield pointed out. "She couldn't have done it alone, anyway."

"You think the boy was her accomplice?" said Collier.

"Well, it looks like that," said the sergeant slowly. "Only— he's a nervous type. I'd have expected him to go to pieces more than he has."

Collier groaned. "These amateur crimes are the devil. Now with that burglary at Hampstead last month we knew Pannikin

Joe was in it because he'd finished a pot of raspberry jam in the larder. Funny how that blighter can't leave raspberry jam alone. They've all got their own methods, and their little ways that help us. With a case like this you've got to learn the alphabet before you can read."

He dropped the stub of his cigarette into the saucer of his coffee cup and beckoned to the attendant to bring his bill. The lights of greater London were showing through the steamy glass. Ten minutes later they were in the Underground on their way to the Yard.

Collier's superintendent had gone home and his report would have to wait until the morning, but he found a large bundle of newspapers waiting for him on the table in his room.

"All right, Sergeant. You get along to Mrs. Duffield and the kids. Be here by nine to-morrow. I'm taking this little lot along with me."

"What's the idea, Inspector?"

"I'll tell you. . . . Mrs. Dene was very much on her guard when I was trying to pump her, but she did let out one thing. She said she had not seen Mrs. Hall for sixteen years. I believe that was the truth. That dates some crisis in her life in which that man was involved. The enquiries our people have made in Chelsea where Mrs. Dene and her children lived with her brother-in-law go back sixteen years, and no further. It looks as if a clean break had been made somewhere for a fresh start. Now this is a bundle of Sunday papers, one of those that specialise in juicy scandals to give an extra flavour to the Sunday breakfast bloater, and they cover that period. I'm going through them to see if anything suggests itself. Rather an arduous job, but I feel it ought to be done."

"You're tired as it is," said Duffield gruffly. "It's close on ten. If I were you, Inspector, I'd get a bit of rest and leave that until the morning."

Collier shook his head. "No. I'm too behind with this case. If I find anything I may have lots to do to-morrow." He picked up the bundle and was leaving the room. Duffield followed him. "I'll help you."

"What about the family? But I won't say no. I can give you a shake down on the sofa in my sitting-room."

They took another taxi to Collier's rooms in Denbigh Street and there they sat up reading until the floor was ankle deep in discarded newspapers. Collier twice boiled a kettle and made tea. "We've nothing much to go on," he had warned the sergeant, "the names may be different. Almost sure to be. We've got the approximate ages. Sixteen years ago Mrs. Dene was about twenty-seven and the elder girl and boy five and four. The younger girl would have been a baby."

"Pretty hopeless," said Duffield.

"I know. Ten to one her trouble, whatever it was, never got any sort of publicity. And yet—it must have been pretty bad or that fellow wouldn't have been able to put on the screw as he must have done after all these years."

It was just after two when Collier uttered an exclamation.

"Gosh. I wonder—Duffield do you remember the Bent case? I was still in the Army. It was this year we're thinking of, nine-teen-nineteen. I read about it."

"I think I do. A rich old lady was boarding with a young couple, a Mr. and Mrs. Bent, somewhere in the Midlands, it was. Bent induced her to make a will in his favour and then poisoned her with arsenic. He nearly got away with it, too, but there was talk in the village and the body was exhumed. He and the wife were both arrested and tried together, but she got off. He was hanged."

"That's it. And it's all here, with pictures of the prisoners in the dock. They hadn't made that rule then about no photographs being taken in court. Look at this, Duffield."

They both pored over the blurred newspaper reproduction of a young man and woman standing stiffly side by side, but it was taken from the back of the dock and the man's shoulder blotted out the woman's face.

"He conducted his own defence. Very self-possessed and plausible, but he seems to have betrayed his complete ruthlessness. It came out that the marriage wasn't really a happy one and that he was planning to go off with another woman with the money left him by his victim. Listen to this, Duffield. Mrs. Bent, interviewed by our representative after her release, said, 'It has been like a nightmare. I only want to go right away and forget and be forgotten. I want to be left in peace with my children.' Mrs. Bent has a little boy and girl who are, fortunately still too young to realise the tragedy that has befallen them, and another baby girl a few months old. That's the usual journalese sob stuff, of course. There must be another picture of her somewhere. I haven't been looking at the pictures. Just run through these last weeks again, Duffield."

The sergeant obeyed and presently held out a page with the caption, "A portrait of Mrs. Bent taken with her children soon after Miss Gully had come to live as a paying guest at The Laurels."

"You're right, by gum," said Duffield. "The elder daughter's grown up the image of her. The only thing is that the hair's done differently. So Mrs. Dene was Mrs. Bent! Well, that brings us a good step forward, doesn't it. Hall knew and was threatening to blow the gaff."

"Yes, we're getting on," said Collier gloomily. "I wish we'd never been called in to the case, Duffield. Blackmail's a filthy business. If anybody tried it on with me I'd lay him out. I sympathise with the Denes. I suppose the boy must have been an accessory if he didn't actually kill the brute. She couldn't possibly have carried the body all that distance from the sitting-room of the lodge to the well without assistance. And that's one of the snags in the case. Would young Dene have called the police if he had any guilty knowledge of the affair? Surely their whole object was to avoid any scandal, or, at any rate, to stave it off until the daughter was safely married to Sir Miles Lennor? But if you rule out Tony Dene you have to assume that Mrs. Dene carried a body weighing close on eleven stone through the house and down that long strip of garden. Carried, not dragged. We should have found plenty of traces if she had dragged him. It's a sheer physical impossibility. And yet—"

Duffield scratched his head. "It's a snag all right," he agreed.

Collier yawned. "Anyhow we've done enough for to-night. We'll turn in now."

Collier seldom allowed his work to prevent him from getting his fair share of rest, but on this night he lay awake long after the rhythmic snoring audible in the adjoining room assured him that his more stolid colleague was sound asleep. He no longer dreaded the coming interview with his superiors at the Yard. He had something to show at last, he could report progress. But he wished the hunt had taken him in a different direction. Had not this woman suffered enough in the past? And her children—why should the sins of their father be visited on them? But, however much one sympathised with them, the hard fact remained that the greater the wrong done them by the man who called himself Mrs. Hall the more likely it seemed that they had combined to rid themselves of an intolerable incubus.

And so the Inspector, who had never learned to harden his heart, tossed and turned and saw the furniture of his room beginning to take shape in the grey light of dawn before he slept.

CHAPTER XX

MRS. DENE SPEAKS

MRS. DENE did not get up until after lunch.

She had been using some sleeping stuff which had been prescribed for her years ago when she was on the verge of a nervous breakdown. The doctor had warned her to take only a very small quantity and to do without it as soon as possible and she had obeyed him. As a result the bottle was still more than half full.

She was glad of it now. It enabled her to sleep heavily all through the night and to lie in a kind of torpor for half the day. She saw no reason why she should not drug herself into semi-consciousness since there was nothing more she could do for Lavvy now. She roused herself with an effort when Parsons brought up her lunch on a tray and propped her up with pillows and left her. She ate without appetite, poured out her coffee from the Thermos jug and lit a cigarette before she reached for the papers scattered on the foot of her bed. Presently, turning over the pages, she saw a paragraph in the social column of the *Morning Post.*

"The marriage arranged between Miss Lavinia Dene and Sir Miles Lennor, of Lennor Park, will not take place."

Lady Lennor must have arranged for the publication of that notice before she sailed for India with her son. But Lavvy had met the young man when she went up to London and had gone about ever since with a little air of secret satisfaction—or was it only bravado? Her mother had been afraid to question her. She was painfully aware that Lavvy had not forgiven her. There had been no more reproaches but she was aloof and civil with the civility one shows to strangers. Mrs. Dene looked round eagerly when the door opened, but it was only Mollie.

"How are you, Mummie?"

"All right. I'm getting up. You might run the water for my bath."

When she was dressed she went downstairs. From her window she had seen Tony and Mollie starting out for a walk with Binkie in the rain that still fell persistently. She was glad to see them go. She wanted Lavvy to herself. As she entered the library where a fire had been lit to conquer the penetrating chill she saw the glint of Lavvy's golden head over the top of one of the easy chairs.

"Reading and toasting?" she said brightly. "Very sensible." She took the chair facing her daughter on the other side of the hearth. Her daughter did not raise her eyes from her book. Mrs. Dene watched her for a moment wistfully. Wasn't Lavvy a little bit fond of her? Didn't she mind her obvious misery? Apparently not. The lovely face expressed no feeling of any kind.

"Lavvy, my darling," she said brokenly.

The girl looked up at last with—alas—with nothing but controlled irritation.

"Mother, I do hope you haven't come to make a scene because I can't stand it. I want to be left alone, please. It's the least you can do after the way you've behaved. I haven't said much, and I'm not going to, but I think it was horrible."

"Lavvy—"

"I've been thinking things over," the hard young voice went on. "I won't go on living with you. You'll have to make me an allowance and I'll share a flat with somebody, Lily James, or Rhoda Harper. That will make it easier for Miles to marry me when he comes home."

Her tone was so wounding that Mrs. Dene's eyes filled with tears, but she blinked them away. "Very well," she said. To ears more discerning than Lavvy's there would have been something terrible in the finality of that acquiescence, but Lavvy, as usual, was thinking only of herself. Parsons came in before she could speak again.

"Inspector Collier and Sergeant Duffield have come back, madam, and want to see you." She stepped back to allow them to pass her and retreated, closing the door after her.

Lavvy stood up. "I think I'll go."

She hated all the policemen who had invaded her home impartially, but being Lavvy she could not help glancing at Collier from under her long glinting golden lashes as she passed him. He met her eyes stolidly and allowed her to leave the room unchallenged. Mrs. Dene was leaning forward to put another log on the fire.

"Won't you both sit down?" she said in her quiet voice.

"Thanks. It's nice to see a fire. It's a cold rain. One of these Buchan spells, I suppose. Where's Mr. Dene?"

"He and his younger sister have taken their dog for a run across the park."

"I see. Well, I want a word with you first. I want to tell you that we've made some progress. We still don't know who Mrs. Hall was, but we know why you let him live rent free at the lodge and lent him furniture and gave him all the money he asked for."

She looked at him and her lips moved but no sound came from them. He would not prolong her suspense. "Your name was Bent formerly."

Her hands were gripping the arms of her chair. He saw the knuckles whiten. He waited. Then, as she did not speak, he said: "Mrs. Dene, you must know that we can have no desire to recall what is past or to give you and yours unnecessary pain. On the other hand I have to do my duty. I have to find the person who killed the man who passed as Mrs. Hall. So far you haven't helped me much, have you? I can't force you to speak, Mrs. Dene. Anything you say may be used in evidence against you. But I don't think you stand to lose anything by telling me the truth. If we have to build up our case ourselves bit by bit we shall be compelled to use every scrap of information we can collect. If you help us we might—I can't make any promises—but we might be able to avoid any reference to a former case."

Her eyes had been closed. She opened them to look at him searchingly. "You mean that if I confess that I killed him nothing need be said about the hold he had over me?"

"Exactly."

"That's not an admission, mind," she said. "I was just asking out of curiosity. And now—if I refuse to say a single word more what will you do?"

"I am afraid I shall have to ask you to come back to Ranchester with us, Mrs. Dene."

"You mean you will arrest me?"

"Yes."

"And my children will be told what—what their father was?"

"I'm afraid so, Mrs. Dene."

"Why do you say afraid?" she asked bitterly. "Don't be a hypocrite. You know you're delighted to have found this weapon to use against me."

Collier flushed. "That's not quite fair. But I understand that any attempt I might make to express my sympathy would sound like an impertinence. Would you like a little time for consideration? I can give you five minutes."

"Thank you."

"Very well." He looked at his watch and then, taking out his note book, sat turning over the pages.

The scratching of the sergeant's pen ceased. For five minutes the room was silent but for the ticking of the clock.

"The time is up, Mrs. Dene."

"I'm so tired," she said faintly, "so tired of struggling. I tried so hard all these years for their sake, and it's come to this. My brother-in-law gave us food and shelter, he had the children educated. I kept house for him. I saved him a servant's wages. No servant would have stayed. He was a tyrant. He was always reminding me of what he was doing for us. Sometimes he pretended to think that I had known what Tom was doing, that I had helped him. He had changed his name too, sold his business, broken entirely with everyone he knew. He was a proud man and a hard man. He never forgave his brother for putting him to shame. He pretended to think I was Tom's accomplice but he didn't really believe that or he wouldn't have trusted me to cook his meals for fifteen years. Then, when he died last autumn and his will was read I learned that he had left all he had to me without conditions. I had not known he was so rich. He wouldn't even let me have a woman in to do the scrubbing. My first thought was to get away from the place where I had been so unhappy. My daughter Lavvy—I wanted to give her a chance. The others thought they'd like to live in the country. I went to an agent. They showed me pictures of this place. I fell in love with it. The neighbours seemed friendly. Of course, I did my best to make a good impression. I subscribed to everything. We were asked out. Then—"

"Yes, Mrs. Dene."

"One day a woman called. I was alone as it happened. She was a big woman, well dressed in black, very much made up. I did not like her much though she seemed pleasant enough. I thought, naturally, that she was someone living in the district, but she said she had come down from London for the day. I began to get a little worried then. There was something sinister about her. I wanted to get rid of her but I did not know how. Then she said. 'I see you don't remember me, Mrs. Dene.' I—I just sat and looked at her. She said, 'I expect you are wondering how I found you out. There's an article in one of the illustrated weeklies on the pageant that is going to be held at Lennor Park next summer. You were mentioned as one of the promoters and there was a portrait group of you and your children on the terrace steps. Quite charming. I might not have recognised you, but your elder daughter is the image of what you were sixteen years ago.' I said, 'I don't know who you are.' She said, 'That does not matter. I am Harriet Hall now. An old friend shall we say. You can tell your children that. A very old friend to whom you owe a debt of gratitude.' I said, 'What do you want?' You can imagine the rest."

"What was his real name, Mrs. Dene?"

"I know no more than you. She was in the court when my husband and I were being tried for the murder of poor old Miss Gully. That is all I can tell you. I had no idea that she was a man masquerading as a woman. I hated and feared her, and had to pretend I liked her. I saw she meant to get everything from me, but she had to do it by degrees. If she had driven me too far I might have done something desperate. She realised that, and it kept her within bounds. I thought that once Lavvy—my daughter—was married to Sir Miles I would put this place in the hands of the agents and get right away from her. She was so grasping. Every day when she came over from the lodge she took something away with her. I did not dare say no to her. My children resented her presence. She was spoiling life for them too, but I couldn't help it. She tried to make friends with them at first, asking them to come to tea with her at the Lodge, but they never went, and after a time she gave it up and just sat and looked at them with her eyes half-closed like a cat watching birds. She had a good deal of money from me. Never by cheque, of course. About three weeks ago she asked me for one hundred pounds. I had given her fifteen only a few days before. The following Sunday she came as usual in the afternoon and sat on the lawn and had tea with us. While the children were out of hearing she told me she wanted a small garage built adjoining the lodge. She meant to have a car. I, of course, was to pay for it. I said I couldn't afford it. She only smiled. I was awake most of that night. The next day I thought I would go and see her at the lodge where we should not be interrupted and try to make her understand that she was asking more than I could possibly give. My son had gone up to Town for the day. Lavvy and Mollie were both out somewhere. I was supposed to be lying down after lunch. I walked across the park thinking of what I was going to say, hoping to induce her to be reasonable. When I got to the lodge I went up the path to the front door but I didn't knock. I heard voices inside. Loud angry voices like two or more people talking at once. I was surprised. I thought she never had visitors. I thought, 'It's no use if there's somebody there.' And I'd been dreading it, so it was a relief in a way to have to put it off. So I turned and came home again. And that's all."

Collier was silent for a moment. He did not doubt that she had told the truth—but was it the whole truth?

"You say you heard voices. Would that be in the room on the right of the front door, the sitting-room?"

"Yes."

"Have you any idea of the time?"

"It must have been somewhere between a quarter to four and the hour."

"How long did you stand there listening?"

"Not more than a minute. The voices were loud and angry. I did not want to be involved in any unpleasantness—"

"But you did not come in again until past five, Mrs. Dene. The parlourmaid says she went up to your room and looked for you elsewhere after she had brought the tea up to the library."

"I know. I was upset. It was a very hot day and I had no sun-shade. I turned aside to get some shade and went up the path to the summer-house on the little wooded hill that shuts off the view of the lodge from the house. There is a seat and there was more air up there. I sat there for some time."

"You have no witness to prove that?"

"No."

"But somebody saw you either going to the lodge or coming away from it."

"What do you mean?" Her voice was not quite steady.

"You know what I mean, Mrs. Dene. Ruby Duncan, the house-maid, had been to the village to post a parcel. She saw you."

"I don't know."

"On the last day of her life she came up to your room and had some conversation with you. We know that from the other servants. What passed at that interview, Mrs. Dene?"

"She said she wanted to leave at once because of what had happened. I told her she must remain until the end of her month or lose her month's wages. She was impertinent, but that was nothing new."

"She uttered no threats?"

"No."

He was formulating his next question when the door was opened by Mollie. Tony was just behind her. They both hesitated on the threshold when they saw the two detectives. Collier stood up and the sergeant followed his example.

"I'd be glad of a word with you, Mr. Dene."

"May I hear?" asked Mollie.

"Better not, I think, miss. I'll see you later if you have any information—"

"I haven't," she flashed.

"Then I think if you don't mind—" he said blandly. He had gone forward and was holding the door for her to pass out. She was very unlike her sister, he thought. There was no trace of coquetry in the look she gave him. It was purely reproachful.

"Why can't you leave us alone? We've done nothing—" Her voice was too low to carry to the other end of the room where her mother lay back in her chair, white and spent, and Tony stood, with his hands in his pockets and his shoulders hunched up to his ears, staring moodily into the fire. The Inspector, who had not enjoyed the last half hour, was goaded into candour.

"I wish to God I could," he said.

He closed the door and went back to the others. He did not sit down again but leaned against a corner of the writing table.

"Your mother has made a statement, Mr. Dene, which will be read over to her presently before she is asked to sign it. There are parts of it which I hope we need not use and I am only going to refer now to one point."

Tony took off his spectacles which had become misted with rain, and rubbed them on his handkerchief. His brown eyes looked strained and anxious. "All right, Inspector. Carry on."

"Mrs. Dene tells us that she walked across the park to North Lodge on the Monday afternoon and that when she came to the door she heard loud and angry voices in the sitting-room, and turned and came away again. According to her this was somewhere between a quarter to and a quarter past four. You were on your way down from London then?"

"Yes, I suppose so. Yes."

"You and Miss Steer both got out at Larnwood at 4.17."

"Yes."

"You had your car in the station yard where you had left it when you went up that morning and you drove away immediately though you must have realised that Miss Steer had not been met. It didn't occur to you to offer her a lift? You had become friendly on the way down and you had learned she was coming to stay with her aunt at North Lodge."

The young man reddened. "I—I'm not proud of that. I just didn't want to be mixed up in Mrs. Hall's affairs. And I thought she would be met. It never struck me that she would have to walk all the way—"

"How long does it take you to drive from Larnwood to the north gate?"

"I never have driven to the north gate. It is never used and the road that used to lead to it from the cross-roads on the Lennor Moor wouldn't be any too good for the springs. But going the usual way round by Lennor village it takes something between ten and twenty minutes."

"Suppose you left your car at the cross-roads on the moor and came on foot to the north gate. How long would it take to cross that bit of the moor on foot?"

"I've no idea. I've never done it."

"A young and active man can cover the ground in nine minutes, Mr. Dene."

"Why ask me if you know the answer?" said Tony. "I suppose you're trying to suggest that it was my voice that my mother heard. But since she has told you that it was between a quarter to and a quarter past four."

"We have no means of checking that, Mr. Dene. She did not return to the house until past five."

"Well, I've already told you that I didn't come straight home. I went for a drive and got back late, about ten o'clock."

"Could you show me on a map where you went?"

"Not exactly. I didn't take much notice. I kept to by-roads where there wasn't much traffic. Twice I pulled up and had a smoke."

"What was your object?"

"I hadn't one. I just felt restless and worried."

"I see. Now about Ruby Duncan, Mr. Dene. On the Thursday afternoon you were not thinking of her at all, were you? You had taken no interest in her?"

"No. Never."

"It was she who, seeing you in the park, followed you and spoke to you?"

"Yes."

"And she told you that she had seen Mrs. Dene coming away from the North Lodge—or going to it—on Monday and that she had not informed the police but felt she would have to do so unless she was well paid to hold her tongue."

"That is so."

"And what did you reply?"

"I told her to go to hell."

"And was that all?"

"Practically. She became abusive, but I didn't stop to listen."

"Was it then that you struck her, or did you meet her again later?"

"I never struck her."

Nobody spoke for a minute. Collier was thinking hard. These two—he had to face it—had not succeeded in clearing themselves. On the other hand, he was reluctant to proceed any further without a little more evidence. There were some negative points in their favour. Tony's finger-prints had been found on various articles of furniture at the Lodge, but that was account-ed for by the fact that he had been there with Amy Steer on the Tuesday. There were no finger-prints of Mrs. Dene, but then there were remarkably few of the late tenant either. It was ob-vious that after the murder a damp cloth had been used to wipe off finger-prints as well as blood stains. Collier decided to talk the case over with Lindo and the superintendent before making any arrest.

"All right," he said. "Just read that over to Mr. Dene, Ser-geant, and we'll ask him to sign it. I'm afraid the fact that there was no truth in your first account of your conversation with the dead girl isn't going to do you much good, Mr. Dene."

"I felt the less said the better," said Tony, "but now that my mother has given you a satisfactory explanation of her move-ments on Monday afternoon I thought it would be all right."

"In short, you tell the truth when it suits you," said Collier, and his tone was grimmer than it had ever been when address-ing the young man. "I'm afraid that rather discounts the value of your evidence. Carry on, Sergeant—"

"What's the use? You don't believe me when I do tell you the truth," said Tony defiantly. "I don't hit girls, even when they try to blackmail me. It seems pretty hopeless." He fumbled over the cigarettes in his case. His hands were shaking.

The sergeant cleared his throat and began to read. His voice was monotonous and he paid no attention to punctuation. Mrs. Dene and her son listened impassively. Collier noticed, howev-er, that they avoided looking at one another. He wished he could be sure.

CHAPTER XXI
THE NEXT STEP

AN HOUR LATER Collier and his colleague were in the Super-intendent's room at the Ranchester police station. Lindo was present. The two local men listened with close attention to Collier's narrative and were evidently impressed by the identification of Mrs. Dene with the wife of the notorious William Bent.

"Why didn't you bring them along, Inspector? They could have gone before the Bench to-morrow and been committed for trial at the next Assizes. The evidence may be circumstantial but it's surely strong enough now. I doubt if any jury would be willing to bring in a verdict of guilty of anything more than manslaughter on the first count. They killed Hall under the most tremendous provocation. But the murder of the girl is another matter. Young Dene will swing for that. His mother may get off as she did before—and break a record. So far as I know no woman has been tried twice in her life on a capital charge. It's your case, Inspector. I'm not interfering, but I can't help wondering what you are waiting for."

Collier was stirring his second cup of tea. It was chilly in the stone-paved passages, but in the Superintendent's room there was a comfortable rug and a faint blue haze of tobacco smoke. Rain beat on the window panes. Looking out he could see over the high wall of the station yard the rooks, black flecks on a leaden sky, battling against the wind on their way back to the elms of the cathedral close.

"You feel certain of their guilt, Superintendent?"

"Isn't it reasonable to assume it? They had the opportunity and the motive. Just now in their statements they each told you a part of the truth."

"Wait a bit," said Collier, "let's look for the points the defence would seize upon if they got a fellow worth his salt. We—that is the prosecution—say that on her own admission Mrs. Dene went to the lodge on Monday afternoon to try to induce Mrs. Hall to moderate her demands. We suggest that actually she, having been driven to desperation, had taken her son into her confidence, and that he had arranged to meet her at the lodge. Do we say that the murder was deliberately planned? I fancy not. We'll assume that there was a violent quarrel and that young Dene picked up some heavy object, probably the brass paper weight, and struck the fatal blow. We shall have to work this out with a time table"—he reached for a writing pad on the table, set down his tea cup and scribbled in pencil. "Here we are:

4.17. Dene left the down train at Marlbourne.

4.35. Dene arrived at the Lodge, having left his car at the cross-roads.

4.35 to 4.45. The crime was committed and Mrs. Dene left the Lodge.

5.5. Mrs. Dene was seen by the parlour-maid crossing the hall at the Dower House.

6. Amy Steer, having walked the five miles from the station, arrived at the Lodge."

The pad was handed round and studied by the others in turn.

"What's wrong with that?" asked the Superintendent. "It allows him an hour and a quarter to dispose of the body down the well, clear up any mess, and make his getaway. Fill in that picture and you'll find there's nothing wrong with it psychologically. I wouldn't be surprised if Hall wasn't threatening Mrs. Dene when her son struck him. Well, the defence can make the most of that. As I said before if it wasn't for Ruby Duncan I believe they'd get off—"

"Wait," said Collier again, "I was wondering if you'd spot the piece that doesn't fit. You've all seen Amy Steer's last statement?"

"Yes."

"Miss Steer says that when she went into the kitchen, about ten minutes after her arrival at the Lodge, she noticed that the oil cooking stove and the kettle standing on it were both warm."

Lindo nodded. "We've assumed that Dene was there for some time. He may have left the cottage by the back door as she came in by the front."

"Yes. But where was his car? She saw no car when she crossed the moor. He might have left it farther off, on the Lennor road where there is a good deal of traffic and a car parked by the roadside would hardly be noticed. But, in that case, what becomes of our time-table? There's another point. Young Dene knew that this girl was on her way to North Lodge. She had told him that she was to be met, and for all he knew Mrs. Hall had instructed one of the Ranchester garages to send a car to fetch her. She might have arrived on the scene long before she did. Is it likely that he would have committed a murder knowing that at any minute Miss Steer might be coming up the path with a chauffeur carrying her suit case?"

"He might if the blow was unpremeditated, struck in the heat of passion," argued the Superintendent. "If you come to that, most murders are improbable from the point of view of common sense. The game's never worth the candle."

"True. But there's another snag. Why did young Dene discover the body in the well the following day and ring up the police about it? What conceivable motive had he for drawing attention to Mrs. Hall's disappearance if he had engineered it himself?"

"The motive of chivalry, Inspector, which would certainly be operative in the case of this boy as it was in the cases of far worse men. Crippen, Seddon. He couldn't endure the thought of leaving the girl alone with that thing mouldering in the well at the foot of the garden, so he took the risk."

"Knowing that he was spoiling his sister's chances of a good marriage and endangering not only himself but his mother?"

"He may not have considered that. He wasn't as calm and cool as we are here."

Collier smiled unwillingly. "I see I haven't convinced you. I don't feel as calm as I may look, Superintendent. I confess I'm worried. I'm building up my case against these two, and I agree with you that it's a strong one—but all the time I can't get rid of an inward conviction that I'm all wrong, that I've missed something that would point in another direction."

Nobody spoke for a moment. The Superintendent was drawing circles on his blotting paper. He thought the Inspector was inclined to rely too much on his inward monitor when the latter conflicted with all the available evidence, but he did not say so. He was aware that in spite of one or two setbacks, Collier had a growing reputation at the Yard. But he had his own Chief Constable in mind. Colonel Boult was growing very restive. He cleared his throat uneasily.

"Then—you are taking no further steps to-day?"

"Unless something fresh turns up. I'm having a description of Hall circulated in the town where the Bent case was tried and at the prison where the sentence was carried out on William Bent. We ought to be able to trace Hall now. According to Mrs. Dene he was present at the trial, or said he was, and that is all she really knew about him."

"You believe she was speaking the truth when she swore she had no idea that he wasn't a woman?"

"Yes, I do."

"What do you suppose was the motive of his disguise?"

"It wouldn't have been so easy for a man to get all that he got from her. It may have amused him to play a part—"

The telephone on the desk rang. The Superintendent took up the receiver. "Hallo . . . yes . . ." he turned to Collier. "This is for you."

Collier took over the instrument. "Inspector Collier speaking. . . ." He settled down to listen while the others waited sitting motionless round the table in the gathering dusk.

Presently he hung up the receiver.

"Well, I've got Hall's dossier. He wasn't really related to Miss Steer. She'll be glad to hear that. He was her uncle by marriage. His name was Harlow. The Steers and the Harlows were neighbours. Jack Steer left home when he was little more than a boy and never came back. Harlow married the sister, another Amy, and he seems to have been a good husband, but she died young. After her death he was employed for some time as a warder at Strangeways prison. He was there while Bent was there and was one of the two who sat with him in the dock throughout his trial. Later he got into bad company and his character degenerated, and he lost his job and left the district. How he lived between then and now they don't know."

"Curious that he should have advertised for this girl. He'd have found it difficult to keep up his imposture with a woman living under the same roof."

"He might. But he didn't lack self-confidence. They said that as a young man he had a great wish to go on the stage. It wouldn't surprise me to hear that he'd done a bit as a female impersonator. I'll have his description sent to some of the theatrical agents. As to his motive he probably meant to marry the girl to young Dene. Well, there's nothing further to discuss for the moment, is there?"

It had grown dark while they were talking. The Superintendent switched on the shaded lamp on his desk. "You think there's no danger of Dene bolting? He must realise he won't be free much longer. It's all very well, Collier, but if you remember Ruby Duncan you have to admit that we're dealing with a man who is both desperate and ruthless. Suppose someone else gets in his way? Suppose he strikes again? It seems to me that you are taking a fearful risk in leaving him at large. If, as a result, another life is sacrificed we should all be broken."

"Not all," said Collier, "only me. I take full responsibility for the delay. You can all bear witness to that. You can say I insisted on it."

"You don't know Colonel Boult."

"I agree that there's a killer at large," said Collier gravely, "but I'm not so sure as you are that it's young Dene. I've done what I could. The household have been warned not to go out after dark, or alone at any time. And three of your men are patrolling the park."

"Only one."

Collier had been turned towards the window. He whirled round.

"What!"

"Only one at the South Lodge entrance to keep out unauthorised visitors."

"How is that? I gave definite instructions—"

"I know it," said the Superintendent, "but the Chief Constable rang me up last night. He thinks the enquiry is taking too much time. I told him—but he wouldn't listen to me. He put me in a very difficult position. I'm very sorry, Inspector, but I really had no choice but to carry out his orders."

There was a strained silence. Collier broke it. "And the question is, what does A do now? Or is it what will B do next?" He took a turn about the room while the others refrained from speech. Duffield was very red in the face. He resented this cavalier treatment of his colleague. The other two looked as uncomfortable as they felt. Collier stopped in front of the Superintendent's desk.

"The Colonel may find that it is easier to call us in than to get rid of us. If he gets in touch with the Yard and asks them to recall me and they agree, I shall go, but not otherwise. I was talking of responsibility just now and assuming it. I take that back. If anything happens to-night Colonel Boult must shoulder the blame. I'm not blaming you, Superintendent. I understand how you are placed. We've worked very well together and I'm grateful for the help I've had from you and your men. I'm going back to the Station Hotel now. They are sending me Harlow's dossier there and it may arrive by the evening post. I'll be round in the morning, but I shan't trouble you before that unless something fresh turns up. Good night."

He smiled as he held out his hand. The Superintendent gripped it hard.

"Good of you not to kick up a fuss," he muttered, "you'd be perfectly justified—"

Collier did not speak again on the subject that engaged them both until he and Duffield were seated before a blazing fire in their sitting-room at the Station Hotel. Collier, who seldom touched spirits had ordered double whiskies for them both. He had asked at the office if any letters had come for him and had been told that the evening post was not in yet. He looked unusually weary and dispirited.

"Well," he said at last, "you've been very quiet all day, Sergeant. What about it?"

"That Colonel—" began Duffield with rather less than his usual stolidity. But Collier held up his hand. "I know. But he doesn't really matter. In a way he's right. Not in over-riding my instructions about the patrols. But in being impatient. Do you believe the Denes are guilty, Duffield?"

The sergeant, now well warmed without and within after his chilly passage through the rain-swept streets, rubbed his hands together and answered thoughtfully.

"I never was one to jump at anything. I'm not built that way. And I don't set up to be a judge of character. If I find a chap's finger-prints on a rifled safe and he can't prove he was somewhere else at the time the robbery was committed I'm apt to take him along to the station even if he has nice blue eyes and is known to be good to his auntie."

Collier laughed. "You insubordinate old devil. Stop pulling my leg. You don't have to tell me you don't jump, but surely you must have crawled an inch or two since we started on this case. Don't forget your function. You're ballast for me. You're not an anchor."

"If you study the map," said Duffield, "you can see that the tenant of North Lodge might have visitors from outside, and nobody be the wiser. The north gate of the park was never used by the family but it was not locked. The baker from the village called at the lodge three times a week, and the grocer and the butcher once. None of them, as we have ascertained, came on Mondays. People could come and go without passing through the village. The country to the north is well wooded and who notices a car parked by the roadside at this time of year when motorists think nothing of driving fifty miles to eat their sandwiches in the shade of a hedge or on a bit of common land? When I look at that map, Inspector, I feel that you're right to hesitate, and that the man who killed Harlow may be somebody who's not been seen or heard of by any of the people here."

He paused and resumed. "Then there's the landlord of the King's Head. He acted as a good citizen should when he rushed over here in his flivver to give us that bit about Dene being seen with Ruby, but he's a nasty piece of work for all that. I wouldn't trust him a yard."

"I agree," said Collier. "We've only one certainty to build on. The murderer was at the lodge on Monday afternoon, and he was within a hundred yards of it on Thursday. We ought to be able to find someone who saw him coming or going. He can't be invisible. But the local police have already questioned everyone they can think of. And, by the way, the gate wasn't unlocked on Thursday, Duffield. Lindo had a padlock and chain put on Wednesday morning when the body was removed from the well."

"It wouldn't be difficult for an active man to climb the park wall. There's a lot of old ivy growing over it that would give footholds."

Collier smoked for a while in silence. Then he said suddenly:

"Has it struck you that Hall does not appear to have made any arrangements for having Amy Steer met at Larnwood? That's rather odd. I can only suppose that he knew young Dene was going up to Town on Monday and that he would be coming down by the same train and that he relied on his giving the girl a lift. It would be part of his scheme to pair them off. I think he had some such intention. It seems the only explanation. He can hardly have expected the girl to walk the five miles from the station. Of course he may have meant to order a car from one of the Ranchester garages and have forgotten to do so. I think I'll go round to Miss Steer's lodgings, Duffield, and pass on the information we have received about Harlow. The name may recall something to her mind. You need not come. I'll be back in time for dinner."

Duffield was glad enough of a respite. He had not yet had time to address some picture postcards of Ranchester he had bought for his wife and children.

Collier resumed his moist raincoat and left the comparative warmth and comfort of the Station Hotel for the darkening streets. He was driven more by the restlessness of frustration than because he really thought Amy could help him. He was beginning to wonder if this was going to be numbered among the growing list of unsolved murder mysteries, the Reading shop murder, the Epsom garage murder, the trunk crime. But he told himself that he would rather admit failure than risk a miscarriage of justice.

He was so absorbed in his thoughts that he passed the house, one of a row of small neat houses, where the mother of P.C. Saunders let a bed-sitting-room. He turned back a few steps and rang the bell. Mrs. Saunders came to the door.

"Miss Steer? She isn't in yet, and it's a wonder she isn't. They can't have been busy at the shop on an evening like this. You're the gentleman from London, aren't you? I've heard of you from my son. Will you come in and wait?" Mrs. Saunders had a proper respect for the Yard.

Collier thanked her but declined to come in. He would walk up to the shop. He might meet Miss Steer coming away.

"She's never been molested on her way to and from her work, has she, Mrs. Saunders?"

"Not to my knowledge, sir. Though after the disgraceful goings on in the town yesterday nothing wouldn't surprise me. But those weren't Ranchester people, just market day riff-raff come in by the cheap day excursion tickets."

"Your son handled them well," he said.

Mrs. Saunders flushed with pleasure at this praise. "He's a good lad."

Collier walked quickly through the rain-swept streets to Luke's Passage. There was a light in the teashop but it was extinguished as he came up and Miss Fraser herself came out. He saw that she was dressed for the street and carrying a despatch case.

"We're closed."

"That's all right," he said. "I wanted to see Miss Steer."

"Miss Steer left some time ago."

"How long? I've just come from her lodgings."

"That's funny. She went over an hour ago. We've been very slack this afternoon."

"She wasn't at her lodgings," he repeated. "Can you suggest where she might have gone? I am Inspector Collier."

"Oh," her manner changed slightly and became more cordial. "I've heard of you from Amy. I know she was tired. I should think she would go straight home in this weather. Besides, she had nowhere else to go. Unless—" She broke off.

"Unless what—" he prompted her.

"I just wondered if she had arranged to meet young Dene and his sister."

"You think that likely?"

"They took refuge here last night, you know, from a hostile crowd. Amy is very friendly with them both."

"You approve of that, Miss Fraser? I understand that you have taken this girl under your wing and offered her permanent employment."

She hesitated. "I liked what I saw of the young man. I can't believe the things they are saying about him, and I know Amy doesn't."

"Yes," he said, "but I don't think young Dene will have come over to Ranchester to-night. She didn't actually tell you she was meeting him?"

"Oh, dear, no. I think you must have missed her on the road. You'd find her at her lodgings if you went back to them now."

"I hope you're right," he said.

She had locked the shop door after switching off the light and they were walking down Luke's Passage together, Collier suiting his stride to her shorter step.

"Why? Surely nothing could have happened to her, Inspector? Do you want me to come along with you?" He declined the offer. Her lodgings were in the opposite direction. They parted in the High Street and he hurried back the way he had come. He was uneasy. Amy had left the teashop an hour ago. It would not take her more than ten minutes to get back to her lodgings. If the evening had been fine she might have gone for a walk but it was not likely in this downpour. The streets, shining with rain, were practically deserted. No one would remain out of doors who was not obliged to do so.

Mrs. Saunders answered his ring at the bell more promptly than before. Her face fell when she saw the detective. "I thought it was Miss Steer. She'll catch her death of cold out in all this—"

"She's not been back then?"

"Won't you come in, sir? My boy's just come off duty and sat down to his supper—"

"I'd like a word with him."

The young constable looked up in some alarm as his mother ushered the Inspector from the Yard into the kitchen, and stood up hastily.

"Sit down, Saunders, and get on with your meal. I haven't come here to disturb you." Collier moved over to the fire and spread his hands to the blaze. Mrs. Saunders was old-fashioned and preferred a kitchener to a gas stove. "More like December than July, isn't it? You were one of the men patrolling the Dower House woods weren't you?"

"Yes, sir. But the Superintendent put me back on my beat in Ranchester yesterday."

Collier bit his lip. "Yes, I know. But there's one man there still?"

"Yes, sir. Harrison was on at the south entrance all day. Baines cycled over about six o'clock as his relief. That's right, sir, isn't it?"

"Quite. I saw Harrison myself when I was at the Dower House this afternoon. I'm afraid I'm making your hearth rug very wet, Mrs. Saunders."

"That don't matter, sir. Tom, the Inspector is worried like about the young lady not being in yet."

Young Saunders, who had just overcome his shyness sufficiently to take another mouthful of sausage and mashed potatoes, replied with some difficulty. "Not in? Then perhaps it was her I saw."

Collier, who by now was standing in a cloud of steam, turned his head quickly. "What's that, Saunders? You saw her? When?"

"It would be round about a quarter to six, sir. I was coming down Paternoster Row, that's the Street that runs parallel with High Street. If you want to get to the Cathedral from High Street you go up Luke's Passage and cross Paternoster Row and through the gate into the Close."

"I know. Go on."

"It was raining hard and nobody about, but I saw a woman come quickly out of Luke's Passage and hurry along in front of me and get into a car some way farther on. Seemed as if she was expected for the car started off at once."

"Make and number?"

"I couldn't say as to that, Inspector. I was a long ways off. It was a small car and not one of the newest type. Bucked a bit before she got going so to speak. I couldn't be sure it was Miss Steer either, but it struck me at the time that it was like her. Sort of slim and moved along easy."

"I understand. It was you who checked a rush by the crowd along Luke's Passage yesterday evening."

"Yes, sir. I happened to be on my way home from patrolling the woods and saw a lot of rough chaps chasing Mr. Dene and his sister."

"I heard about it, and I think you did very well."

"Thank you, sir."

"You saw them off in their car, didn't you, when the crowd had dispersed?"

"Yes. I brought it round from the parking place behind the picture house to Paternoster Row. I went with them down the Passage and saw them start."

"Could it have been their car that you saw this evening?"

"No, sir. I don't think the young gentleman'll be coming to Ranchester again in a hurry after what happened yesterday. He kept a stiff upper lip, but he was proper shook up. And I could see the young lady'd been crying."

"They didn't ought to've gone to a comic picture that afternoon of that poor girl's funeral," said his mother, "not that I hold with the lot that chased them. Cowardly brutes."

"There's still a man on duty at the south gate," reflected Collier. "What were his instructions in the event of Dene going out in his car?"

"He was to go to the post office in the village and ring up the station which way he'd gone."

"But you're fairly certain it wasn't the Denes' car you saw an hour ago?"

"Quite, sir. It was smaller. One of those Babies." After a moment he added, more doubtfully. "Of course I was at the end of the street, and the light was bad."

"Then you're not certain?" said Collier sharply. "Well—I wouldn't like to swear to it, not if a lot depends on it," said Saunders, looking rather unhappy. "Is it anything to do with this case, sir?"

"I don't know," said Collier, "but I don't like it." He looked at his watch. Duffield, stolid as he was, would be wondering at his prolonged absence. His own uneasiness was increasing. He did not understand this latest development. That sixth sense of which he was sometimes aware seemed to be warning him that much might depend on his next step.

CHAPTER XXII
AT THE LODGE

DURING THE AFTERNOON a gipsy woman with a basket of clothes-pegs had come into the shop, offering a penny for a bag of stale cakes. When Amy explained that they had no stock left over the grimy hand adorned with a brass wedding ring had turned over the clothes-pegs and produced a crumpled bit of paper.

"That's all right, lady. God bless you—"

The gipsy had gone out swiftly, leaving Amy staring at the pencilled message.

Will meet you with car Paternoster Street six o'clock. Say nothing to anyone. S.

These were her instructions. The man who called himself Smith had promised that if she did what she was told Tony Dene would be cleared. How? She had no idea, and she had lain awake for sometime the night before wondering what her part could be. And what had he meant when he said that he had been sent down from headquarters to work on the case, unknown to the men who were already engaged on it, because there was something wrong? Amy, like most of her fellow countrymen, had a childlike faith in the integrity of the police. Could that ambiguous phrase refer to the burly, authoritative men who had been ordering her goings and comings? It was like seeing what had seemed to be solid ground crumble. Something wrong!

She had time to think, for customers were few. Miss Fraser noticed her pallor and her evident depression.

"You look tired out, my dear," she said anxiously, "I hope the work isn't going to be too much for you."

"Oh no. But my head aches. I wonder if I might go a little earlier—"

It was a quarter to six.

"Of course, child. If anyone comes now I can attend to them. Away with you. And in your place I'd go to bed and have a good rest."

Amy put on her raincoat, adjusted her beret, and hurried off to avoid being asked questions which she would not be able to answer with truth. She saw the car parked at the bottom of Paternoster Street and went towards it. Smith leaned out of the driver's seat and opened the door for her.

"Well on time, that's good," he said. "Jump in."

The car leaped forward with a grinding of gears and a jerk that threw her back in her seat.

"Funny old bus, isn't it," he said, as if he read her thoughts. "Talc windows and a mouldy smell. But if you stop to think you'll realise that I can't go about in one of the flying squad's cars here and keep my incognito. This aged Tin Lizzie is a part of my disguise. And the engine's not too bad."

"Is—is it safe to go so fast round corners?" she ventured.

He laughed. "Are you nervous? You needn't be."

He did not speak again for some minutes. She sat listening to the rain drumming on the tarpaulin roof and wondering how he managed to see through the windscreen without a screen wiper. They had left the town behind them and were following a road between fields.

"Where are we going?" she asked a little doubtfully.

"To the North Lodge."

"Oh"—she shrank a little. "Why?"

"There are several points that will be easier to settle on the spot. I want to stage a reconstitution of what took place. A favourite stunt with the French police. It ought to be rather amusing."

"Oh!" Amy glanced at Mr. Smith's sharp profile and thought, not for the first time, that there was something rather ruthless about this emissary from Scotland Yard. Perhaps they had to be like that—cold blooded—to get to the top so young. Inspector Collier was more human.

"I don't think it will amuse me," she said.

"Wait and see. I've got it all planned. I'm producing this show."

"It's going to prove Mr. Dene's innocence?"

"You bet it is. Absolutely. Completely. A pail of whitewash couldn't do more for him." He laughed again with evident enjoyment of his own wit. "And now, if you don't mind, we won't talk any more. I don't want to get into a skid."

Amy subsided. The car was draughty and she felt chilly and uncomfortable. And Mr. Smith's high spirits were not infectious. He did not improve on acquaintance. He laughed too much at his own jokes.

They were on higher ground now and meeting the wind. It was difficult to see much through the talc windows but Amy guessed that they were crossing Lennor Common.

He stopped the car presently and turned to her, raising his voice to make himself heard above the drumming of the rain on the tarpaulin roof.

"We get out here and walk across to the north gate."

"Couldn't we have come round through the park?"

"No. Be quick, please."

He had silenced the engine, and was holding the door open for her. She got out reluctantly, and he took her arm and hurried her along the rough track. The water in the puddles splashed up to her ankles for he gave her no time to pick her way.

"It's rather important that we shouldn't be seen," he explained. "Not that any one is likely to come along this road in this weather."

When they reached the comparative shelter of the park wall he released her arm and produced a tool from the pocket of his overcoat. "I'm pretty good at locks, but you couldn't keep a child out with the padlock the local bobbies have put on here," he said contemptuously. "It's a cheap standard pattern."

Amy shivered as she looked about her. When she had first come that way the sun had been shining and she had hardly noticed the desolate and uncared for appearance of the park. Now as she peered through the bars of the gate she thought how gloomy it looked in the falling rain. She noticed the acrid scent of the dying nettles by the gate posts. The police had trodden them down when they were carrying out their search after the finding of Ruby Duncan's body. She remembered hearing that the second murder had been committed within a hundred yards of the lodge. Perhaps the killer had lurked behind one of those trees.

Her companion had got the gate open. "Quick," he said again. He was glancing about him and she saw that he was uneasy. "We're too much in the open here."

He had taken her arm again. His grip was quite impersonal, but she resented it though she lacked the courage to protest. He rushed her up the little garden path to the front door.

"I've got a key for this as it happens. Go straight into the sitting-room."

She obeyed. Already the place smelt musty and there was dust on the furniture. She wondered how she could ever have thought it a cheerful room. The superficial gaiety of the bright flowery chintz covers was horrible, like paint on a dead face. Smith had left her. She could hear the rapid light footsteps in the other rooms and the opening and shutting of doors. He was making sure that there was nobody else in the cottage. But surely, she thought, others were expected. He had talked of a reconstruction of the crime. That could not be carried out without witnesses. He had promised that Tony Dene should be cleared. How could that be done if the authorities were not present?

"The others aren't here yet," she said, trying to speak naturally as he came in.

"No."

He took a cigarette from his case and lit it without going through the form of asking her permission. Inspector Collier, she thought, had better manners. She sat down in a chair by the table.

"The fire's laid in the grate. Do you think we might put a light to it?" she asked. "I'm wet, and it's so cold here."

"No, it wouldn't do. Somebody might see the smoke from the chimney. Otherwise I would," he said, "my hands are numbed." He rubbed them together as he spoke. "We need not wait for the others though. That's quite unnecessary. Suppose you begin by telling me how you came here in the first place."

"But I've been through all that so often," she objected, "to Sergeant Lindo, and then with Inspector Collier. They've got it all written down."

"But you didn't tell them what Mrs. Hall had said to you about her nephew," he reminded her.

"No. I forgot that. It was stupid of me."

He looked at her with the rather fixed smile that never seemed to reach his eyes. "It was rather," he said gently. "And now for the whole story."

She complied, telling her tale clearly and with every detail she could think of. He listened closely and with evident interest.

When she had finished he made no comment but stood with his back to the fireless hearth rocking himself gently, first rising on his toes and then sinking back on his heels, his hands in his trouser pockets, a cigarette between his lips.

Her heart sank. Was this all he had brought her here for? And it would be dark before long. "I thought you said I could help—" she ventured. "I mean—the police have known all this from the beginning."

"Yes. There was only one piece missing. Would you like to know what really happened here before you arrived?"

"You mean how she—he was killed and who killed him?" she faltered. "Was he—was it in this room?"

He nodded. "The floor must have been wet in that corner when you arrived."

"Yes—it was."

"Can't you imagine why?" His voice changed. "Who would have thought the old man had so much blood in him? Don't look so scared. It's only a quotation. Macbeth. You don't seem to know much about your father's family. I'll enlighten you.

The person who introduced himself to you as Henrietta Hall was a man named Henry Harlow. He had married your father's sister, Amy, so he was your uncle by marriage. Your aunt died young and after her death he knocked about a good deal. He was warder in a big prison for a bit. He lost that job and he tried several others. He'd always had a liking for private theatricals and dancing and singing and dressing up, and he and a young nephew of his toured in the halls with an act that had a big success for a while. Harlow was pretty good as a female impersonator and they did an eccentric dance together. The young fellow, Syd Harlow, had the greater talent of the two. If he'd been given his chance, he'd have made a big name. But the older man was jealous. There's a hell of a lot of that in the profession—and he queered the boy's pitch every time. Spite and envy, that's what it was. Spite. And the end of it was that a first class act was ruined, and they were out of a shop and a black mark against their names in the agents' books."

Amy was puzzled by his growing excitement. She said nothing. He resumed. "After a bit the uncle got to hear of Mrs. Dene living down here. He knew something about her that she wouldn't care to have published. After that he was on velvet. Naturally. She couldn't say no to him. He'd been in a bit of trouble and wanted to make a fresh start and it seemed to him that it might be pleasanter all round if he was a woman. And Mrs. Dene toed the line. Henrietta Hall was introduced to the family as a dear friend who'd laid her under an obligation in the past. As I said just now he was on velvet."

He threw the end of his cigarette into the fender and lit another.

"What about the nephew? It was the old man's obstinacy that had ruined their act and spoilt his chances on the variety stage. You'd think the least he could do would be to go fifty-fifty when he had a bit of luck? What hopes. Did he say, 'Come along, Syd, there's enough for both of us.' Did he say that? Like hell he did. Doling out pound notes and warning him not to come too often. Grasping, he said. Grasping! That was funny, wasn't it, coming from that old bloodsucker. Damned funny."

Amy sat very still. Her lips had gone dry. She had to moisten them before she could speak. "You're—you're not—"

He finished her sentence for her. "One of the Big Five? You fell for it, didn't you? It was risky, but I like risks. And I had to stop you somehow from talking about the nephew, hadn't I? I'm Syd Harlow, the chap he said he'd done with. He sent me a final twenty pounds and told me to stand on my own feet. I laughed. Well, I ask you! I came down Monday week to have it out with him. Left my motor-bike in the usual place along outside the park wall. There's plenty of cover. I said, 'You've got a hold over this dame and what you say goes. The elder girl's booked. Okay. I'll have the other.' He wouldn't listen. We had a regular dust up. I was sick of his blasted ingratitude. But we both calmed down after a bit and he gave me a couple of quid and I went back to where I'd left my motor-bike in a dry ditch along the park wall. I could show you the place. It's about half a mile farther on. When I got there I felt tired. You remember what a hot day it was. A regular scorcher. And it was the hottest part of the afternoon. I lay down and smoked a fag thinking things over, and then I fell asleep. When I woke up I decided to go back and make the old skinflint part with a bit more than he'd given me. After all, if it came to a showdown I was fifteen years younger. But when I walked in at that door he was lying partly under the table, with his head in a pool of blood. And if you want to know who did it, that's the chap."

He pointed to the placidly smiling brass Buddha seated cross-legged on his lotus on the bureau.

"He was on the floor too beside my uncle, and not as clean as he looks now. Well, it was a bit of a facer, and I had to do some quick thinking. Who had laid him out? I could make a pretty good guess. But they'd got cold feet and left the job half done. I decided I'd clear up the mess and give them something to think about when they came creeping back as they were bound to do. And when they knew what I knew about them I'd be on velvet too. So I carried him down the garden and shoved him into the old well that I'd used before as a hiding place for the stuff I collared on a couple of jobs I did in this neighbourhood in the Spring, and I warmed some water and washed the floor and wiped every surface I could think of. I'd just about finished when I heard the click of the garden gate and looked out and saw you coming up the path. I didn't know who you were. Uncle hadn't told me he expected you. Just a young woman with a suitcase."

He took another cigarette from his case and struck a match.

"That was a surprise, and not a pleasant one. Yes, you made a mess of my plans, butting in where you weren't wanted, my dear young cousin Amy. Blast your eyes."

Amy was watching his hands. He used them a good deal to gesticulate while he was talking. They were lean and sinewy and the fingers were stained yellow with nicotine. His hands filled her with horror.

"Butting in," he repeated. "I had a right to share in the doings. You had none. He brought you down here to spite me. Well, now I've brought you back to amuse myself by telling the truth. It isn't often one gets a chance to do that."

She sighed unconsciously. He glanced at her sharply. "Not bored, I hope. I flattered myself I should retain your interest. I wanted time to think over the position. Instead of going back to London I went on to a friend of mine at Southampton. She and her brother run a garage with a repair shop. Most of their customers are men on shore leave. Their garden goes down to the water's edge and one can land there in a row boat at high tide. They run some profitable side lines, and the police haven't got on to them yet. I came over here every day, and always in a different car. I had to meet Ruby on her afternoon out. I always met her when I came down to see my uncle. I'd come across her by chance in the first place and we got pally and I'd let out more than I should have done. Girls like Ruby are always asking questions and one can't be always on one's guard. I was waiting for her in the usual place on Thursday. I hadn't made up my mind— not quite—but it seemed to me she knew too much to be safe. She came along and she said, 'Hallo, Syd!' I said, 'Hallo, Ruby.' I kept my hand on what I'd brought with me in my coat pocket. A big stone, it was. She said, 'Have you brought that wrist watch you promised me?' I said, 'No.' She said, 'Maybe I'll get one from someone else. I had a parcel to post Monday afternoon, and I got leave to take it down to the village. I made a bit of a round on the way home.' I said, 'Let's get a bit further away from the path.' She said, 'None of your rough stuff, Syd,' and laughed. She went on first and I hit her on the back of her head. She didn't cry out or anything."

Amy shuddered. He stared at her with his fixed smile.

"That wasn't just lack of imagination, you know. If you'd seen our turn on the stage you'd have to admit I've got imagination. One of the critics said a touch of macabre genius. I've got the cutting somewhere. It was too much for some of the audience. There was generally some fool of a woman screaming. Ruby had to be killed the same way to convince the police that the same person was responsible for both jobs. I resented the necessity. It was a clumsy and inartistic method. Brute force unallied with intelligence is always dull. I hope to manage your little affair much better."

"Mine—" she faltered.

"Yours. My dear girl, you're not such a nit-wit that you can't see that you are even more in my way than Ruby was? You don't really imagine that I should have told you all this if I had meant you to go back to Ranchester to repeat everything I've said to your friends in the police? It's got to be, and I won't pretend I'm sorry. You've been a nuisance from the start. You spoilt my graft. But for you I'd have had the Denes where I wanted them, and money to burn."

He was coming towards her. Amy had been paralysed with fear, but as he approached she sprang up and ran round behind the bureau.

It was useless, for the other end was blocked by the settee and he was still between her and the door. He had her hemmed in a corner from which she could not escape. Despairingly she picked up the heavy brass Buddha and hurled it at him. Her aim was poor, it missed him completely and smashed a window pane.

"You little devil," he said angrily.

He gripped her arms and forced her back against the wall. She heard herself screaming like an animal caught in a trap.

The last thing she saw was his face distorted with fury. She had ceased to struggle and hung a dead weight in his grasp. He let her slip to the floor and stepped back, breathing heavily. She looked very small lying huddled there at his feet in the narrow space between the bureau and the wall.

"You've asked for it," he said thickly, "getting in my way."

CHAPTER XXIII

HELP!

TONY WAITED in the morning-room until Collier and the sergeant had gone. Then he went back to the library. He switched on the lights as he went in. His mother, who had been bending over the fire, warming her hands, shrank a little from the light.

"Must you, Tony? My eyes are so tired."

"I'm sorry, but we've got to talk and we've been in the dark long enough."

"If you think this is the right moment to bully me—"

"Lavvy can hurt me," she was thinking, "not the others—"

"Mother, if you take that attitude you make things even more difficult than they are already. I know it must be painful but wouldn't it be better to tell us exactly what the hold was that man had over you? We're not children any longer. Whatever it was we can face it and—and try to make the best of it."

"Have you talked this over among you?" she asked in a hard voice. "Are you speaking on behalf of your sisters, too?"

Tony was hurt by her tone but he answered steadily. "We haven't discussed it but I know Mollie feels as I do. I can't answer for Lavvy."

"Lavvy's leaving home. She told me just now. She's going to share a flat in Town with a friend. I'm going to make her an allowance. If you and Mollie have made any plans I may as well hear them before I go upstairs. My head aches. I'm going to bed."

Hopeless, he thought. They were talking round the subject as usual and with the usual increasing irritation on either side. "What do you want us to do?" he asked.

"Does it matter what I want?" she asked bitterly. He had known she would say that. "Sixteen years of self-suppression and humiliation and drudgery for your sakes, and this is what I get for it."

"Mother, for God's sake try to be reasonable. We know what you've done for us, how much you put up with from my uncle, and we aren't ungrateful. We're ready to do our bit now. Anything you say—"

"Very well," she said coldly, "I'll take you at your word. I'll ask you to refrain from harassing me with questions. Let me have some peace if only for a few hours."

"Oh—all right," he said.

He would have helped her to get up from her chair for he saw she was trembling, but she signed to him to stand back. He went to open the door for her. She passed out without looking at him.

When Mollie came into the library five minutes later she found him sitting with his head in his hands.

"Tony—what's going to happen now?"

He jumped up and began to walk about the room. "God knows. I think my immediate future is provided for, but I'm worried about you, old girl."

"Can't I be with you?" she asked wistfully. "I thought we were going to stick together."

"Yes. But they think I'm the—the man they want. I could see that just now. Collier's shillyshallying because, in spite of everything, he likes me rather. But it can't go on much longer. They'll fetch me to-morrow."

"Tony! They can't be such fools!" she cried indignantly.

"Can't they? You watch them."

Mollie's dog had followed her into the room. She lifted him on to her knees. "Binkie darling, you're the only one with any sense. I believe I'd die without you."

Binkie licked her cheek.

"Lavvy's up in her room packing."

"Is she? Mother said she was going to share a flat with a friend. Well, let her, I say."

"You were in here with Mother, Tony. What did she say to you?"

"Nothing useful," he said wearily. "The Lear touch. Our base ingratitude after all her sacrifices. Oh damn, I know she made sacrifices. But she won't talk things over quietly. She maddens me. All the same I'm fearfully sorry for her. The way Lavvy has turned on her is a knock down blow. She doesn't mind you and me." He kicked a stool out of his way. "Oh, hell. I'm going out."

"Oh, Tony, don't. It's dark and it's still pouring, and—"

"And I might meet the murderer? What hopes. Don't be an ass, Mollie. I'm not going to try to get pneumonia. I'll wear a mac. I've just got to have some exercise and get away from things."

"May I come with you?"

"No!" he shouted. Then he said, more quietly, "Can't you understand, after to-morrow I may never be alone. I've read about it. Warders sit up with you—"

He felt better when he had banged the house door behind him and was out in the windy darkness. Should he take the car and drive as he had driven that Monday evening, trying to get away from himself and his troubles. No. He would almost certainly be held up by the policeman on duty at the south gate. He was to all intents and purposes a prisoner already. He remembered a story of Poe's in which the walls of a cell had closed inch by inch relentlessly on their victim.

"But I'm innocent," he thought, "they don't hang a man unless he's proved guilty. Proof. I can't prove where I was when either of them was killed. If it wasn't me I'd say, 'That chap's story's pretty thin.' The evidence against Norman Thorn wasn't much stronger and they hanged him. Poor devil. But he cut the girl up. I didn't do that. Oh God! I must keep a hold on myself."

He walked quickly, tramping over the sodden turf. The gale roaring through the tree tops was beginning to fill him with a vague exaltation. His spectacles were misted with rain. He took them off and slipped them into his pocket. He strode on, with his head up, watching the racing clouds and the dark swaying masses of the wind-tormented woods on the sky line. For the moment he was one with the night and one with the storm. He had transcended the short-sighted, nerve-ridden youth who was about to be drawn in among the wheels of the machinery of the law. No use struggling. He'd be like the man down at the farm caught by the chaff-cutter. Screams and blood. No. Stop thinking of that. A star gleamed for an instant through a black rack of flying clouds. Help. Four angels round my bed. Four angels at my head. Matthew, Mark, Luke and John.

He stood still, leaning back against the wind, and covered his face with his hands. He heard the thudding of his overdriven heart, the wailing of the wind, and, far off, a shrill and long drawn cry.

He dropped his hands and turned and stood, dazzled by the white glare of a car's headlights. The car stopped beside him with a grinding of brakes, and a man jumped out and gripped him by the arm.

"What are you doing out here in this weather, Mr. Dene?"

Tony began to laugh. "I know the answer to that one. Acting in a suspicious manner."

Collier looked at the white haggard face and the over-bright eyes. "All right," he said and his voice was suddenly kind, though he did not relax his grip of the young man's arm. "You've had about all you can stand, I know. But wandering about in the rain won't help. Now listen to me. Did you arrange to meet Miss Steer to-night?"

"No."

"Well, we can't talk here. Get into the car."

Tony went with his captor obediently for two or three steps. Then he began to hang back. "Wait a bit. Look here, Inspector. I heard a scream just now. Very faint and far off, but I'm pretty sure it wasn't my imagination. I think we ought to do something about it."

Collier's eyes narrowed. "Where did it come from? Which direction?"

"Over there, I think."

Collier glanced at Duffield, who was leaning out from the driver's seat. "To the north, eh? We'll drive that way."

They got into the car and the sergeant, who had not yet spoken, let in the clutch. He stopped the car when Collier touched him on the shoulder and they all three got out. The north gate was a hundred yards away, its iron scroll work just visible against the strip of open moorland and the sky. The lodge on the right of the grass-grown road lay in dense shadow, but as they looked towards it a dim light flickered for an instant in one window and was gone.

"Did you see that, Sergeant? There's somebody there. Switch off our head lamps, quick. That's right. Now stand by to switch them on again if you hear me shout. Do you get that?"

"Yes, sir."

The Inspector turned to Tony. "I'm going to have a look round. You'd better remain with the sergeant."

"Can't I come with you?"

"Do what you're told," snapped Collier.

He moved forward and they lost sight of him almost at once in the black shadow of the high laurel hedge. After a minute they heard the click of the gate and that was all.

Tony fumbled for his box of matches and found them too wet to strike. "Can you give me a light, Sergeant?"

"Better not, sir. Not just now."

"Perhaps you're right. I can't make head or tail of this. There can't be anybody in the lodge. I say, what did you come back for?"

"Miss Steer's missing. That's why."

"Miss Steer? Amy?" Tony became excited. "Since when? Oh, for Heaven's sake get on with it, man."

"She left the tea shop in Luke's Passage at a quarter to six and was driven off in a car that was waiting for her. Unfortunately Saunders, who saw it, was too far off to get the number or describe it. The Inspector thought it might be yours and so we came back here but when we got to the house your car was in the garage. We saw your sister and she told us you'd gone for a walk. You must be fond of walking," added Duffield.

"Amy? In a car? But she hasn't any friends here. Sergeant, you—you don't think anything's happened to her?"

"Let's hope not," said Duffield.

"The Inspector's a long time gone."

"He's coming back now," said Duffield, who had been thinking the same thing himself.

Collier came back to them and flashed the light of his pocket torch on Tony. "All quiet and dark, but there's a pane broken in the sitting-room window. Were you coming away from the lodge when we met you just now, Mr. Dene?"

"I was not. And I wish you wouldn't dazzle me with that thing."

"Your sister said you'd been gone over an hour. Plenty of time to come here—"

"I was just walking about."

"All right," said Collier, but he sounded dissatisfied. "Bring him along, Duffield. We've got to get to the bottom of this. That window wasn't broken last time I was up here."

The sergeant's huge fist closed like a vice on Tony's arm. The young man protested. "I'm coming. Damn it all, it was I who brought you here, wasn't it? I heard—Oh, Lord! That couldn't have been Amy, could it?"

Nobody answered him. Collier was leading the way up the garden path. "The door's locked. Where's the key, Sergeant?"

"At the police station."

"It would be."

"The window's broken. I can put my arm through and open the casement."

"Good. Do that."

There was more shattering of glass, the casement swung back, and the three men scrambled into the sitting-room. The white ray of light from Collier's torch wandered from point to point.

"Seems okay. Light the candles on the mantel-piece, Duffield. The lamp's no use. The girl burnt it out that night she spent here. Wait here."

They heard him going about in the other rooms. He was back almost immediately. He prowled round the room, stooping once by the window to pick up something that lay there. "The brass paper weight. There's a dint here in the window-frame. It strikes me the window was broken from the inside. Interesting. Practically no broken glass here. That means it fell outward. Obvious, of course. I could do with a cigarette. Could you spare me one, Mr. Dene?"

"Certainly." Tony proffered his case. Collier took one and stooped again to gather up something lying in the fender.

"I've noticed you always smoke cork tipped, Mr. Dene."

"Yes. What about it? I say, aren't we wasting time?"

"I hope not. There were five cigarettes ends here, smoked so recently that they are still moist. You have three in your case, all of a different make to these. I haven't said I doubted your word, Mr. Dene, but corroborative evidence is always useful. Two people have been here lately. They were both very wet. This hearthrug is damp and so is the seat of that chair. They were here. What's become of them? Why was the window broken? I don't like it."

Tony, following his example, was wandering restlessly round the little room. It seemed to him, too, that something had happened recently within those four walls.

"I can't stick this place," he said, "it's got a bad aura. I—what's that?"

"I don't hear anything."

"It's stopped. Now it's beginning again."

Collier listened, and shook his head. "It's the rain. There's water dripping everywhere. No use staying here. We'll have a look round the back though before we go."

They passed into the kitchen, Duffield carrying the candles from the mantelpiece to light their way. Here again Collier looked about him carefully.

"Duffield!"

"Yes, sir."

"You were with me the last time when I went through this place?"

"I was."

"Did I leave that table drawer an inch open?"

"It wouldn't be like you."

Collier grunted. "As you say. We'll have a look." He pulled it open. "A job lot of knives, forks and spoons, two lead pencils and one slate pencil, two-pence three farthings in coppers, a pack of playing cards, a screw driver and a corkscrew. I went through this little lot before. What's missing? Something is—"

Tony was fidgeting. "Does it matter?"

"It may—" he checked himself. "You're right, Dene. That's a funny noise. It isn't water." Tony went to the back door and opened it. "It's out here somewhere—"

They could all hear it now, a faint intermittent fumbling and scraping.

"It's more like a branch rubbing against the house wall," said Duffield. "Or a starling fallen down the chimney. They do sometimes."

"No." Tony was peering out into the darkness. "Now it's stopped. But it was just here on my right. Bring the torch, Inspector."

Collier joined him and the light flickered over the coal shed, the drenched currant bushes, the wet brick pavement of the yard. "On your right. Great Scott. Look there, just at your feet—" They both stared at the hammer lying among scattered two inch nails. "That's what I missed from the drawer."

He stepped out, crossed the yard and came back again. "Do you hear anything now?"

"No. But I'll swear it wasn't a bird."

"And there aren't any branches," said Collier half to himself as he flashed his torch over the walls and roof. "Was this rain water butt drained off, Duffield?"

"Yes, sir. But I daresay it's filling up again in this downpour."

"Just take the cover off and see."

"Very good, sir," said Duffield briskly, and then—"I can't move it. Seems to be stuck."

"Has it been nailed down?"

"Seems like it."

"My God," said Tony huskily, "you don't think—"

Collier steadied him by giving him something to do. "Fetch a knife from the kitchen and a poker. Anything you can lay your hands on that will serve to lever it up."

Tony rushed to obey and they all worked feverishly. Presently they were rewarded with the sound of splintering wood as the nails that had been driven in were slowly forced up again. The cover was lifted off and Collier flashed his light inside. All three saw the girl's body lying huddled at the bottom in several inches of water.

Following Collier's directions they turned the butt over on its side, drew her out and carried her into the sitting-room where they laid her on the settee. Collier produced a pocket flask and moistened her lips with brandy.

"Her heart's beating. She'll come round in a minute."

Tony knelt by her, chafing her cold hands. Collier stood at the end of the settee, looking from one to the other thoughtfully. He had felt the back of her head and assured himself that there were no outward injuries.

She opened her eyes. They looked unnaturally large in that small white face, pinched with cold and fatigue.

"Oh—Tony—" she whispered and made an instinctive movement towards him. Collier, watching closely, was aware of rising spirits. That let young Dene out.

"Tony, I had such an awful dream. Or was it—is this the lodge?"

"Yes. But you're quite safe. You're all right."

"My hands hurt," she murmured.

Collier looked down at the bruised and blood-smeared fingers and torn and blackened nails. His face hardened as he visualised the frenzied efforts she must have made to escape from her prison. If, by the mercy of God, they had not been there to hear her he could guess what the outcome would have been.

"We must get her away from here. Bring the car up to the garden gate, Duffield." He bent over her as the sergeant hurried out. "Drink this"—he held the cup of his flask to her lips. She sipped obediently and choked a little.

"It burns my throat—but it's nice and warm. Tony—"

"I won't leave you, darling. I'm holding you."

She tried to smile. "I was so terrified."

Again Collier intervened. "Who brought you here?"

"Don't worry her with questions now. It's brutal," said Tony fiercely.

"I'm sorry, but we've got to know."

"He called himself Smith. He said he was sent down from Scotland Yard because the police were making a mess of things. I was a fool, I suppose," she said faintly. "I believed him. He said I could help him with a reconstruction that would clear Tony. Then, when we got here, he talked quite differently and I got more and more frightened. He told me Mrs. Hall's real name was Henry Harlow, and that he was a nephew. He was here that Monday afternoon. He pretended he found his uncle lying dead, but he admitted that he killed Ruby. And then he said I'd got in his way from the first, and he came towards me and I threw the paperweight at him and broke the window, and I screamed for help, but nobody came. And I don't remember anything more."

"A nephew—"

"Yes. Mrs. Hall spoke of him when I met her at Victoria. I forgot to tell you. He's been staying at Southampton and coming over every day in different cars. He boasted a lot of being too clever for the police."

"The devil he did," said Collier grimly. "And now the car's at the gate. Do you feel able to walk?"

"She needn't," said Tony, "because I'm going to carry her."

CHAPTER XXIV

THE LAST TURN

THERE WAS SOME inevitable delay at Ranchester. Collier had driven first to Mrs. Saunders' house and left Amy in her charge. Tony had been left there, too, at his own request, to run errands and open the door for the doctor, while the landlady, who had been a nurse before her marriage, hustled her patient upstairs

for a hot bath and heated the blankets for her bed. Constable
Saunders was added to the party and then Sergeant Lindo,
who heard the latest developments from Duffield while Collier
was busy at the telephone. They were off at last, but it was past
midnight when they were stopped just outside Petersfield by a
young policeman who stepped forward from the shelter of the
hedge, his cape shining with moisture.

"From Ranchester, sir? A car answering the description sent
out to all stations passed through here at ten to eleven. She was
going very fast and I didn't get the number. An A.A. scout who
was along just now says he saw a similar car by the roadside
on Rake Common, apparently being repaired, but the driver
jumped in and got away before he came up."

"Which way was it going?"

"Towards West Meon."

"Would that be the road for Southampton?"

"You can get to Southampton that way."

"Good. Thank you, Constable. Drive on, Sergeant."

Lindo was at the wheel with Collier sitting beside him. Rain
was still falling and he drove carefully, his eyes on the patch
of road made visible by the headlights, while the wiper moved
steadily to and fro on the blurred windscreen.

"Do you suppose he knows we're after him, Inspector?"

"Can't say. It all depends on the margin of minutes between
his leaving the lodge and our arrival. He must have been in a
hurry at the last or he wouldn't have left the hammer and nails
where he did. If he got right away before we drove up he must be
feeling fairly safe. But the wicked flee when no man pursueth."

"Southampton is a large town," said Lindo, who, being chilly
and tired, was in a pessimistic mood. "If he dodges the patrols
it'll be a job looking for him. His friends have a garden running
down to the water's edge. That means he may get away in a boat.
Fancy telling the girl all that. He must be a fool."

"An exhibitionist," said Collier. "Lots of crooks are. And you
must remember he didn't mean her to live to repeat his stuff."

"Would she have died in that butt?"

"I think so. Your chaps drained it off last week, but there was about a foot of water in it when we got her out, and it was running in all the time from the roof. She must have been unconscious when he put her in, but she came to and made some efforts to get out. That's the noise we heard. If we hadn't been there—"

"He must be a cruel devil," said Lindo.

"Yes."

Lindo drove on through the darkness. Once they met a heavy lorry laden with market produce, and once an owl, dazzled by their headlights, dashed itself against the screen. Duffield and Saunders slumbered on the back seat. Collier spoke occasionally, knowing that if he did not there was some danger of Lindo falling asleep at the wheel.

Once they stopped to consult a map. Soon afterwards Collier pointed to some lights in the distance. "What's that?"

"Southampton. We're coming into Woolstone." He reduced his speed. "There's a steep bit just here. Damn these road surfaces. They're like glass."

"What's the gradient?"

"One in five. And there's a sharp turn at the bottom, if I remember rightly, and I'm not sure that there isn't a railway arch. Hallo—"

They stopped with a grinding of brakes as an A.A. man in his yellow waterproof signalled to them and came forward. "I've instructions to stop all cars—"

"That's all right. We're police. Is there any news?"

"There's been a nasty accident. A car coming down the hill. The driver must have lost control. Instead of taking the turn he crashed through a fence at the bottom. It's soft black mud out there and covered with water at high tide. Nobody saw it happen—it was about an hour ago—but the man who owns the little grocer's shop at the bottom of the hill is on the 'phone. He had been awakened by the crash and he rang up the police. They're down there now with a breakdown lorry, and some of the chaps are rigging a crane to lift the car out. They've located it, but there's only a bit of the roof showing."

Collier looked at Lindo. "Can this be our man?"

"Sounds as if it might be."

"We'd better have a look see."

At the foot of the hill Collier and the two sergeants got out of the car stiffly, for all three were cramped with cold, and walked forward, leaving Saunders in the car, to join a group of men standing in the gap where the board fence had been broken down.

The headlights of three cars and a lorry were concentrated on a patch of shining black mud that was just being left bare by the receding tide. The gaunt arm of a crane had swung over it and the hook at the end of the chain was groping like some sentient thing over the submerged car. The mud smeared tarpaulin roof might have been the back of a hippopotamus wallowing in the slime.

A tall man in a Burberry joined the newcomers. Collier introduced himself and his companions. The tall man shook hands with them.

"I'm Detective Sergeant Withers. We've got all our men out after Harlow, Inspector. I fancy he's put paid to his account."

"You mean you think he's here?"

The crane was in action. There were curious sucking and gobbling noises as the mud quivered, reluctantly yielding up its prey. "Look out!" shouted Withers. He was too late. As the car was lifted into the air the body of a man that had lain huddled among shattered glass in the driver's seat, slid out and fell back with a splash into the mud. The crane worked on, but the centre of interest had shifted from the car to its occupant. Planks were hastily fetched from a neighbouring wood yard and laid over the quaking mud.

"Is it safe?" asked Collier.

Withers shrugged his shoulders. "Farther along it would be. All the urchins bathe there at low tide. But this is a bad patch. You see we've got boards up marked Danger. Still, it's got to be done. I'll call for volunteers."

"No. I'll go myself."

"No need for that, Inspector."

"I will. I'm at least a stone lighter than any of the men you've got here. I'll just slip a loop of rope under my arms, and you can haul me back if I sink."

Duffield said nothing. He knew better than to interfere when his superior officer had made up his mind, but he had turned rather white. Silence fell on the little group of men at the edge of the narrow margin of shingle beach as Collier stepped quickly along the first plank. It sank into the mud as he left it. The second plank tilted sideways, nearly throwing him off his balance. He could only recover himself by springing on to the next plank. A fountain of muddy water spirted up all round him as it settled down under his weight. He was crouching, stretching forward, grasping at the arm of the dead man floating in the water that had filled the hole made by the car.

"All right," he shouted. "I've got him, but I can't lift him. You'll have to haul us in together."

Getting back to land was a messy, slithering business, and the strain on Collier's arms was so severe that as willing hands divested him of the cord about his middle he toppled forward in a dead faint.

He was still rather pale when he came into the Superintendent's room at Ranchester police station that afternoon, but he was as spruce as ever. Colonel Boult acknowledged his arrival with a grumpy nod.

"You're late," he remarked with a glance at the clock. "I had suggested five as a convenient time for a final conference."

"Sorry, Colonel. There were various things to be done at Southampton. I had been afraid we should have to take Miss Steer over to identify the body, but I was lucky enough to find somebody who had known him in the days when he and his uncle were touring the halls."

"And that's why you kept us waiting?" said the Colonel acidly.

Collier had come to the conference determined that he would not allow the Chief Constable to irritate him into losing his temper.

"I'm sorry, sir," he said patiently, "but this Mr. Isaacs kept me waiting. He's the manager of the new Gloria Picture Theatre below bar, but he used to be manager of a music hall in Stafford. He knew most of the artistes on tour ten years ago. He remembered the Harlows and their turn. The elder man was a female impersonator. They called themselves High and Low on the bills. He said their show was clever—they ended up with an acrobatic dance, a sort of Apache affair that was definitely sinister. In fact, it sometimes upset the more squeamish members of the audience, and as they didn't seem able to modify its more objectionable features they were not re-engaged when their contract was at an end. I took him round to the mortuary, and he identified the dead man as Syd Harlow. After that I hardly think it will be necessary to subject Miss Steer to the ordeal of seeing him."

"And he made a statement to Miss Steer admitting that he murdered Ruby Duncan as well as his uncle?"

"Ruby Duncan. Yes. He said he left the lodge and came back to it and found his uncle's body," said Collier drily.

Colonel Boult nodded. "Pretty thin. He might as well have confessed to both while he was about it. Well, he's saved the ratepayers the expense of a trial at the next Assizes, and that's that. You and your colleague will be returning to Town to-night, I suppose?"

"Yes, sir."

"Well, I've no doubt you did your best," said the Colonel handsomely. He hesitated. "Strictly between ourselves, Collier, I suppose these Harlows had some hold over the Denes?"

Collier looked at him woodenly. "That hardly arises, sir, as we have satisfied ourselves that the Denes had nothing to do with the murders."

"No. No. Quite," said the Colonel, his red face rather redder than usual. "Well," he got up to go, "I'm glad it's over. A very unpleasant scandal. Very unpleasant indeed. I think it might have been cleared up earlier and I'm not going to congratulate you on your handling of the case, but I shan't stress that when I communicate with your superiors at the Yard. To err is human, what?"

He held out his hand and Collier took it. "Remembering the bruised reed," he said, smiling. And the Colonel, who did not react to literary allusions, took his departure looking slightly puzzled.

"You mustn't mind the C.C.," said the Superintendent when he had gone, "and, look here, must you go back to-night? You're all in, and no wonder."

"Thanks, but the Colonel was right. The case is over. And I've got to report. I shall sleep in the train."

Two hours later Collier and his colleague, having packed their bags, settled their bills at the Station Hotel, and paid a final visit to the Cathedral, where they formed a part of the small congregation for evensong and heard an organ recital, were alone in a third class smoker going back to London. "Well, the locals were pleasant to work with," said Duffield summing up, "all but—"

Collier's lips twitched, "All but the Colonel, you were going to say."

"Pompous old ass," said Duffield with unusual heat.

"With everything handsome about me," murmured Collier. The rain had ceased but the sky was still grey. Duffield stared at the sodden fields and dripping woods in the gathering dusk. "I suppose Syd Harlow got a kind of a kick out of telling that girl the truth because it was ugly and would shock her."

"Exactly."

"But why did he mix up lies with it?"

"What makes you think he did that?"

"Well, he pretended he hadn't committed the first murder. I mean—his uncle. Why not confess to that?"

"Why should he if he hadn't done it?"

Their eyes met. Duffield drew a long breath. "I see. Then you think—"

"Hardly that. I merely wonder. I doubt if in any case we could have proved the other person's guilt. And the provocation was so enormous. Sometimes the proverb about letting sleeping dogs lie is just an excuse for laziness, but not in this case."

"Those children mixed up in the rotten business," said Duffield, who had boys and girls of his own.

"The sins of the fathers," said Collier. He yawned. "I can't keep my eyes open." Five minutes later he was asleep.

EPILOGUE

"AND THIS is our drawing-room." The manageress, opening the door, afforded prospective guests a glimpse of four women, all elderly and grey-haired, playing bridge. She shut the door again gently.

"They seem absorbed."

"They are very keen players."

"Poor darlings. I suppose it's their one interest in life. So terribly sheltered and secure. I suppose nothing's ever happened to them." The manageress led them along a passage.

"You could have this bedroom."

The bridge players had finished their game. "They're late with the tea as usual. The service here gets worse and worse."

"Well, I hope the water boils to-day." The speaker broke off as a sulky youth in an evening suit spotted with gravy pushed in a tea wagon. "Has the afternoon post come in, Carter?"

"Yes, madam."

Mary Dene hesitated. If she went down to the hall to see if there were any letters for her in the rack the toasted scones would all be gone before she came back. There were never enough to go round. She poured herself out a cup of tea and helped herself to two pieces of scone. It was a mistake to miss tea. The dinner was often uneatable like the fish last night. The others were discussing the latest murder case. They enjoyed murders. How she hated these old women. Miss Gregson, with her parrot nose and her trick of prefacing every remark with "In my opinion—" Miss Cotter, with her knack of securing the most comfortable chair nearest the fire. Miss Lewis, who asked prying questions and fingered one's letters.

She ate her scones quickly and went down to the hall. There were two letters for her in the rack. One from Tony and one from Mollie. They had remembered her birthday. Lavvy had not written. She went up to her dreary little back bedroom to read them undisturbed.

Tony had married that girl. He and she and Mollie had joined forces with some old Scotch woman to run a tea garden in the New Forest. Apparently they were making a success of it.

She glanced through Tony's letter without much interest until she came to the postscript. "I expect you've heard from Lavvy herself. She played a small part in a film at the Elstree studio and that has led somehow to her getting a Hollywood contract. She sailed last week and she's to be away three years. I dare say she'll be more in her element than she would have been married to Miles Lennor and playing the lady of the Manor. Dearest Mother, don't worry over Lavvy. She can take care of herself. She always could."

Mollie was brief, affectionate, and uninforming. Mary Dene tore up both letters and dropped them in her waste paper basket. Then, laboriously, she picked the pieces up again. It would be better to burn them in the drawing-room fire before the others came in after dinner. She could slip out before the last course. It was always stewed prunes and custard on Thursdays. That pain in her side was worse. She would not see Lavvy again. Lavvy wasn't grateful. She didn't care. Of course she didn't know all. Mary Dene's hands clenched on the rail at the foot of the bed— but it wasn't a rail, it was a brass Buddha sitting cross-legged on a lotus flower. The Buddha, gazing up at her placid and un-moved, through the blood on his smiling face. For Lavvy. And Lavvy hadn't been worth it.

"Are we having our game of bridge to-night?"

"I suppose so."

"You left the dining-room so early. I was afraid you weren't feeling well."

"I'm quite well, thank you, Miss Lewis."

"Where's the hearth broom? It looks as if somebody had been burning paper."

"Shall we cut for partners?"

"Are you quite sure you want to play, Mrs. Dene? You don't look very well."

"She's all right," said Miss Cotter, who did not want to miss her game. "It will do her good."

Miss Cotter was dealing. Mrs. Dene picked up her cards and looked at them rather vacantly. There was a Buddha in that antique shop next to Boots. She saw it in the window every time she went to change a book or buy aspirin.

Lavvy.

THE END

AFTERWORD

CASES OF transvestism occur in Golden Age detective novels, although the incidence appears to be small. Immediately coming to mind from British mystery are Gladys Mitchell's *Speedy Death* (1929), Brian Flynn's *The Murders Near Mapleton* (1929) and Agatha Christie's contribution to the collaboratively composed Detection Club detective novel *The Floating Admiral* (1931). (Josephine Tey's *To Love and Be Wise* was published two decades later, in 1950, making it post Golden Age.) In Brian Flynn's novel the cross dressing seems to be merely a matter of criminal convenience, while in Gladys Mitchell's the eonism—in this case a woman dressing as a man, a world-famous explorer—appears to be a genuine case of cross gender identification. In the case of Agatha Christie, the matter is not so clear cut, with Christie explaining in notes to her rather tongue-in-cheek book chapter that while the man dressing as a woman in her contribution has a definite criminal purpose in mind in doing so, he, a former actor, nevertheless "takes an artistic pleasure" in vamping the various beaux of the neighborhood, who evidently find his feminine company strangely intoxicating.

Far less appealing is Harriet Hall, the titular character in Moray Dalton's *The Strange Case of Harriet Hall*, the other characters in the novel finding him (or her as the case may be) distinctly off-putting, even repellent. Young Amy Steer deems her supposed aunt "rather alarming" and tries "hard not to shrink away" as Mrs. Hall leans in, with her "somewhat overpowering aura of combined Nuit d'Amour and Turkish cigarettes," to kiss her cheek. After the birth sex of Harriet Hall is revealed at the coroner's inquest on her (his?) death as decidedly masculine, with all sorts of titillating accompanying details (e.g., "The underclothing was of pink silk trimmed with lace"), the author informs us that the "livelier Sunday papers" run stories about the affair in which the strange case of Mrs. Hall is "compared with that of Savelette [sic, Savalette] de Lange and the Chevalier D'Oex [sic, Chevalier d'Eon] and certain theories concerning Queen Elizabeth. . . ." Here Dalton, who of course herself masqueraded under a male pseudonym, evinces awareness with historical cases of men who for decades dressed as women (allegedly and improbably in the case of Queen Elizabeth I). Likely she had read Bram Stoker's *Famous Imposters*, a book published in 1910, when she was 28 years old, which included chapters on both Queen Elizabeth I and the Chevalier d'Eon (who may have been inter-sex).

Like Mademoiselle Savalette de Lange and the Chevalier d'Eon, Henry Harlow deceives a great many people in his guise as a woman. As a female impersonator he once performed an "eccentric dance" on stage with his nephew, one which "sometimes upset the more squeamish members of the audience," Inspector Collier explains late in the novel, as the two men seemed unable "to modify its more objectionable features." Although Henry Harlow, aka Harriet Hall, no doubt was correct in his insistence to Mary Dene that his blackmail scheme would be easier to carry out with him adopting the guise of a woman, one cannot help but conclude that Henry/Harriet derived great enjoyment from his imposture, until an end was put to it for good with a violent blow from a Buddha statuette.

Curtis Evans